Z JEFFRIES

Gamble: One Champion Wins

Dedication

For Richard. I wish you could have seen it.

Gamble: One Champion Wins

Book Three of the Hide & Seek Chronicles
By Z Jeffries

I

Part One

The Fall

Chapter 1

C hapter 1

She hovered in her cloud, a queen bee orbited by her hive. I'd say she was standing straight and tall, if she were standing and not floating. In the yellow and black jumpsuit, she cut a very feminine figure that made her featureless, matte black, elongated head that much more unsettling. The helmet was impossibly narrow and gave her an insectoid appearance.

But Captain Miss was no robot. She was my very human enemy. She took my team away from me. Stole the love of my life. And beat me at the only thing I've ever been good at.

A cluster of her bees returned to her, and the mysterious inhuman captain disappeared.

The Atomic Seeker drifted through the air, splitting the distance between Harla's disappearance and me while following the gentle white edge of the Atlantic Ocean. I was holding my breath, safely hidden behind an invisible shield within a concrete bunker until the blob inched by. Suddenly, the oversized atom halted and shot a projectile from its nucleus down the beach and out of sight.

CJ's voice filled my helmet. "Captain Awesometown is out."

Captain Miss rematerialized, this time only ten feet from the opening of my bunker. Of course, she hadn't actually disappeared; her mirrored nanobots simply bent the light around her, so instead of her queen bee floating figure, there was only sand and rock and sea and air. Reigning champion of DARPA's Military Camouflage Challenge, Captain Miss was good. She was the best.

And in this game, the only player Captain Miss, Harla to her friends, had left to beat was me.

The randomly selected arena for this MC Squared was a beach in Normandy, France. It reminded me of grassy parks they divided up for kids soccer fields on weekends. Only this field was full of overgrown craters; green bowls in the earth anywhere from a couple feet to deeper than I was tall.

Past the green, there was a steep drop-off where the grassy area hit the beach. Not tall enough to be a cliff but rockier and higher than a dune or natural seawall. And dotting the drop-off, every quarter mile, were concrete bunkers; most were intact, but several were bombed out.

There was always shock when you first saw a new arena, but it wore off quick. And now, two days into this spring MC Squared, the reverent presence of the men who lost their lives here fighting for the world's freedom in World War Two had dissipated. Now, I was in the zone, playing the game.

Aiden Run, or Captain Awesomepants, or whatever, just got out, tagged by the Atomic Seeker with a smart nanobot made to mimic a paintball. The boy in the mech suit was tagged nearly two miles away at a concrete bunker stronghold on the only hill (if you'd even call it that) on the other side of the arena.

But I wasn't just hiding from the Atomic Seeker. Captain Miss played so aggressively, it was imperative to avoid her, too.

Still behind my invisible shield of bots, I backed out of the bunker. Captain Miss was more athletic than me, and she had a more complete support team — I should know, I used to lead that team. But I had the money of one of the biggest corporations on Earth backing me up, and my tech was superior.

Unlike the Atomic Seeker, which was a sad copy of Miss's ScatterSwarm, my tech was unstoppable. Innumerable. Self-replicating — able to continue creating more and more of itself with virtually any material. It was no swarm or oversized atom. It was the Regalia, fourth generation shape-shifting tech passed down from my Grandad.

Aside from forming my shield, I also had thick layers of bots covering my person. Not a flight suit like those other suckers who'd already been eliminated had. More like a muscle suit. Suited up, I looked like Batman, a whole five inches taller and looking about fifty pounds heavier. In it, I could run faster, lift heavier objects, and launch myself into controlled propulsion. I could fly.

And ten steps out the back of the bunker, I did just that, absorbing the shield into the Regalia, warping light around me, and zooming off to another hiding spot.

About a quarter mile away, the Atomic Seeker stopped again, this time its protons slowing to a halt.

Crap, it must've seen me. Even in lightwarp, there was a chance the Seeker could detect me thermally. I ducked down into the nearest crater, a big one, laying out on the bottom and disguising the Regalia as overgrown grass.

"Atomic Seeker is over a thousand feet away, seems to be headed in your general direction; if he keeps on this course, he'll just sweep up the ocean side and miss you." The overly intense dorky dramatization was Todd Fowler, the guy so weird, it's easy to forget he's the fourth richest person alive. But, he was a decent navigator, plus CEO/president/founder of my sponsor corporation, so when he asked to be on the team, we didn't have a choice. Also, it was just me and CJ now, so I couldn't be picky.

What a beautiful day for a game, I thought. There were so many moments waiting, so much time spent in the MC^2 when absolutely nothing was happening, and that was good news, but usually it was spent cold, hungry, overly dry or drenched or in some other extreme condition thought of beforehand. But this, this place which housed a turning point in European history, where thousands died and changed the course of the world, was sunny, warm and breezy.

And suddenly across the cloudless blue sky streaked a dark figure. Black with yellow trim. Captain Miss was on the move. Fast, without camouflage, and headed straight for the Seeker.

What's she doing?

I sent a cluster of Regalia up and out, disguised as a dragonfly, to see what that crazy girl was up to. I couldn't help but laugh. Harla - or rather, Captain Miss - would hate it if she heard me calling her a crazy girl. She'd say it was ableist and sexist.

"Changing view to drone cam," the billionaire on the comms said, although he didn't have to since I was the one who sent the drone and I could see that my helmet's view changed. Needless chatter during the game. But I wasn't about to tell *Todd Fowler* that.

Above the level of grass, Captain Miss sped. She held a

runner's pose as if frozen mid stride, knees and arms in a series of right angles. The swarm around her wavered, lighting her and propelling her toward the sea at a...healthy pace.

She wasn't headed after the Seeker, the half-submerged atomic model dredging along the ocean. She was headed to cut the Seeker off at the pass.

What was she doing?

"Finally!" Fowler's voice cracked a bit, giving away his frustration like mine. My view zoomed in. The giant atom ceased spinning, electrons halting. A piece of nucleus shot out from the sheet toward Captain Miss, who was bearing down quickly.

I had no idea why Harla would be giving up like this. She was the most competitive person I knew, annoyingly so. Why would she be forfeiting like this, especially when we were so close?

Harla Gamble had had a stick up her butt about this game since I've known her, how unfair it was, how rigged she thought it was, all of the conspiracies she imagined made the big decisions. And yes, maybe there was one Seeker that almost killed two contestants during one game, and yes, there was one contestant who may have been kidnapped, cryogenically frozen, and impersonated. But I thought Harla's — Captain Miss's — theories were pretty out there.

Was it possible she was eliminating herself from competition in some sort of protest? Sticking it to the man? Handing me the championship just to show how little she cared about it?

The gray splotch shot through the air, headed right for Miss's chest...and missed. It passed right through her, whizzing by my dragonfly drone.

"Search for triangulating projectors," I commanded. It

was just like the projection technology the Regalia used for camouflage— if enough projections crossed paths in an area dense with dust, smoke, or, say, nanobots, you could make a hologram.

Why hadn't I thought of that before?

CJ answered, "Good call. We found some."

"Some?" I'd expected three projectors to triangulate.

"Yeah, fourteen I can see."

Of course. She used extra projection stands so she could hide among them. Captain Miss was in one of those projectors.

"Where?" I asked.

My display converted abruptly into a 3-D computer rendering of the playing arena, a rectangle of mostly grass, bordered on one side with beach and sea. I was the flashing green triangle in the grass. The fourteen flashing red X's making a circle that filled the arena square were the projectors. She was in there somewhere...

"She has me surrounded."

"Wait. What's she going to do?" Fowler was a smart guy, but he ran hot and cold. Even if he appeared so stoic in the media, he was prone to panic in the excitement of the game. I understood; this was his hobby, his trip to the movies.

For me, this was a two-year-long chess game against my nemesis.

"Chay-Z." The voice came from outside my helmet. Loud. Booming. She was blasting this from her projectors. "I'm giving you an out. You and I forfeit, right here and now, and we go talk to the FBI about the Council. My evidence ain't enough; we need a witness. We need you. I'll leave Emily out of this."

As if I'd ever let Emily get involved in this. I finally got a girlfriend outside of this crazy world of the MC2 (well, we met here, but she was officially retired), and now Captain Miss was going to leverage that against me during gameplay? Heck no.

"Thirteen more dragonflies." I barely breathed the words.

"Oh, hells yeah," CJ said. I could hear her laughing. It was as if the game's been boring to her up until now. Last game, CJ was all nerves, but she was trapped in the arena with me and a deadly Seeker. Now that she was safely away, CJ was letting her hair down, so to speak. Her hair was pretty close shaved, so it didn't actually go down. Her attitude this game almost got a chuckle out of me. This was a doozy of a team I had.

Without needing any more direction, CJ sent fourteen dragonflies off toward fourteen projector towers hidden beneath bent light.

"Don't do this, Chay-Z." She wasn't supposed to use my real name, or any mispronouncing of it, during gameplay. But Harla was a hypocrite, always worried about everyone else cheating. "You better come with me now, or I'll take you out."

Over comms CJ updated, "Dragonflies closing in. What are we thinking? EMP? Blow their fuses?"

But before I could answer, Harla pleaded, raising her voice, "Don't be like this, fool!"

Calling me a fool to do what she wants. While not very smart, it was just what I expected, knowing her.

I was about to tell CJ to disrupt her light warps, but that was before the name calling. "Corrosives," I whispered.

CJ lets out another chuckle, this one less swept up in humor and more resigned. "If you say so, Cap."

BWOOOOH

We're interrupted by a noise. No, louder than a noise, a force that hit like a punch. My hands flew to my ears, though they were under my helmet. A booming noise, a vibration that shook through my body, made the ground tremble. The entire arena erupted in a full blown earthquake.

Harla's speakers. They weren't projectors with PA capabilities— they were sonic canons that happened to project.

The sound went on forever, but then suddenly it was gone, and the silence was more jarring. Fowler was screaming over my comms, but I couldn't hear him. I couldn't see straight. My breaths stuttered, and I rolled over. Beside me, the Regalia had become a pile of dark gray ball bearings.

I gasped and gulped air, then coughed and retched. I threw off my helmet, my ears ringing and my eyes stinging with tears. The ringing faded, and I shook uncontrollably, a hollow, humming weakness throbbing in my joints. I fell to the fetal position, eye to eye with the bobcat face of my helmet.

Ahead, someone called out to me, "Captain! Captain!"

It was so confusing; Harla wouldn't call me captain. Was there someone else in the arena? Was Diamonds here? Was Diamonds calling for me? And suddenly I was panicking for the first time this game.

Though my nose was thick with snot from dry heaves, I caught a whiff of a stinging odor. I smelled smoke.

"Captain!" It was Fowler's voice, only distant. No, not distant, but coming from my helmet in front of me. Controlling my hands took focus and strength, but I clutched the helmet in front of me and pulled it over my head, just in time to hear Fowler shout, "You've got to get to the water, Captain!"

I reassembled the Regalia around me, pumping in fresh oxygen, cooling me off and hydrating me. There was one command that we'd programmed into the Regalia, one of its emergency forms that was possible, but we'd never tested it out. It only existed in theory.

"Rocket Man," I commanded the team.

It was an advanced shape CJ and I programmed into the Regalia, one that was entered but never tested.

CJ giggled maniacally in response.

"What is Rocket Man?" Todd Fowler asked.

I didn't answer. No unnecessary chatter. Maybe he caught on because he didn't push it as the white tube formed around me.

Fire rushed toward me just as I was fully encased. Harla was out of control.

"Engage." I blasted off within the rocket into the smoky air, seeing the extent of Harla's tantrum. The entire arena was on fire. But it didn't feel as hot as it should have.

I slowed the rocket to a stop and flattened it beneath me so I could catch my breath. From underneath, she'd only see the sky. From up here, I was on all fours on a sheet of glass a hundred feet in the air.

"Where's the Seeker?" I ask.

"Northeast corner, as far out in the water as he can get."

Good. Was it staying away for its own safety, or was someone controlling the Seeker and letting us fight?

"Did any of the drones land a corrosive?"

"Nah, they were ripped apart by the ultrasonics. Ope. Nevermind. One got through. Eating away at a stand on your eight."

The nanobots that made up the Regalia were self-replicating, which meant you could set them into a concrete wall, and they'd break it down to make more and more nanobots. But if you set them to corrosive, they just ate through things. Chewed up the concrete and rebar and spit out dust.

The queen bee, Captain Miss, wherever she actually was, had divided up the swarm into the fourteen parts capable of projecting light, sound, and evidently, Hellfire.

She'd flipped the game. The Seeker was in the corner, unable to search through the flames, and now I was hiding from her. Aggressive to the point of bending the rules. If I was found by the Seeker, I could run from it, outsmart it, or outmaneuver the blob. But could I outmaneuver Harla?

"Set it back to replicate."

If Harla was going to play this aggressively, fine. Hit me with an ultrasonic cannon? The Regalia would eat the dang ScatterSwarm. In for a nickel, in for a dime.

"We've got to find her!" Fowler was back to full tilt panic.

CJ kept it together. "Should we disperse the extinguisher?"

"Nah, that'll just give us away. Plus, it ain't real fire. She'll give up on it."

"It ain't real fire?"

"No, that's completely projection."

CJ chimed in, "One of Miss's projectors has been disabled. Dispersing bots to the nearest two projectors."

"Nearest four."

"Four? I'm not sure how effective-"

"Make it so," I insisted.

Harla wouldn't wait to smoke me out while I attacked a third of her tech. She would panic. And without Diamonds on her team, no one could calm her down once she got agitated.

The smoke cleared and the fires died down, revealing burnt grass and evenly scorched ground. So the fire wasn't completely projection.

Of course, Miss vented heat from her tech across the arena to hide her thermal signature. But that's what you got from cheap tech that wasn't meant to shape shift. So I switched my vision to thermal. Hot air and smoke blinded my screen red, pulsating out to take up the entire field of vision, then ebbing erratically, giving peeks of the arena.

There.

I tapped the Regalia board beneath me, essentially a giant screen I was riding like some magic carpet. Bingo. There was her heat signature, a blur of red shaped like a person. I shifted the Regalia into a shape not unlike the rocket, now plummeting through smoke into the ground, crashing nose and head-first.

Tunneling capabilities had been CJ's idea. She must've been really happy back at mission control as I was a good four foot down now with a drill for a helmet and conveyor limbs. Pretty much flying underground, like Bugs Bunny, or some kind of sandworm.

Half my view was a digital read of the arena representing me as a green arrow flashing its way through the ground. Had to use that to steer clear of craters. The other half showed me two more of Miss's mini-towers falling. I'd flush her out eventually, I thought as I swerved around a huge crater.

Something grabbed my leg.

How? I was four feet underground. Plus, my leg was pretty much coated in conveyor belts. But something, or someone, had somehow clamped down on my calf.

"What's that? What happened?" asked Fowler.

I ignored him and commanded the Regalia, "Boosters."

Usually that would send the majority of my nanobots to my legs to form a pair of synced rockets. But underground, the Regalia suit and helmet demanded a larger percentage of the bots, plus the ones making up the drill ahead of me. I couldn't fire myself into the dirt.

So what resulted were mini-boosters formed around whatever still had me by the leg.

"Put more bots on the drill; your boosters are working for crap." Of course CJ wanted me to use the boosters.

I shouldn't have listened to her, but I did. I turned my boosters off and sent the bots up the outside of the Regalia suit to form the drill head. But as I did, the thing holding onto my leg pulled.

It didn't just pull. It *launched* me.

I was flung legs first out of the dirt, flying through the air at an astounding speed. Grass flew by, but the G-forces were too great to even let me look down at my feet to see whatever it was that still had a hold of me.

As if he could read my mind, Fowler changed my vision to a wide angle. The best way to describe it, I was manacled to a missile flying toward the Seeker. Behind me, the towers converged, and Captain Miss materialized, arms crossed, her curvy hip cocked to the side, and even though she was in her blade-shaped helmet, I just knew she was smirking.

I send bots from my suit to start working on the manacle. "Status on replication?" I asked.

But instead of an answer through my helmet comm, I got my answer from the playing arena.

Harla roared. My replicating bots were breaking her tech down. The missile on my leg faltered, not a hundred yards away from the Seeker.

Her cocky pose broken, matte black bits of Harla's suit sloughed off. Her helmet cracked, and shards fell away, a swath of her face now visible— dark complexion, furious brown eyes, and groomed eyebrows giving away just a touch of fear.

The Regalia was on her suit, corroding it, turning it into more of my bots.

The Seeker finally caught up on what was happening, understanding that the dangerous threat of the fire was gone. It halted again in firing mode, then shot.

Not as fast as projectile paintballs at first, the blob of bots the Seeker sent out gained speed as it flew right for me.

The manacle at my foot gave way as the Regalia ate through it.

I shifted my drill head to boosters and ignited.

The Seeker's bots whizzed by Harla's missile as I pushed off to fly free.

She was far away now, almost a half mile away. Harla pulled off her helmet and was desperately shooting a freezing ray onto the ripped parts of her suit. But she could only slow the Regalia down now; she could no longer stop it.

Her busy little bees rushed to save her, abandoning their structures as the towers. Clouds of the Swarm enveloped her, protecting her exposed skin.

She was on the ropes, and I wasn't about to quit. I threw everything I had at her. Literally.

I ejected from the missile, falling out of the tube, falling out of my own suit made of bots. And I sent the whole thing right at her.

"Set it all to replicate."

"Captain, the Seeker's still on you."

I smiled. Of course it was. But even out there, in the arena, at the very climax of the game, I knew what the judges would say.

Her swarm had collected completely, encasing her like an armored statue, black with yellow flecks. My Regalia missile didn't hit her, didn't collide with her, it splashed against her.

The impact knocked Captain Miss on her ass, now covered in the sticky mass of bots. Dull gray bots the size of ball bearings attached to the black and yellow bees of the ScatterSwarm.

And Harla, no longer the anonymous Captain Miss with her mean mug exposed, sat coated in the viscous gray goo.

The tagging pellets from the Seeker didn't burst, they just shot right into the tangle that was both Regalia and ScatterSwarm.

"Game's over," Fowler spoke breathlessly.

"Captain, you're not going to believe this," CJ began.

I didn't even need to hear CJ finish her sentence. Across the arena from where Harla sat in a mud hole of techno sludge, I already knew what had happened. I planned it. So I caught everyone else up.

"They need more time to decide who's won."

Chapter 2

C hapter 2

CJ paced back and forth. The little conference room was too small for her, especially when she was this anxious. Todd Fowler wasn't that much better, strumming his fingers on the table, constantly shifting, fidgeting with his hoodie strings. But at least he wasn't really in the room, only his hologram. CJ was present, lumbering about and huffing in the same air as me.

Who knew where billionaires like Todd Fowler set up their telecommunications hubs? If it were a joke, the punchline would be "wherever they want to."

But Todd Fowler was no joke, even if he was thousands of miles away. He started his own company, Powers Limited, in his garage, and spent billions of dollars sponsoring my team and investing in my tech. I never knew what the prizes for first place were, but they had to be worth it. The Throne and its later models, the Scepter and the Regalia, were not just bleeding edge tech, they also ran on enough kilojoules to power a small city. Enough to invest another fortune into the Lack, the portable power source that may be a doorway to alternate dimensions. So Fowler was as deep into this as me.

And if the guy who footed the bill that let me fly the greatest tech in history wanted to sit in on the team, I pulled up a chair for him. It didn't hurt that he was mass-producing my invention, the floatboard, just in time for Christmas this year.

If CJ could actually build some of the tech Grandad had planned, I'd be winning games for Fowler and Powers, Limited for years.

The stuff Grandad left behind, schematics and prototypes he and Harpreet couldn't build, was always on my mind. I'd only had access to his official training footage, no files. And his only engineering partner, Dr. Harpreet Verma, was now chin-deep in lawsuits with Fowler and his mega-corporation, Powers, Limited. So that was the prize Fowler gave me for letting him on the team: access to Grandad's pipe dreams, his brainstorms, his big ideas. His old hard drive.

And it was because of those big ideas that I wasn't worried about the outcome of the game. Plus, I was enjoying a really good sandwich.

CJ was talking it through out loud. "She was in possession of the tech when it was tagged, and possession is like fifteen sixteenths of the law."

"That's not the saying," Fowler corrected.

"If I had access to my computers, I could see how much Miss's tech was still intact and what percentage the Regalia had replicated."

"And what about the raw materials the Regalia had already broken down?"

"And what about raw material? What percentage of all that... goo was raw material the Regalia hadn't put to use yet? Why are they taking so long to decide? And why are you so damn calm, Captain?!"

"Ceej," I said between bites of a sandwich. Honestly, the first thing I ate after a hard-fought game was always the best tasting thing in the world. This was a hot ham and swiss. "If they're not in here, then they're in there with her...to let her decide. And Harla Gamble has a choice."

I took another bite. Dang, this bread was soft. "Either she gets the tech — both the ScatterSwarm and the Regalia — which means she gets the Lack, by admitting she was tagged." I wiped mustard from the corner of my mouth. "Or she can win."

Either way, I had Grandad's theoretical tech to fall back on for game tech.

"Is that why you insisted the Regalia self-replicate?" CJ was catching on.

I smiled and took another bite. It was a tech competition, after all. If I couldn't beat Harla at her aggressive gameplay, then I used tech that would. She must have been livid.

But, I wouldn't have to wonder about her thought process. Me and my billionaire buddy had Harla Gamble bugged to the gills. I could always go back and listen.

And I always went back to listen.

* * *

So while I enjoyed my sandwich, in a conference room identical to ours, Harla Gamble, Luis Escondido, General Wilder from NASA, and Secretary of State Esau Holter sat around the table as Harla got angrier.

"He wants me to choose to lose to him! Tell me how much NASA wins with first place, and I'll tell you whether I was tagged or not!"

General Wilder had an overly calm voice, like podcasts designed to put people to sleep, "Those budgets aren't out, Captain. And income to NASA won't affect the team's budget."

"So there may not be any money for another Swarm," Escondido warned, leaned back in his chair, arms folded.

"That's fine. I could beat those fools naked with one arm tied behind my back!"

"Harla." General Wilder furrowed a brow to show he thought that was too far.

"Fine." She stuck a finger out at Holter and continued, "If I say it's mine...and lose... NASA gets all the tech?"

Holter said, "Our crew managed to separate some of the... mass."

"How much?"

"There's about fifteen um...bees, identifiable tech you'll get back no matter what. And fifty pounds of identified Regalia."

"Fifty pounds?" Harla dumped. "So he gets his tech back no matter what?"

"He does get that back."

"And how much...gray goop?"

Holter checked a report in front of him. "The mass is about one hundred fifty pounds."

Escondido chimed in, "And that should be all Regalia soon, if the bots have continued replicating."

"We froze them," Holter assured everyone. "With temperature as well as a magnetic field."

"Can I see it?" Harla asked.

"No," Holter answered.

"Can I look at last year's team budget?"

"No," Holter answered for General Wilder and NASA.

"And you can't tell me anything about the prize."

"No. But I can tell you that if you don't decide in the next minute," Holter shot his cuff and looked at his expensive gold watch, "I'm rescinding the offer to make that decision and taking it to Captain Kiddo."

"This is some BS, and you know it. Chase came at me knowing the Seeker would take him out. You can wear your fancy uniform and use your official words, but you were a player too. And you know he did me dirty out there!"

"That's why I came to you to decide."

Harla paused in her pacing, hunched over, and put her hands on her knees. The dilemma put a pained look on her face.

Escondido broke the silence. "So what is it, Harla? Do you win the game, or keep the tech?"

"Damnit Chase!" She clapped her hands violently. Quietly, more breathing than speaking, she said, "I'll take the loss. The tech comes back with me to NASA."

And she left the room for her post-game physical by the team's new medic, Dr. Bird.

✳ ✳ ✳

The award presentation was always such a solemn affair. Sure, there were a good amount of audience members in attendance, all politely clapping for each name read at the podium (after all, captains, their support teams, and liaisons for sponsors add up with ten separate teams), but this was no World Series win. No one would be charging the mound for a hug. No one would be crying as they slide to their knees or ripping off their jerseys. No one announced they were going to Disneyland.

After the last couple of years with teenagers entering the game and making it to the dais as a part of the top three, there'd been a little more celebration, but the award presentation showed that at its heart, the MC2 was a boring military exercise. Even if I walked through fire, fought a missile, and tunnelled underground at 60 miles per hour to win.

By now, I was used to this rigmarole: portal from the arena back to DARPA headquarters (or the new one since the last MC2 destroyed the previous HQ), go through another physical, and change for the award presentation. Of course, there were more handshakes after winning. The team even had some champagne I wasn't allowed to drink. I never knew exactly how much prize money I was bringing into Powers, Limited with a win, but it was enough for Todd Fowler to open a bottle of booze older than all three of us combined.

I had on DARPA med regulation scrubs over my knee-length white wetsuit and bobcat helmet. I threw on my gold cross necklace Mom had given me on my last birthday and mustered up some swagger as we took the elevator to the presentation.

I'll admit, the room noticed when we entered. Good. The expansive theatre had teams spread out and seated in three row clumps. NASA, Harla's team, immediately stopped talking and turned, all of them cool in shades and black masks. Well, I thought they looked pretty dumb, wearing sunglasses inside.

I hope they hated seeing me win. I hope Harla ugly-cried, and Diamonds had to comfort her over the phone, lie to her, tell her she was still good at the game, as good as me.

We grabbed seats by the front, as far away from team NASA as we could. Besides, I had to be close to the stage to claim my victory.

"What do you think of these vids?" Fowler always had footage cued up to show off. Under secret Twitter handles and YouTube channels, someone had been uploading videos from previous games and developing a following.

I never knew exactly how the MC Squared paid for itself. I know it was a patent machine, making the camouflage of the future, of tomorrow's tomorrow. But who was buying these? Who was spending millions of dollars to outfit one soldier?

Of course, there was some shadiness around the game; it was full of soldiers and spies, after all. Maybe it held some secrets people didn't want found. Even with the game back in the hands of the Department of Defense, all the attention must've been making higher-ups, Secretary of Defense Holter included, anxious.

One thing Harla and I agreed on was we both thought Fowler was the leak. She'd claimed it was me for a while, but that may have just been leverage to move me against the Council. But the fact was, too many videos were out now. It was too large an operation for me to do it anonymously. There was someone super smart or super rich putting those videos out, and Todd Fowler was both.

My guess was he figured the US government couldn't keep a secret like the game the way the old Council had. And, of course, Uncle Sam couldn't risk showing their military secrets on YouTube. So when that day came, my bet was Todd Fowler was putting himself in a position to take the game over.

In the theatre, the hall of the awards ceremony, the footage he was showing me was pretty badass — Harla throwing Aiden

Run into the ocean, Harla shooting flames out of her hand onto the grassy arena, Harla sending her swarm into a crater to blast me out of there with a land-to-air missile.

Holter took the stage. In his dress uniform, he'd filled out a bit. Retirement from the game looked good on him. Last time he was onstage for one of these, he got in a fight with a naval officer. Now he took the officer's place, announcing each of us by our captain and team names while handing out ribbons.

Harla strutted to the winners' platform with all of the swagger of a hip hop billionaire. You would have thought she won instead of placing second behind me. But her whole team - Escondido, Dr. Bird, New Doc, Kevin the Intern, and Brandi the intern (Kevin the Intern wasn't an intern anymore, but the name and title fit him like a suit) - were all in black hats, hoodies, sunglasses, surgical masks, and slick black Adidas pants. Harla herself had on a shiny black robe, like she was a boxer. Her faceless helmet was retired for the day, so she was in a black surgical mask and aviators, all under a hoodie.

They called my name, and I made sure to cross her line of vision as I took my spot at the top. Okay, maybe I was staring her down a bit. But she didn't look back. In fact, as I scaled to the top of the platform, Harla walked offstage.

I don't know what I expected. Maybe to see her hurt, to show me a little respect, but when I saw the backs of her whole team, I couldn't take it.

Yawning the wildcat mouth open to expose my face, I grabbed the mic from General Holter.

"I just wanted to take a moment to thank all of the competitors."

It worked. Harla paused a few feet up the aisle, her team waiting at the back of the theatre. But none of them turned to face me. Fine.

I spoke at the back of Harla's head, the closest to the stage.

"The MC squared is getting better and better each game, and it's because of y'all."

From the aisle at the back, it seemed like Escondido was about to say something, but Harla raised a hand to keep him quiet. I was getting to them. So I twisted the knife a little.

"And especially, I want to thank Captain Miss. I believe she has proven since entering the competition that she is a leader to be reckoned with."

At this, Harla surprised me. She turned and faced me, still sporting sunglasses, face stone-still and unreadable.

I don't know why I liked to poke the bear so much. After the previous game, I thought I wasn't mad anymore. I'd gone too far to win, crossed a line I couldn't go back from. And I was genuinely sorry. I knew it was wrong.

So why did I have to insult Harla after I forced her to lose to me? Why was I like this?

"It is an honor to compete with you and to consider you my peer. It's an honor to compete in the game at all. And whoever is leaking footage online is breaking a sacred honor and..."

Surprisingly fast, Harla sprinted into the edge of the stage. It was so fast, it felt like she was rushing me, but then she walked around to the front of the stage. She stopped to stand below me, and for a moment, I thought she was going to shake my hand. I relaxed. Was she going to say something in the mic? Would I give up the mic and let her?

Instead she pulled my feet out from under me. I awkwardly flailed and landed on my ass and lower back, then tumbled backward behind the winner's platform.

It hurt. My back and my pride.

There was laughter in the audience.

Lying there uncomfortably on my neck, legs still in the air, I wanted to punch Harla in the face. Or push her. Or scream. Or something. For a second, I wished I had killed her two games ago.

I took a breath, still awkwardly on my back.

Now, everyone would see what a bully Harla was. Heck, everyone did see. As my teammates and some DARPA officials came over to me, I took my time. I played it up; maybe I'd hit my head. Maybe I was concussed. Everyone had seen it, I was attacked. While Harla and her team moseyed out of the theatre with second place, everyone else was worried about the innocent victim who was attacked. The champion.

* * *

Well, I wasn't attacked in front of *everybody*. Diamonds wasn't there. They were never going to step another foot in the game again. Or at least that's what they said.

The game had a way of sucking us in, no matter what we wanted. Maybe Diamonds was right. Maybe it was destiny.

And they hadn't managed to separate themselves from the game completely. They still cared. More than they wanted, I bet.

All of the rituals were to keep them calm. They tried getting Harla into rituals herself, but to no avail.

In the exercise room, they'd change the screens away from their dad's sports and stock market presets to their screens of music videos. Yoga. Stretches. Two miles on the treadmill.

Forty minutes jiu jitsu. Mat work. Weights. Heavy bag. And then five hundred meters breaststroke in the treadmill pool.

Getting out of the pool, toweling off and removing a swim cap, Diamonds checked their phone again. Nothing.

The game was still going on.

They went onto more jiu jitsu. It was new to them and used muscles they didn't know existed. Dr. Bird had recommended a place.

This was just like Diamonds. They had to find a way to stay in control. They had to. Otherwise, panic attacks. Total breakdowns.

I caused their last anxiety episode. It was the worst mistake of my life. Remembering it, it didn't even seem like me doing it. Like I was watching someone else, like I was as helpless as Diamonds, tied down to be a decoy. It was easy to see that waiting to hear Harla was safe at the end of another game was triggering to Diamonds.

More jiu jitsu.

Another mile on the treadmill.

Purging the anxiety through sweat and work.

An alert dinged and slowed down their stride. Stumbling, they almost bit it while clamoring to get off and to their phone.

Dinged again. But Diamonds knew that alert wasn't a text message.

There'd been another leak. Another piece of footage anonymously posted. This was on a 4chan thread about US military conspiracy theories.

Since the leaks began, Diamonds had set out algorithms to do the looking for them. All major social media sites with video posts. They ran image searches for Harla in her game gear. Escondido had provided them some gameplay images to search for the other players and their tech. And, of course, they set their computer to search for images of me.

But it wasn't me they found. It was Harla, tearing it up on the French coast, the game that just ended, or that was still going on as far as Diamonds knew.

This was different from the other leaks. This video was long, uninterrupted footage from a distance, the wide view.

Despite working out for the past few hours, Diamonds only had a flush on their cheeks interrupting their cream-white skin. But seeing Harla in the game...and on 4 dang Chan? Diamonds went fully red faced, fists curling in on themselves.

When they were watching the video for the second time, it froze, interrupted by another alert, a little clip from a Fall Out Boy song.

That was an alert for a text from Harla.

"He set me up. Lose to him or lose the swarm."

Diamonds didn't wait to find out any more. They must have known what Harla picked. In a furious spin, they whipped their arm with a low, grunting roar. The phone sailed across their family's home gym and lodged into the nearest flatscreen tv.

That's where the feed ended. My access to Diamonds depended on Powers, Limited's ability to access their phone.

Chapter 3

C hapter 3

"Now Chase, just calm down and have a seat. Drink your water. You sure you don't want lunch? They can portal anything here. *Anything.*" General Esau Holter had a much calmer demeanor in his cushy office than he'd ever had in the arena. The kind of calm that was just making me angrier in my current mood.

"You had a room full of soldiers, but they can't stop a fight? An attack?" I was pacing, gesticulating wildly. I'd held it together while being humiliated in front of the entire theatre of participants. But once that door closed, I laid into Holter. The old man could take it. He still owed me. He would until the end of his days, as far as I was concerned.

"They're soldiers, not bouncers," Holter said. "They'd shoot you before they broke up a fight."

"Then why isn't there security at these events?"

"It's a top-secret classified event."

I let out a forced laugh. "Tell that to the millions of views I get on YouTube."

"We're tracking the leaks."

"That's what you said six months ago."

"You know, some people actually treat me with respect," he said, gesturing to the medals and pins on his chest. He was still in his parade dress uniforms or whatever they're called after the award ceremony. "Once I reached a certain level, I thought I was done getting chewed out. At least for things that I didn't do."

"And how do we know *you're* not the leak?"

"Chase, I am the highest ranking soldier in the US armed forces. If I'm not to be trusted, we're all up the creek."

I sat in a slump. It was obvious Holter was just talking me down to shut me up. He wasn't going to do anything about Harla's attack.

"If the next leak is of Harla flipping me on my ass during the awards ceremony, I'll quit."

He angrily raised an eyebrow in reply. "Chase, I don't understand the falling out between you and Captain Miss, but you two are the leaders in this...new age of the MC Squared. If I'm going to keep the game safe and use it to develop camouflage technology to keep our soldiers safe, I can't have infighting. And like it or not, the profile on our little game is rising. If the world's first impression of the MC Squared is a couple teenagers in a fistfight, we're going to get shut down. Again, I don't know what happened, but I'll tell you this much: I don't care. You two are the best captains we got in the game. You don't have to like each other, but you have to stop fighting."

I dropped my voice. "Have I been the one who's fighting?"

"I watch gameplay, Chase. Both of you are taking this too far."

"I'll take this as far as I have to in order to win. Are we done here?" I stand, acting like I wasn't the one who demanded to talk.

"You can leave whenever you like, Chase. Thanks to your little scuffle earlier, I have a full day ahead talking everybody down."

There was something he'd stopped himself from saying.

"Is Harla here?"

"I spoke with you Chase. You had a chance to speak your mind. She gets a chance, too."

"Why does she need talking down? Seems like she blew off all the steam she wanted at the ceremony."

"Well, some people have more concerns than that."

So that's what this was about. Harla wanted the opportunity to talk to Secretary Holter one-on-one about her conspiracy theories. She was still convinced her mysterious "Council" was pulling the strings, even with DARPA taking over the game again. Maybe Harla didn't care about the newest leak. Maybe the attack was just about getting a sit-down with the Secretary.

She attacked me knowing I'd flip out and insist on her being reprimanded. She used me. And I was so predictable.

"There anything else, Chase?"

"No, sir." I made the attempt to leave cordially and professionally. "Thank you for your time, and I look forward to the next Military Camouflage Challenge."

"We look forward to seeing what you and your team come up with. And be careful- not just with the tech. There are some who prefer the old days of the Council running things." The three-star general led me to the door, grabbed the knob to open it for me, then paused. "Oh, before I forget...did you still want that letter of recommendation?"

Damn. I still wanted to be mad, but Holter knew he had me. A letter of rec from the Secretary of Defense was my ticket into any college I wanted.

I softened. "If you're offering, that'd be great."

"I'll mail you a couple copies today. What schools have you narrowed it down to?"

"If I told you, I'd have to kill you." I winked at him. Now that he wasn't my mortal enemy, I kinda liked the old General.

"Atta boy."

So I left his office and goopgated back to the lab at Powers, Limited. It was where we built the Regalia, and where we were building my next tech, Grandad's last invention he never saw made into prototype. Thanks to Harpreet's schematics and CJ's programming, we'd managed to assemble the impossible technology of the Crown.

We didn't know what it did or how to work it, but we knew it was the culmination of Grandad's life's work. And I was going to figure it out.

* * *

"Harla Gamble." When Holter dropped his voice down and took his time, he grinded the words into dusty gravel more than said them. "Harla. Freaking. Gamble."

Stone-faced, looking at nothing in particular dead in front of her, she raised an eyebrow.

"Why is it that every single time there's trouble outside of gameplay directly linked to gameplay, your name comes up?"

"Ain't you supposed to address me as Captain?"

"No ma'am. You are a civilian, and I'm not on your team. I'll call you Sally Tuesday if I please. Now what is it going to take for you to fly straight and stop disrupting events around the game?"

"What is it going to take to stop gameplay leaks?"

"I'm tired of hearing about it, Harla!" Holter's face turned crimson, and his jowls shook with the loud, angry grating of his words. "I have offered solution after solution, and nothing is good enough for your team."

"We all know who's doing it."

"Then where is the proof? Harla, no one was happier than me when DARPA took the MC Squared back from the Council. And then a week passed. And you spent that whole damn week tearing me a new one about what I *should* be doing and what you *think* is happening. And when it wasn't you, it was you sending your attack dog Lieutenant Escondido after me. And I asked you for one thing."

"To find the leak?"

"To play the game, Harla. To play the game and nothing else. But you had to keep sticking your nose where it didn't belong. You and your team of civilians." He spoke it like a curse word. Sometimes it seemed like Holter barely tolerated Harla Gamble.

"Why you talking like this? What's happening?"

The General pulled out his phone and started to play classical music loudly as he spoke quietly.

Did he think I wouldn't still be able to eavesdrop? With *my* tech? But thinking was never the General's strong suit.

"No one's happy about the new leaks. There's been talk of pulling the plug on the whole program."

"Crap. Ain't there anything you can do?"

"I'm not happy about the leaks either, but I can't do anything without proof. You getting a hunch Chase is involved isn't enough. Besides, he saved my life."

"*We* saved your life."

"Fine, we all saved each others' lives! I'm not going to keep him out of the game without proof. With all the attention, there are some people pushing to privatize the game, sell it, and cut our losses. Contract it out to a third party."

"That would be just like the Council running things again!"

"I'm not sure. But I wouldn't be able to touch the thing, and I'd worry about safety more than ever. So, I've been trying to float a new idea that I hope can save the MC Squared."

Why hadn't Holter brought this up with me? I was the dang reigning champion and he didn't think I'd like to know that the whole game was in jeopardy? What was it about Harla Gamble that made people open up to her like this?

"What?"

"Declassification. Just like the other DARPA programs. We could release footage under our own control, show the world what we're up to."

"But wouldn't that give away the tech?"

"Maybe. But if we don't, the leaks will. And who knows when the leaks will include tech schematics or a player's private info?"

Harla clenched up. The idea of losing anonymity on a large scale always scared her. I don't know why. Who cares? We're nobodies.

"This way, we control the flow of information."

"And you edit one of the games into a season of reality tv?"

"Have you seen yourself play the game, Harla? You're making this a full-contact sport. And the games are much shorter since you've begun playing."

"How long until y'all start feeding me lines or asking me to take a fall? Or stop in the middle of a hot pursuit and do some toothpaste commercial?"

"That's not what we're talking about here."

"Yet," she corrected him. "If this turns into something that makes money, then someone is going to try to change it to make more money."

"That's not what *I'm* talking about here."

"And you ain't going to be around forever."

"Thank you."

"What? *I* plan on playing for years. Decades. And these decisions y'all make now could make life real tough for me once you're gone and the next guy's here wearing that suit with all these broaches."

Ugh. The thought of competing against Harla for decades was exhausting.

One of the General's hands went up to the medals on his uniform. "I'm just trying to keep us open for business at this point. There's nothing stopping us from shutting everything down, classifying it as top secret, confiscating all tech, and selling it off to third world freedom fighters."

"Man, don't even joke about that."

"It's not what I want, Harla."

They sat in silence.

"Can I get something to eat?"

"Y'all got fruit or pb and j or nuts or something?"

"Got any allergies?"

"Lactose intolerant a little."

"I got spicy peanuts." He slid a bowl across his desk to her.

"Thanks. So when do you think they'll decide what to do?"

"We," he corrected. "I get a say in this, too."

"Who all is deciding then? Any civilians? Are you sure this ain't just the Council version 2.0?"

I imagined Todd Fowler would be a voice in the room when it came to big decisions. And if I played my cards right, did everything asked of me, it could be me one day, calling the shots.

"You wouldn't believe who's involved if I told you," he said, dead serious. "I'm going to suspend the game and force the Pentagon to make a decision. Otherwise, these drama queens'll drag their feet until there's a budget emergency and they have to make an impulsive decision. No, I'll force their hand and suspend the program. But you didn't hear that from me."

"So should I plan on a spring game?"

"I'm hoping we'll decide by then, but who knows?"

"K. I'll keep training then. Got marathons coming up anyway."

"When did you start running marathons?"

"This year. I got a fifteen mile mud run in two weeks. 'S why I got to keep eating. These are fire, by the way." She took another handful of peanuts.

"Harla, if you want to have a long career captaining in the game, you need to adjust your style a bit. Go easier on your own body. Go easy on yourself. Just take it easier than you have been. And maybe lay off the relentless pursuit of the truth. Right now, there's someone out there who has a problem with you and the solution they settled on is leaking footage of you. Maybe it's because you always think folks are against you. You're always fighting no matter what. Let sleeping dogs lie. The Council's been disassembled, removed from their perch, but these are still powerful people. Dangerous people.”

“Yeah. Thanks for the tip, big guy. I’mma keep training, getting in shape for spring. I’mma get you your proof, too. Hopefully, we can cut the problem out of the game, and there won’t have to be a drastic decision.”

“I’m afraid we’re past that.”

“I don’t care. I’ll get you your proof. And then, no matter who’s running the show, I’ll be out here shutting down fools. The Queen. And I’m not gonna let you yell at me and disrespect me like that next time.”

“Yeah, sorry, I was just speaking to Chase, and he got me all wound up.”

Good.

“He alright?” Her voice dropped. “He hit his head?”

I almost wondered if she hit *her* head, asking about me.

“No, I think he faked it.”

“Little punk. You know he’s with Emily now? Miss Mars?”

“Are you serious? No. I don’t believe you. Why would you even say that? It’s not funny. It’s not. Holy crud, he is? Is that what this vendetta of yours is about? Are you jealous?”

“Hell no, fool!”

“Do you think he’s under her control?”

“He may well be. But he’s done plenty on his own to know to stay the hell away from me.”

“I remember when you two were friends.”

“Do you? Cause *I* don’t remember that. And I definitely don’t remember seeing you around back then.”

“Just cause I wasn’t there doesn’t mean I wasn’t listening.”

“Creepy.”

“You play hide and seek with adults for a living.”

“And I’m the best at it.”

"Then I say good luck to you...whenever the next game is."

"Make sure it's soon, Esau."

"Keep your head down, Harla Gamble. Trouble's too good at finding you."

"Bye, Esau."

* * *

The spa was ultra-swanky, the bottom two floors of a luxury hotel in San Francisco. They'd all gone as a team thanks to Escondido's recommendation back in Harla's first game. She'd always had a tough time with stress, piling it onto herself, clenching her broad shoulders until they looked like they were up past her ears.

Evidently, Harla liked something about the spa. She and Diamonds went after every game now. Even though after games, she had to point out every bruise and tender spot that her deep brown skin tone didn't give away to the masseuse.

As they settled onto their massage chairs, Diamonds played DJ, choosing K-Pop ballads on their phone while Harla poured almond chai for the both of them.

"To another game survived," Diamonds said as they tapped their plastic cup against Harla's.

But Harla wasn't having it, she wasn't relaxed and judging by her chewing her lip and patting her head, she had enough nervous energy to power the ScatterSwarm. "I know you worry about my safety, D. But I don't play to survive. I don't want no participation trophy."

"And that's what you consider coming in second?"

"You don't understand, D. Wonderbread tricked me, he-"

"Can we have a nice day without talking about Chase Hawkins?"

"Sorry, D. I just get so mad."

Was it just me under her skin? I'd like to think so, but maybe these leaks she and Holter talked about were beginning to wear on her.

"I know, Harly. That's why we do spa day."

"You're right."

The masseuses got to work. It had been easier to book a couple's massage, and they settled into silence...or K-Pop rather. And even I had to agree it was nice to see the two of them relaxing without talking about how much they hated me.

* * *

Each in towels, Diamonds' hair slicked back, Harla's in a shower cap, they sat in the steam room.

Diamonds said, "Did you ask for a letter of recommendation?"

"The convo didn't go great."

"No surprise there. He's a stubborn old man used to giving orders, and you're no good at taking orders."

"We do get along at some level."

"You're both great competitors."

"Yeah, too bad we never had a chance to ball. Maybe he'll come out of retirement." Harla took a deep breath and changed the subject. "When do you go back to Boston?"

"Monday," Diamonds rolled their eyes. "Don't remind me.

Oh, that reminds me, I need to fill my prescription before I leave."

"Sure. You want to come have dinner with my folks tonight?"

"Sounds good."

Harla settled back against the tile wall, eyes closed, then peeking one open at Diamonds and laughing. "You know, if you're gonna check me out, you can at least mention how skinny I look."

"I wasn't..." Diamonds flustered and blushed. They began again, talking slower. "You're lip's split."

"I know."

"I didn't know you broke your nose."

"Technically, you can't break your nose because it's cartilage."

"You broke your nose." Diamonds said, met with silence. They kept their eyes on Harla. "And you don't dress to show your shoulder anymore."

"What? How can you tell?"

"I haven't noticed the scar before. You had shoulder surgery."

"So?"

"So? You used to tell me these things. I didn't have to notice them."

"I used to see you every day, too. I'm sorry. I didn't want you to worry."

"Ha. Good luck."

"You notice too damn much."

"I notice you aren't code switching as much anymore."

I gasped just listening. Harla always made race such a thing. Why would Diamonds get into a conversation about race with

Harla *on purpose?*

"Is that woke for 'I don't talk black enough for you'?"

"It's woke for 'you're relying less on the defense mechanisms against uncomfortable situations by talking more like your Dad, who is your ideal for a dominant force.'"

"Diamonds, how much longer are you going to be studying psychology?"

"Like at least seven years."

"You can't cut me up like that for the next seven years. Anyway, you're way off. Mom's much more dominating."

"I said 'ideal.'"

Harla stared at Diamonds stone-faced for a second before relaxing back again. "You're going to be a delight at dinner."

* * *

Now in fluffy white robes getting pedicures, one or both of them seemed to be asleep until Diamonds said suddenly, "Snap, I can't do tonight. I'm supposed to grab dinner with Luis."

"For what?"

"Just to catch up. Haven't seen him in a while..."

"Tell him I say hi. You can come Saturday or Sunday, too. We sit down for dinner every night."

"That's the weirdest thing I've ever heard."

"Really? Not the land cephalopod?"

"Point taken, D."

They sat in silence as women finished with their feet and toes and showed them to tables for manicures.

"Well, *I* think I look skinny."

"If that makes you happy," Diamonds said as they picked out a color. Black. Go figure.

It got quiet again.

Then Diamonds' phone beeped an alert.

"Oh snap, they just posted a new vid." Harla knew exactly what the alert meant. There'd been a lot of videos leaked, a couple while she was with Diamonds. Harla took a breath to steady herself. "You think I'm in this one, too?"

"Of course," Diamonds said flatly. "You're in all of them."

They looked at each other for a moment, the only movement the frantic hands of the pair of manicurists.

With a quick apology to her nails lady, Harla pulled her hand back, wet nails and all, and grabbed Diamonds' brand new phone, streaking smudges of red fingernail polish like windshield wipers spreading bug guts.

"Oh my God, that's my face. That's my face! That fool showed my face. Do you think anyone will recognize me?"

Harla's theory of Todd Fowler running a conspiracy against her had grown to include me as the game's leak. After all, she was in the leaked footage, not me. She thought since we became rivals at the time the leaks began, it must have been me. It wasn't. But that didn't stop her or Diamonds from feeding into the fantasy.

"Most likely, but it may be localized. I'm going to run some searches off the image from the vid and see if anything pops up." Diamonds went to work on their phone.

"You can do that?"

"It's just Google."

"Are you finding anything?"

"Basic racist Google, confusing your picture with dozens of

other black women..."

"And?"

"And your photo doesn't show up until like the twenty fifth position."

"But I show up? I'm going to kill him."

So much for a day between Harla and Diamonds without me being hated on. But even I had to admit, the leak seemed obsessed with Harla.

"I'm looking at those now. It may not be as bad as you think."

Another alert. This time, Harla's phone blasting country music. "Oh crap, that's my sister."

"There's no way it's about the video."

"Of course it's about the video." She dramatically answered, "Ahem, Hello?"

Her sister's voice was pitched high and fast. "Tyler said you're in a video with a flamethrower and you shot a guy with a missile?"

"What? Who said that? That's wild. A flamethrower? That's crazy. And I'm sure I didn't hit a guy with a missile."

"Harla."

"Nakea."

"You know I have to tell Mom and Dad."

"Hold up, you ain't gotta say nothing!"

"Harla, don't talk like that; it dumbs you down."

"Don't talk to me like I'm stupid, Nakea."

"Don't shoot flamethrowers on YouTube, Harla."

"Is that what you called me for? Did you even watch the video?"

Nakea clicked her tongue. "Like I have time to watch your dumb YouTube videos."

"Like you're so busy."

"You better watch that mouth."

"I'd like to see what you'd do."

"Whatever," Nakea said, suddenly shifting her tone to uncaring. "Anyway, I'm coming by for dinner tonight. Is there any ice cream in the house?"

"No, Mom doesn't let Dad buy it anymore."

"Not even frozen yogurt?"

"Naw."

"Alright. I'll bring ice cream."

"Cookie dough!"

"Shut up, Harla, ain't nobody wants to eat no cookie dough!"

Her sister hung up, and Harla looked at her phone for a moment, zoned out.

Diamonds gave a chuckle, trying to lighten her up, "You're not supposed to eat ice cream, are you?"

Harla didn't answer, just clamped her lips shut, put the phone away, and put her nails back for the manicurist to fix the Pollack painting on her hand.

Parents didn't always understand, but I didn't get why Harla was always so down about the leaks. They made her look like some kind of super hero. I wished I had badass videos of me all over the internet. She didn't understand how good she had it. All the good stuff about fame without anyone knowing her name.

Diamonds tried again, "Well, that sounded like it went well. What? Harla, what? That went well, didn't it?"

"She's going to tell Mom and Dad tonight."

"Well, what do they know about the game?"

"Next to nothing. They call it my, like, soldier girl thing."

"Well, that's dismissive."

"You've met my parents."

"They're not dismissive!"

"Not dismissive to you."

"Do you ever think you're just being hard on them?"

"Literally never. But I always think they're being hard on me."

"Are you sure this isn't post-grad pressure you're putting on yourself?"

"Well, I definitely ain't had post-grad pressure back in kindergarten. And that's the first time I remember Mom being disappointed in me. It was a smiley face sticker on my report card."

"What's wrong with a smiley face sticker?"

"As Mom says, 'The Gambles aren't a smiley face sticker family; the Gambles are a gold heart sticker family.'"

"They said that to a five year old?"

"No, I got out of kindergarten by the time I was three."

"It must have been so weird being a kid genius."

"While being treated like a kid underachiever, yeah. Weird."

"They just want what's best for you."

"What they *think* is best for me. And that doesn't include military exercises."

"What do you think they'll say?"

"I don't care what they'll say, what they'll do is pull me from the program."

"So what? You're almost eighteen. You may be by the time the next game comes around."

"And in the meantime, I'm supposed to let my family drive me crazy, huh?"

"That's a little ableist. I think you're driving your own anxiety and projecting a little. Maybe taking some time to prioritize your mental health wouldn't be the worst thing in the world."

"Today's my spa day. This is what I do for my mental health."

"Oh cool, add denial to the list."

"And how long until you're a full-blown therapist? I'm not going to like it when I have to pay for these sessions."

"You've got a while. But unless you're a runaway trans teen, I don't think you'll fall within my expertise."

"Well, it ain't too late for me to run away," Harla said with a heavy sigh, then chuckled to herself. Pretty soon, the both of them relaxed into laughter.

"So does this mean you're feeling better about the leak?"

"Not really. Moms might kill me. But at least the leaks never say who I am. That's what I'll tell my parents. If I'm not named, it ain't that big of a deal. But when's it going to end? Holter's nowhere near to stopping them. And I bet the closer we get to Christmas, once Chase's floatboards hit the shelves, vids from the game will be everywhere."

"Are you saying they're connected?"

"I'm saying they're two opportunities for Todd Fowler to line his pockets."

There wasn't much talk about the game after that. If Diamonds was getting tired of the subject matter, they weren't letting on, but Harla didn't bring it up again. They parted ways, Diamonds heading to meet Escondido for lunch across the Bay while Harla goopgated home. She got pulled over by police, failure to signal a lane change when she was positive she did. Harla got pulled over all the time. Maybe it was her Dad's Tesla she was driving.

By the time Harla got home, she was angry and late for

dinner, and the light outside the front door was on, though all the rooms visible from outside were dark.

Everyone was clanking plates in the dining room when she walked in, and she made a wincing face as she tried to close the door quietly.

"Harla?" Her mom called out loud enough to hear outside. "Is that you? Are you home?"

"Damn," she whispered before saying, "Yes ma'am."

"Well, quit cursing to yourself and have some dinner while we finish our ice cream."

"Are y'all finishing all of the ice cream?"

"Young lady, you can come into this room to address me."

The table was set, complete with candles burned half down. The entire family was there, but only her pregnant sister Nakea was still eating. Harla immediately clammed up.

"What were you asking before, young lady?"

"Nothing, ma'am."

"Well, have some chicken. And don't just load up on gravy, eat some green beans, too."

"But they're cold."

"Harla." The name and the eyebrow were all it took for Dr. Gamble to shut Harla up.

Her dad, overly cheerful, was obviously acting extra to lighten the mood. "Nakea stopped by to tell us some news."

Harla was about to get busted for a video she didn't leak and fame she didn't even appreciate.

Chapter 4

C hapter 4

Her dad was smiling too much, her very pregnant sister was taking bites behind a sly look, and her mother appeared to be vibrating, she was so full of energy.

Was Harla about to get chewed out? She visibly stiffened. Whatever good the massage did to relax her shoulders had been completely undone by her dad's overly-positive words.

With an evil grin, Nakea savored a spoonful of mint chocolate chip ice cream. Harla hated the combination of mint and chocolate, and I was sure Nakea picked the flavor to get under her skin.

"Well," Nakea basked in the attention of the family, "I was scrolling around on my phone today..." She paused for extra effect.

Harla was noticeably cringing, eyes down on the hardened drops of candle wax growing at the base of her mom and dad's crystal candleholders. These were the good ones, usually reserved for big anniversaries or graduations. Having graduated without fanfare through a private tutor, none of Harla's special days had ever warranted the use of the good candle holders, a point she'd brought up on several occasions.

"And then I saw a message from a friend. And it turns out," Nakea caught her sister's eyes across the table before finishing, "I'm going to be the youngest professor in school history to get tenure."

The words struck Harla wonky, and she tilted her head, puzzled as she crossed the room toward the kitchen. "Tenure? But you was just complaining about their terrible maternity leave."

"Were," Dr. Gamble corrected her daughter as the door closed behind her.

"Well," Nakea kept on, shouting at Harla through the kitchen door. "They've offered to let me telecommute for a couple semesters once my leave is over. I'll be teaching classes from home or at least from a room at the library."

"That's so great, sweetie," Mr. Gamble said pleasantly beneath his huge smile.

"Not just great, it's unheard of!" Dr. Gamble clapped her hands in excitement. "They're bending over backwards to keep you there. I was never offered a chance to work from home."

"Yeah," Harla came back to the table with a plate of chicken, gravy, and two green beans. "You had Dad to take care of us."

That was most definitely a dig at Nakea's fiancé Tyler being in the army. It was a sore spot for the family that they didn't tie the knot before shipping out. And nobody could aggravate a sore spot like Miss Harla Gamble.

"Harla," Dad said in a low warning, "be happy for your sister."

"You didn't tell her to be happy for me when I won a

Pentagon contract for NASA! I don't care about tenure!"

That drew some angry looks. Nakea slapped her hands on the table, pushed off, and left in a huff.

"Inappropriate!" Dr. Gamble pronounced it like it was a prison sentence to someone on trial.

"Harla, please apologize to your sister." Dad's approach was a little softer, but only a little.

"What? I didn't mean anything by it!"

"Oh, and people aren't going to get their feelings hurt because of what you mean?" Dr. Gamble got up and followed her oldest daughter out of the room and upstairs.

Slumped, Harla pushed green beans around a pool of gravy with her fork.

"I saw the video." Her dad spoke quietly. "You alright?"

I gasped. This was it. The hammer was about to fall on Harla. She was going to find out which pressure was worse — her parents' expectations or knowing someone was revealing Harla's identity, one video at a time.

Her big, teary eyes flashed from her plate up to her father.

"Don't worry," he said, "I ain't telling your mother. This military exercise always so dangerous? The way you went on about it, I thought it was more like beta testing computers."

"It's not usually that bad."

"I know you can handle yourself; I just need to know what you're getting into."

"Yes, Dad."

"Once you turn eighteen next year, we won't be stopping you, but it ain't a good idea for you to go back to this competition anytime soon."

Harla looked up like she was going to say something, to plead her case, but she kept quiet. Slouched in her chair, she looked like a little kid at that big dining room table.

"If your mom finds out, she gon flip. You have to realize your actions don't just have consequences for you, they affect all the people around you."

"Yes, sir."

"Harls." His word had an authority that snapped Harla out of her punished-kid daze. Enunciating sharply, he said with immense care and power, "Don't 'yes, sir' me. *Listen*. Learn. I know you. You're going right back to this soon as you can, and we can't stop you. But you need to protect yourself and those around you. No more showing your face."

"K, Dad."

"Promise?"

"I promise."

They each went back to their plates, eating in silence. Upstairs, a bedroom door creaked, and two sets of footsteps came down the stairs. Just before her mom and sister made it back in the room, Dad flashed his eyes to his daughter and muttered before a big bite of melted green ice cream, "Pretty badass, though."

Stormed. Nakea and her mother stormed into the room. They were mirror images of each other: flailing, all elbows, both of their voices at the same pitch of indignance.

"Harla, you apologize to your sister right now."

"I don't appreciate your implications that I need a man!"

After smacking her lips, finishing a hastily shoveled mouthful of chicken, she looked to her sister and said in a very nonplussed way, "Sorry."

Two sets of big brown eyes blinked, expecting more.

The only thing that came was more of Harla's bored look. And then a bite of macaroni and cheese.

"Anything else?"

Breaking off a hunk of buttered roll, dipping it in gravy, then stuffing it into her face, she just shrugged.

To be fair, Harla was an incredibly disciplined dieter in training. Every day, she had one hundred twenty-eight ounces of water, 4 ounces of chicken breast with brown rice or veg, and two shakes that looked like they'd just come out of a human body and probably didn't taste much better. But in the two weeks after a game? Harla was a human garbage disposal.

"I can't believe you disrespected me like that," her sister said at the same time her mother nodded and spoke, "Well, thank you for your apology."

"Nuh-uh," Nakea had the tone of a teenager, although she was nearly thirty. "She can't act like this when I come home with good news!"

But the apology was enough for Dr. Gamble. "Baby, take what you can get."

"You two can't do this constantly," Mr. Gamble added.

"Congrats on your little job." Harla wiped her hand and face on her napkin. "Oh, by the way, the military camouflage challenge has been postponed indefinitely."

Mom furrowed a brow and resumed eating ice cream. "Oh, I'm sorry, honey."

But her father kept quiet, leaning back in his chair and playing with his spoon on the side of his bowl. Nakea's mouth fell open, then pursed hard. Harla was stealing her sister's opportunity to rat her out.

"Yeah, I'm going to keep working on the tech, though. I'm still employed by NASA."

"But honey," her mom said gently, "this sounds like the perfect opportunity to head off to school."

Her Dad butted in, "Wanda, we don't have to do this right now."

"What am I doing, Harold? She couldn't go to postgrad because of this little soldier girl exercise, and now that it's over, there's time."

Harla added, trying to get into the conversation now between her parents, "I'll still take my online classes."

"Honey, that is no kind of school to get a degree."

Nakea added, "It's true, Harla, academia looks down on these purely online schools."

"Now wait just a minute," Mr. Gamble began.

Harla interrupted. "Then I guess academia will have to kiss my a–"

Mr. Gamble interrupted, "Oh, come on Harla."

Dr. Gamble got to her feet. "No, ma'am, you're not going to disrespect me like that in my own house."

"I wasn't talking to you, Mom; I was talking to Nakea."

"I hear how you talk to your sister, and I want you to guess whether or not I'm okay with it." The woman was standing, legs wide like Superman staring down a locomotive. Harla didn't flinch, but she certainly didn't say anything back to her mother. "Now, this is an opportunity for you to begin a graduate degree at a physical university, and you will not pass up this opportunity, young lady."

"But my team," Harla muttered, twirling her fork on her plate balanced on one tine.

"What's that young lady?" her mother fumed.

"Wanda, take it easy."

"My team is expecting me to help with the maintenance and redesign of our tech. Because I work for NASA, remember?"

"Harla." Her mother made explicit eye contact with her

father, and then carefully chose her words. "We are very proud of what you're doing, baby. We are very proud of both of you, but it is not a competition. We expect each of you to work hard at what you want to excel at. But you also have to be smart. Have fallbacks. Degrees."

"Nakea doesn't have a fallback!"

"I don't need one."

Harla said calmly, "I don't see a violin in your hand. There is no shame in the life you're leading, but there's also no shame in admitting that being a professional violinist didn't exactly work out the way you'd planned, right, Nakea?"

Their father defused the stand-off. "We love you both so much. I don't think it's too much to ask if Harla reduces her online university coursework and applies to start postgrad."

"I can help you find a school."

"Thank you, Nakea. Now what do you say to that, Harla?"

"We got any ice cream that ain't mint?

* * *

General Wilder smiled warmly as he shook Harla's hand. The big guy put a hand on her arm, rubbing her tricep in a kind and safely distant mini-hug. He looked like he'd give her an actual hug if he was confident of its appropriateness.

"Have a seat, please." Wilder was an overly-enthusiastic guy, from hugs to polite chit-chat. "How are you feeling? It looked like an especially athletic game this year. Congratulations on placing silver! We're all so proud of the work you and your team managed. Y'all are absolutely great, and we're very pleased with the results game after game."

"Wow. Uh, well, thanks, General. It's nice to be appreciated. I did want to talk with you…"

"About the suspended game, right? So sorry to hear. I understand the challenges of keeping up team morale in the meantime. I'd recommend regimented scheduling. Stay just as busy as if you were prepping for another game. Except, you know, indefinitely."

"Yeah, General, that's kind of what I wanted to talk with you about."

"It is quite unfortunate. But maybe necessary? These leaks are awful; protecting team captains is absolutely paramount."

"Well that's just it, General. I don't know if I can be team captain."

"Excuse me?"

"I need to take some time. At least until I'm eighteen next May."

"But the game's suspended indefinitely. There won't even be a Spring game."

"I understand that, but if you expect the team to prep until the game comes back, I'm not going to be available."

"Not available? Are you taking a trip?"

"Nope."

"Getting a job? Going to school?"

"I haven't decided."

"Then, Gamble, why throw away a good thing?"

She shrugged. Her voice cracked, betraying emotion, "It's not my choice."

"Oh," he sat back in his chair and said quietly, "I think I understand. I imagine that once you turn eighteen, you'll be free to make your own decisions?"

She paused for a second and that pause said more than she could...or would. Harla was getting the same sneaking suspicion I had once it was obvious the leaks were targeting her: someone was gaining control over Harla. She may have been free to make her own decisions now, but for how long?

"That would be correct," she said in an attempt to convince Wilder or herself.

"Well, I'd be lying if I said I wasn't disappointed, but I understand that these things happen. We don't always get to do what we want."

"Thank you, sir."

"As you venture out into decision making, Gamble, I'd love to put in a good word for the United States Air Force. We can put in the calls to get you fast-tracked to officer's school."

She was all smiles and polite thank-yous, but I didn't think Harla took the offer seriously.

Before she left, General Wilder insisted on writing Harla a letter of recommendation. She faked a smile and thanked him.

Harla Gamble was actually walking away from the game.

* * *

When Harla was moping back to her car, she got a new voicemail. She didn't even listen to the entire message before she hung up and called back Brielle Ward, associate dean of admissions to Mr. Gamble's alma mater and historically black college.

"Ms. Gamble, thank you for calling me back, my name is Brielle Ward, I run admissions and financial aid programs for

Roland College. Do you have a minute to talk?" Her voice was smooth and confident, but to the point. This lady spent her time getting things done.

"Um, sure?"

"Thank you, Ms. Gamble. I'd like to talk to you about a scholarship for a soft enrollment here at the school. Soft enrollment is a new program that hasn't been completely defined, and in my opinion, that makes it a great opportunity for incoming graduate students. We'd admit you, let you attend at any caseload of your choosing — even if you just want to do three credits every academic year — but most likely, you'd receive credit for lab hours for out-of-university work."

Harla was never the most trusting person, but this must have set off some serious red flags. "Hold up. You're asking if I want to go to your college. For free. And take as many or as little classes as I want?"

"As many or as few as you'd like."

"And what do y'all get out of it?"

"A student of your caliber. Hopefully some media attention if we could get academic papers of yours published. And ultimately, you'd be asked to assistant teach."

"You're clowning. You funny. Hold up, you're serious?" The silence on the other end of the line got Harla clearing her throat. She took on a more professional tone and said, "I would like a little background on how you came to the decision to recruit me. Like, how'd you even find out about me? Who'd you talk to? How'd you get this number?"

"Well, your state homeschooling scores — specifically, standardized math tests — are public information, so you've been on our radar since then. But your old tutor, Dr..." She shuffled some pages. "Laura Bird, had submitted your transcripts when you graduated three years ago. A quick search showed me you've earned an undergrad degree since then? And you're listed as an R & D consultant for Powers, Limited as well as project manager at NASA. So, needless to say, we're impressed and excited about offering you this opportunity. Ms. Gamble, I'd love to bring you in and speak with you face to face about this. Would you be able to make it to campus any time in the next few days?"

"I don't know. I've got a lot of training to do. Marathons. Plus, I'm needed at the lab. In fact, I'm real busy this week."

"Well I'm sorry to hear that. Let me just say, Ms. Gamble, that we are very interested in recruiting you to attend our school. Let me know what we can do to get you to withdraw applications from other programs."

"I currently don't have any applications out..." Harla didn't sound so sure of herself.

"This is not the busy season for me, so if you'd like to stop by my office in the Admissions building anytime in the next week or so, I'll be in my office from nine to five."

"Cool, cool. Well you have a nice day, Miss..."

"Brielle Ward. You can call me Brielle, Ms. Gamble."

There was a hesitation, a pause that sounded like Brielle expected Harla to extend the same courtesy.

"Well, ok, Brielle...bye."

And as fast as Harla had given up the game, another opportunity had fallen into her lap. But Harla Gamble didn't trust things that seemed too good to be true.

* * *

For the agreed-upon dinner, Diamonds showed up at precisely 5:30 pm with a bouquet of flowers and a bottle of Cabernet. All the Gambles fawned over Diamonds, even though they were way early for dinner.

"Diamonds, thank you for coming," Dr. Gamble gave them a big squeeze as she took the beautiful arrangement.

Mr. Gamble took the bottle. "And wine? You didn't have to bring that? There's no label, what is it?"

"Oh, it's a Cabernet Sauvignon from France. They think it's from the 19th century."

"The nineteenth century?" Mr. Gamble suddenly held it out like it was a baby about to vomit.

"Yeah, from the cellar of an old hotel my dad bought. An old monastery that was some deacon's."

"That is dope." His smile spread wide just like Harla's.

"Yeah, I hope you enjoy it!"

"Thanks for coming," Mr. Gamble said warmly.

"Thanks for having me."

Dr. Gamble led them into the dining room, all fancy with crystal, lace, and competing glass china cabinets. The Gambles and Diamonds sat and began serving themselves food. After Dr. Gamble said, "You know, Diamonds, I have to say, it's great to see you like this. You've grown into such a confident, strong young-"

Harla interrupted, "Mom."

"...Person."

"She doesn't mean anything," Harla whispered to Diamonds.

"I do," Dr. Gamble insisted. "You look good."

The spread was amazing, but Harla's dad never disappointed. Every meal had bread and salad, but this one was whole wheat rolls and a blue cheese wedge. Mr. Gamble agreed with his wife, passing the roast sweet potatoes down, "You've got a good energy about you, Diamonds. For real."

"Thanks. It's the meds."

Dr. Gamble dropped her fork which clattered loudly onto her plate. Harla swallowed back a spit take. The room got awkwardly silent. She scrunched her eyes in embarrassment as her parents looked at each other. Only Diamonds kept moving, spooning farrow and polenta onto their plate. Dr. Gamble shook her head, and Mr. Gamble shrugged.

Diamonds salted their polenta. "It's okay. I don't mind talking about it. It's important to fight the stigma of psychological medication. I'm on meds, and I'm in a better place. My anxiety was out of control; I needed help, and I got it. And if you guys ever have questions about what I went through or want to talk about what you're going through, I'm here." They spoke with a cheery brightness as careless as offering a neighbor to borrow a cup of sugar any time.

"Thank you, Diamonds," Dr. Gamble said, "that is quite kind of you to say."

Mr. Gamble added, "You're going to make a great therapist."

"Psychologist, right, Diamonds?" Dr. Gamble interrupted. "Gotta get that doctorate, and if you've got the stomach, that MD. Do you see yourself practicing in an academic setting? The resources are fantastic–"

Harla cut her off. "Chill, Mom."

"You'll be great at whatever you want to do," Mr. Gamble assured them.

"Honestly, I'm flabbergasted at how mature you've become, Diamonds," Harla's mom said. Was that a dig at Harla? Based on Harla's pouting look, it was. Dr. Gamble closed her eyes, joined hands around the table and said, "Now let us pray."

Whether Diamonds knew the Lord's Prayer or not, they didn't speak as the Gambles recited it in unison.

Mr. Gamble gestured to the blue cheese crumbles in a small bowl. "I did all of the cheese on the side. Lactose intolerant, right?" Mr. Gamble asked, as if he'd studied a file on Diamonds.

"I am, but I took a pill. I'll be fine."

"Harla doesn't take a pill."

"Dad!"

"And we can do ice cream with chocolate shells for dessert."

"Sounds delicious." Diamonds looked about the table, maybe a bit overwhelmed.

Harla asked, "We got cookie dough?"

"Cherries Garcia," her Dad said.

"Weak."

Harla's and Diamonds' phones went off simultaneously. They both reached for their pockets.

"Girls..." Dr. Gamble warned.

Mr. Gamble cleared his throat and lightly corrected, "Kids."

"Oh, yes, I mean," Dr. Gamble stuttered. "I'm sorry, what I meant...I meant–"

"Mom!"

"It's okay," Diamonds said. "It's fine."

"Well, we don't look at phones at the table."

"Are y'all for real? Not even let us look? What if it's an emergency?

"Then they would call. Everybody's in-case-of-emergency contact is the landline."

Harla's phone began ringing.

Diamonds' phone pinged again, a different noise. One alert

was a text and the other was email.

Dr. Gamble loudly stabbed at a square of sweet potato. Harla's phone kept ringing.

"You guys," Harla said, "what if it's the lady from Roland College who wants me to attend?"

"Say what now?" her mom reacted, head cocked and squinting.

"You applied to Roland?" Mr. Gamble was obviously excited at the prospect, scooting up in his seat.

Harla's phone kept ringing.

"So can I answer it?"

"When were you planning to tell us about this, young lady?" Dr. Gamble didn't share her husband's excitement.

"It's great news! Tell us what happened. Who's the lady you talked to?"

Her phone stopped ringing, and Harla slumped. "I got a call about taking classes there on scholarship."

"Scholarship, that's great, princess!"

"To go there full-time?"

"However many classes I want."

"Wow, this is a cause for celebration! Diamonds, would your parents mind if you had a sip of wine to toast? We should have used the nice candlesticks!"

"With whom did you speak at Roland?"

"My parents wouldn't care—"

"Is there a minimum of credits?"

"— but I'd rather not. Thank you, though!"

While Mr. Gamble busily grabbed a wine opener from a drawer and Dr. Gamble grilled her daughter, Harla's phone rang again. And I could tell it was really starting to tick her off.

"Can I answer it, please?"

Her mother's fork clattered again. Now Dr. Gamble was getting fired up, but her husband laid a gentle hand on her shoulder and spoke. "Harla, take it to the living room. Diamonds, could you excuse Mr. Gamble and I for a second? I'm sure you'll want to check your phone, too."

They were out of the room almost before he finished talking.

Harla's screen told her it was Loo-Weezy. Escondido.

"Luis?"

"This is BS, Harla. I'm going to kill someone."

Her mouth hung open. Nobody had heard Luis Escondido speak like that before. He was so cool, so polite. So official. But now he was reduced to expletives. If he'd seen someone else do it, he'd call them out for showing weakness.

"What is?"

"And now it's on TV! Are you watching this?"

Shaking her focus out of a fog, Harla squinted and asked, "Say what now? Luis, have you lost your damn mind?"

"Harla, you haven't checked your email?"

"No. No phones at the dinner table."

"BS."

"I know, it's some bullshi-"

"No, Harla. We're in it. Turn on your TV right now."

Harla headed toward the door.

"Which channel?"

"Any channel." Escondido gave a tired laugh. "They interrupted all of them."

On TV, Todd Fowler stood behind a clear podium

The crawl at the bottom of the screen read *Powers, LTD settles w Fed; will dissolve*

"I stand before you all today a humbled man but proud of our past and excited about our future. And that's only if time exists. I am here to announce I am dissolving Powers, Limited. To avoid any further investigations into antitrust laws, we will be breaking up Powers, Limited into three main companies: PowCom, PowTech, and SuperPowers, Unlimited.

"Powers Communications, PowCom will own our telecom infrastructure and continue to provide internet service across the globe. Powers Technologies, PowTech, will become a brain trust and institution of higher learning funded by every tech patent we own. I will sell my controlling interest of these subsidiaries and relinquish my board memberships of PowCom and PowTech. And thus, I embark on a new venture. A new entertainment streaming service, *SuperPowers, Unlimited.* We will stream and produce STEM-based film, episodic and educational programming, and video games.

"But the crown jewel of SuperPowers, Unlimited will be part reality television and part professional sport, all in a high-tech package. It is my honor to introduce the world to the Military Camouflage Challenge, the MC Squared."

Chapter 5

Chapter 5

As far as family dinners went, Diamonds wasn't attending one of the Gamble's best. I couldn't really talk, I found ways to avoid sitting down to dinner with Mom and Dad was off living his life, keeping touch through a phone.

In the Gamble house, Harla dropped her phone. Her jaw about hit the floor at the unveiling of the MC Squared to the world. Diamonds rushed into the room, their hands slapped over their mouth.

The TV screen went black. Then a sweeping drone shot over the plains of Africa. Among a galloping herd of gazelles in the tall grass, the brush shifted and moved unnaturally. Against the backdrop of a rising sun, a clump of grass ran. It was a man in a gilly suit.

"We've been doing this for years, secretly."

It was my voice-over, my voice, and hearing it sent Harla and Diamonds into a rage.

Diamonds face-planted onto the huge leather sectional couch. Harla squatted into a crouch and covered most of her face.

I continued, "Figuring out how to make our soldiers disappear on the battlefield. Keeping our service people safe. If we can make one mom or dad or daughter or son come home who wouldn't have, then it's all worth it."

Another slow motion shot showed off the light-warping function of an old stealth shield. This tech was years behind the game now, but in super-slow motion, the vanishing effect was pretty cool.

"We've been playing this game for so long, I'm excited for the evolution. I'm excited to see where it goes."

And then there it was, the gameplay footage of Harla, her face showing as her helmet was consumed by the Regalia. But it wasn't the same as the leaked footage. This was a close-up, her twitchy, wild eye incensed. Then it switched from one view to another to another as Harla unleashed a spray of flamethrower across the overview of the Normandy beach.

"It's a game, and it's a technology trial, but we're very competitive."

On the screen, the Regalia splash-crashed into Captain Miss, eating away at her, the screen filled with her seething face in epic zoom.

"I've gone against the absolute best, and I came out on top." And then there I was in a darkened locker room, wearing a boxer's robe, hood up. My face glistened with sweat. I looked directly into the camera, and said, "I'm here to prove I'm the best to ever play the game."

Harla threw the remote at the screen. We probably signed away the rights to our images somewhere in all the paperwork we'd filled out as Captains. It was a part of us they owned. And they were using hers against her will in front of the world.

Diamonds was now pacing. "So what, one fraction of Powers sponsors Chase while another runs the game and owns the TV rights? That's not fair. What was the point in breaking them up?"

Harla paced as well. "Or did that fool just buy the whole damn thing? Torpedo the program by leaking footage then swoop in to buy once it was damaged goods?"

"What's going on in here?"

Just as Harla's parents came into the room came the hero shot in the last game, me standing across the field, Regalia bots dripping her helmet off to show Harla's determined, ticked-off mug. Her parents gasped. Her dad was stunned, and her mom yelled, "And who is that? Because I know goddamn well I didn't raise a damn fool for a child!"

"Wanda!" Mr. Gamble chided.

"Streaming available right now. It's the MC Squared: The First Twenty Years. And next year, the season premier. Can Captain Oman retain his championship? Find out only on SuperPowers, Unlimited. Subscribe and start streaming today."

And then the voice listed all of the other classic movies and shows available on the service. But Diamonds and Mr. Gamble were focused on the burning stare between Dr. Gamble and her daughter.

Dr. Gamble yelled. Loud. "What the hell kind of science program is my baby girl in? Developmental testing of soft-military tech?"

"Oh, so now it's not my little 'soldier girl thing.'"

"Harla..."

"You watch your tone, young lady!" Dr. Gamble warned.

Harla stormed off, and before her Mom followed, she managed a smile, "Diamonds, I am sorry that we are airing some of our laundry, but my daughter and I need to speak. Feel free to help yourself to dinner."

"Thank you, I will," Diamonds said. "I'd like to talk to Harla after all of this."

Mr. Gamble made small talk as they both poked at the food on their plates. "So this means your friend Chase turned on you two? I know Harla was always talking about people in the game cheating."

"He's not our friend."

"Oh, well, I didn't mean to bring up a sore subject. It's just…"

"He's Harla's rival and most likely always will be as long as she's associated with the MC Squared, which may not be at all anymore. But he's my ex, and I don't see us ever being friends again." They went back to eating.

"Oh. Well, I'm sorry to hear that. With Harla out of the… what did you call it?"

"MC Squared."

"Right, MC Squared. With Harla out, do you have to find a new team or a new captain, or will they just assign you?"

Diamonds furrowed their brow. "I've been out of the game for a year. Just finishing up school and getting on with my career."

"Oh. So like, the game was holding you back from school and growing up?"

"No, I wouldn't say that. I've made my best friends through the game. Without it, I'd never have figured out what I wanted to do with my life. Honestly, I can't really picture what it would have been like to not have this game to constantly look forward to."

"But you didn't play."

"I did, and I didn't. It's complicated."

"I see."

"Well, I guess you'll be able to see enough pretty soon. Maybe you can watch the last game and see what it is she does and how good she is at it."

"To be honest, Diamonds, I'm not sure I'd be able to watch my baby girl in danger like that."

"Understood. It's easy to forget that everyone out there is someone's baby."

"Yep. But hey, like you said, most likely you've participated in your last MC Squared. So how much school do you have left for your career goals?"

* * *

Upstairs, Harla stared into nothing, offering her busy, pleading mother no answer or emotion.

"Listen. I know you, baby. I understand what you're capable of. Believe me, I know you are a fierce, strong woman, but if I had known, I would not have let you do any of that. Guns and missiles and flamethrowers?"

"There ain't any real guns."

"Young lady." Her mom's pursed lips made the rest of her point for her.

"I'm really good, though." Harla got up off the bed and paced around her room, around her mom, posters of Einstein, SpaceJam, Serena Williams, and Katherine Johnson. "Like for real. I've come in the top two for three games in a row. NASA says I'm welcome back to work with them at any time. NASA,

Mom! I've wanted to work for them since, since…"

"Since your father and I wouldn't let you go to space camp."

"Exactly!"

"But this game ain't sending you to space, it's sending you onto a battlefield." Dr. Gamble sat and quieted her tone. "You're too good to be someone's guinea pig."

"I'm no one's guinea pig. I'm a star athlete in a technological and athletic competition."

"Lord, child, you starting to sound like the commercial."

"Because it's true. I dominate. When I lose, it's from technicalities or loopholes or cheating. Chase Hawkins knows I'd wipe the floor with him in fair competition!"

"I don't care, Harla. I am not Chase Hawkins' mother!"

Harla slumped onto the bed to hold her mother's gaze. "And I'm not some kid."

They sat in silence on the bed for a moment, each woman's eyes threatening tears. Finally, when Harla spoke, it was gentle and apologetic. "I don't know who I am without this game."

Dr. Gamble grabbed Harla's chin and forced her daughter to look at her. "You stop that. You are Harla Lynn Gamble, math and science genius. You are not defined by your job, your sport, your rank, your socio-economic situation-"

"Mom…"

Harla tried to turn away, but her mother wouldn't let her. She said more quietly, warmer, "Child, the things you are capable of far exceed what your father and I have been able to do in our lives."

"Nakea, too?"

"Not everything is a competition, Harla." Dr. Gamble cradled her daughter's head and embraced her, then added,

"Besides, Nakea is about to find another world of pressure and responsibility raising a baby by herself. She'll need us to help, not try to always outdo her."

"So, Mom?"

"Yes, child?"

"What if...what if we put the game on hold for now, and maybe wait and see what it turns into with the streaming channel, and then I'll decide what to do?"

"Harla, you're about to be a grown woman who does what she pleases. And I'm not going to try to make your decisions for you. Hopefully, we helped teach you enough to make them on your own. But you have to realize, these people running this media company, they intend to use you to make money. And that is as far as they care about your well-being. If it's what you want to do, sweetie, I'll understand, even if I'm not happy with your choice. But that still leaves the question — what would you do with yourself in the meantime?"

"Well, I guess if I have to go to any college, it'd be cool to go to Roland like Dad did. And I guess...well, having some extra time to help out Nakea wouldn't hurt."

"Who are you, and what have you done with my daughter?"

Harla sniffed and wiped a tear, managing a laugh. "What?"

"You want to help your sister? Without me yelling at you? That's a first."

"I know, right? Well, I ain't never gonna have kids, so I guess this is my opportunity."

"Never say never, sweetheart."

"This better not segue into you trying to set me up with a boy. I swear to God, if you ever try that again..."

"Hey, I didn't know any better! And a trip to the aquarium at age thirteen isn't a 'set up.' Besides, I already have a few young ladies in mind I'd like you to meet once you're eighteen."

"Mom! No. For real, though. I mean it. No. Don't even play like that, ain't no one laughing."

Her mother cackled, flopping back onto the bed. "Double negative. So someone is laughing. And that someone...is me!"

"Man, I ain't even playing." Harla laid back with her mom. For a second, they sat there laughing together.

"So. Real talk. Are you sure you even want to consider going back to the game now? Things'll be different. And not just keeping your face hidden. They have to make ratings and sell ads, and I guarantee some producer somewhere is going to start meddling."

"I don't know. I don't even know what the game is going to be. It was never fair, always fools messing with the rules or influencing things, but now...now everything is skewed to help him from the jump."

"Who, baby?"

Me.

"It's like, I don't even want to say his name, don't want to give it any power. I don't know, it don't make sense."

I was the one so detestable she wouldn't even say my name.

"Makes sense to me. Young lady, and don't tell your father I said this, but you're a serious badass."

Harla gasped and her eyes went wide as she overacted shock. The hint of a smile pulled at the ends of her mouth.

"Powerful as all hell. Sometimes stubborn, yeah, but that's good. Flexing your powers. And you can't give them away. You can waste them trying, but ain't no one gon wield Harla Gamble's power except Harla Gamble. And whatever you focus on, you'll tear it up." She kissed her daughter's forehead.

* * *

I watched it live with Mom and Emily.

Thankfully, Emily was always quiet when she came over. I wasn't ashamed of her or anything, she could just be a little... odd. I didn't want my girlfriend to intimidate my mother, after all.

"Chase, this is great! You look so handsome on TV! Right, Emily?"

"Yup."

"Oh, you're down-playing it. Chase, you looked great! So cool. Super cool. You looked...Chase I mean it, you looked cool."

"Thanks, Mom."

"Okay, fine. Your uncool Mom will stop embarrassing you in front of your girlfriend."

"You're not embarrassing, Mom," I lied.

"It's fine. Emily, what time are you getting picked up?"

"Nine-thirty, if it's okay."

"It's fine. I'm old and tired and embarrassing," Mom said, yawning and stretching. She kissed me on my forehead. "I'm going to bed. With the door open. I'll see you in the morning, my cool TV star."

"Am I going to Dad's tomorrow?"

"Nope. Sorry, kiddo."

I shrugged. "Night, Mom. Love you."

"Love you."

As soon as she was around the corner, Emily said quietly, "You're talking too much."

"To my mom?"

"On TV. About the game. You're ruining any chance you have of a mental edge."

"Mental edge isn't really my thing."

"Did you just call yourself stupid?"

"What? No! I'm just...I'm just confident. That's my brand."

"Is that what Fowler told you?"

"No, it's what I said."

It *was* what Fowler told me. I'd been doing pretty much everything he suggested — appearing on ESPN, signing with a sports agent, even wearing the clothes he told me to wear.

"What's confidence going to get you in the arena? Unless you go cocky. Cocky helps. Confidence is lame."

"It's not just other competitors. We have an audience now. We have to get people interested in the game. We need people to watch."

"Ugh." Emily rolled her eyes and acted like she would make herself vomit, like she did to make fun of things. I laughed. I always laughed at it, but I don't know why; it wasn't funny. Emily's funny was always poking fun and laughing with me. "So why aren't you going to your Dad's?"

"I don't know. I guess he's going through some stuff."

"Like what?"

"I don't know. Maybe the divorce is like just now hitting him."

"Do you ever get the feeling that instead of a person, you're like, this lab experiment of your parents where they tried out a bunch of theories on you and then they just observe and evaluate you constantly now?"

"What? No. I just feel like...like they're both so busy, which is fine, I'm not a little kid, but... sometimes I feel like a roast. In the oven. And they're checking the temp, poking, turning, but they've got stuff going on outside the oven. Their whole lives are outside the oven. I'm just the roast."

And then we turned the sound up on the TV and made out pretty much until she got picked up.

By the time I was laying down to sleep, I was sad and couldn't figure out why. Everything was going so great...but it was so much. The girlfriend, the network, figuring out the Crown, all of the attention. When I thought too much about it, I cried. I thought too much about it for that whole night.

Meanwhile at Harla's parent's house, after the half hour it took to convince Diamonds to leave and that she'd be okay, Harla ordered the new SuperPowers, Unlimited streaming service and watched the condensed four hour version of DARPA's Military Camouflage Challenge year one. The exercise was timed, the players given one week. They hid from a pair of black ops marines tethered to one another. All participants were soldiers from different branches of the military, each in unique, but standard, military-issue camouflage. The tethered marines got everyone out within five days.

Harla would have likely flushed everyone out within the first ten minutes. But instead of talking trash about all the "white bro" soldiers, she just shook her head. She shook her head the entire four hours she watched.

Chapter 6

C hapter 6

When Escondido walked angrily, which was almost never, his limp was more obvious. He may have test-flown jets for the marines, but I don't know of anything that got him more fired up than disagreements with the brass who ran the game.

"Do you really think they're going to let you walk away?"

For once, Harla was the calm one. "It ain't the same game, Luis. If they want to play Ninja Warrior in mech suits on their little network, that's their prerogative, but I ain't gotta join in."

They were arguing on the tarmac. Luis Escondido had a cool blue flight suit and jogged to catch up with Harla in her bright white and orange visitor's flight suit. Everyone at the airfield knew Escondido, and he kept up appearances, only ever looking either uncaring or intensely angry. "If you leave like this, after Chase manipulated the judges, then they win. We should have a team meeting before you go in and talk to General Wilder."

"I'm sorry, but I already went in to talk to Wilder before Fowler even had his little presentation. I'm done with the game, Luis. But you know, I'm good with it."

They got to the trainer jet, and Escondido let out a deep sigh of defeat. "I don't know why you're acting like this isn't a big deal. You need to look back over your contacts to play. They own the rights to your image, anything you worked on while you were captain... you may not even be able to quit like this! I'm sorry, I don't think you should pilot today."

"You're letting me pilot?"

"I'm not! I mean, you've got the license and the hours."

"Then I'm piloting."

"No, you're not!"

Captaining an MC Squared team always had benefits and perks depending on the sponsor. In Harla's case, she got to tour every NASA facility in the US and was shown aboard a shuttle (even if it wasn't in space). But the coolest part was once a month, Luis Escondido, using Harla's NASA perks or his own contacts in the Marines, took Harla up in some kind of super-cool state-of-the-art jet plane.

Sometimes, I can be jealous.

He sat behind her in the cockpit and spoke between teaching pointers, their air masks adding gravity to everything they said.

"So why don't you go back?" she asked in between the mask's Darth Vader breaths.

"Go back where? Keep your nose up."

"Back to the game."

"Nah, I'm retired."

"Come on, former champion? They'd plaster you all over TV."

"Is that supposed to convince me? Tighten up a little, you're flailing."

"I'm fine, we're fine. Don't change the subject. Why not come back? There's an opening at NASA."

"Listen, it's a different game now."

"No fair! That was my excuse."

"No, I mean now that you and Chase changed it. This game used to be about hiding. When SteelCut came along, it became about tech. Now, it's about control. You two are so aggressive. And no one stays in their vehicles these days, either. And I want to just...pilot planes and jets and, and..."

"Stickbugs?"

"Stickbugs with cockpits, yes! I don't want mind control over some flock of flying robots."

"You don't? It's pretty cool..."

"You know what's pretty cool? Inversion. Let's invert. Right here, right now. Pull back."

It was another subject-change, but Harla didn't seem to mind.

A high pitched squealing came from somewhere within Harla as she pulled back, the plane climbing higher and higher, until their nose tipped past vertical and the squeal turned into a full-body "Woo-hoo!" They were soon flying straight for the ground.

If Escondido had any teaching pointers, they went unheard as Harla laughed uncontrollably, pulled up out of the dive, and leveled off their flight path.

Finally, he couldn't take it anymore, and laughed along with her.

"This," Escondido said. "This is better than flying around with your little bees. If I could pilot something state of the art like this in a game, I'd go back in a second."

"Yeah, it's pretty amazing. So what you gon do?"

"About what?"

"The game, fool?"

"I don't know. Maybe stay on the NASA support team. Or I could always switch to the Marines' team."

"What if they make you do interviews and have camera crews following you?"

"Then they'll see how boring I am and they'll stop. What will you do?"

"Finally get my postgrad. Stopping by Roland College after we land."

"Oh, I'm sorry. Is a ride in this billion-dollar jet boring you?"

"No, Luis. You are."

"You know, I don't know how much longer we'll be able to do this if you're no longer working for NASA."

"I figured. Can we barrel roll?"

"Are you serious?"

"Please, Luis? Diamonds told me not to ask. Said no way you'd have the balls for it."

"That doesn't sound like Diamonds," he said incredulously.

"Come on!"

Of course, he agreed to it. Escondido was weak like that. A tough facade with a gooey center. And they both whooped and hollered and Harla was still a mile in the air even after they landed.

I was impressed with her restraint once she was driving a car again. I'd probably have been speeding all over the place. Harla drove the exact speed limit all the way to Roland College, although she did get pulled over anyway.

Roland College, nestled into the trees in the Appalachian foothills through a brick and stone entrance was a modern campus in miniature. Clusters of brick and stone buildings, a few ugly concrete structures from the 60's.

And, of course, Black students everywhere. Hundreds of students rushing here and there, talking and laughing in cliques, all in shades of brown.

Harla stood back and watched the quad from the corner, taking in the school, and most likely, demographics of the student body. In fact, she stood there for a couple extra minutes taking it all in.

Then she practically skipped to the admissions office as she hummed a tune from Top Gun, "Danger Zone."

The office was expansive. Parquet tiled floors, high ceilings, and crown molding. It was an old building, and Harla looked about with wide eyes, tiptoeing like she was afraid to get caught. The administrative building was busy with staff and students, but the hall to the admissions offices were empty. Even stepping softly, Harla's gait echoed.

She found the plastic marker 'Mrs. Brielle Ward' by a door that was slightly ajar. She knocked delicately.

"It's open."

With braided hair in a melon-sized bun atop her head, the woman in the vibrant sweater behind equally bright blue and purple reading glasses didn't look up from her paperwork as she waved Harla to the desk.

Ward took her time finishing what she was reading, one long finger with deep maroon-painted nail held up to buy her some time. Harla sat in the chair, at the edge of her seat, still buzzing. Her hair hadn't been done since the game, and now tufts of fro escaped her rows of fuchsia braids. Her white button-up was rumpled from getting stuffed in an airfield locker, yet despite it all, she sat quietly and properly straight. Harla was there to make a good impression.

Ward finished reading and addressed her guest, "Hello, yes. Oh." The woman was startled that it was Harla. "Ms. Gamble, I wasn't expecting you."

"Oh, you told me to stop by. Is it okay?"

"Yes, it's fine." The woman got to her feet and closed the blinds on the tall, oversized windows.

Harla shrunk down in her seat a little.

"It's just that," the woman checked through slits in the blinds thoroughly before returning to her desk, "your profile has been significantly raised since we last spoke."

"My profile?"

"Surely, you've seen the commercials for the MC Squared?"

It was weird hearing a civilian say the name of the game. Awkward.

"Oh, that? Yeah, of course."

"It's just that you're a celebrity now."

"Not really. They don't even say my name."

"Sure, but you're recognizable to the public."

"And is that a problem?"

"Well, Roland College has only a minimum of courses available online."

"That's fine, I don't need classes online. I'm sorry, is something wrong?"

"Well, Ms. Gamble, celebrity status does put some extra pressure on a student attending school. Our number one concern is the safety of our students. All of them."

I could see the moment it hit Harla that this visit wasn't going well, that all these ideas she'd had in her head — dreams, plans — weren't built on a solid base.

But she held it together, I was surprised to see. But I felt for her seeing how she struggled to hold it together.

Harla cleared her throat. "What are you saying?"

"If you're still interested in attending Roland College, we will be asking for you to provide your own security detail."

"Security detail? Like bodyguards?"

"*Like* bodyguards. You'd have to coordinate with the dean, department chairs, and head of campus security to work out specifics."

"I...I don't think I can afford bodyguards."

"You don't personally have to pay. You could always suggest it to your game sponsor."

"But...I'm leaving the game to come to school. You called me. You begged me to come and talk to you."

"Ms. Gamble, I did not beg..."

"Well, you were pretty damn convincing." Harla took a breath and lightened her tone. "I'm sorry. I'm just upset because I thought that this would go different."

"And I'm sorry to disappoint you, but a celebrity on campus can bring mobs of fans, stalkers, and who knows what else, Ms. Gamble."

"Just Harla." She said it like she was giving up.

"Harla, this isn't my decision, but I understand why it was made. We don't have any high-profile students. We don't even have a social media influencer enrolled. But off the record, you should know that this was a hastily-reached decision. The MC Squared announcement just dropped, and people panicked. I think once things settle down, maybe after you sit out a game or two, folks will see more clearly."

"I thought you recruited me because I was in the game."

"I'm sorry, Harla. That was before the game became a television show."

She cussed my name the entire drive to her sister's new house. But I wasn't the one controlling the game. I didn't sell it or buy it to turn into a streaming network. But I knew who had.

* * *

Harla scrolled through old games to find one she hadn't seen before. It was afternoon, but she was still in her pjs on the couch.

The doorbell rang.

From her phone, Harla checked the front door cam to see a lanky, smiley, freckled black kid.

"I'm here with your shake, Miss Gamble!" He held up one of those shaker bottles to the camera.

She unlocked the door from the couch and yelled out once he opened it, "Kevin? What are you doing here?"

"Oh, I'm sorry, didn't you hear me? I'm here with your shake. For post-game tests. Dr. Bird says that because of the nuclear energy some of the vehicles were running off, the testing in the physical will be more...extensive. Didn't you get her email? You have to drink this for some machine to look at your insides better; it's all in the email. I'm going to bring you one every other day, then daily up until...you know what, Captain Miss? I think it'd just be better if you read the email."

"Thank you, Kevin. You don't have to call me Captain anymore."

"Oh. I don't? Why's that?"

"I've left the team."

The boy, older than Harla, began to pout. His bottom lip jutted out and quivered as tears shook at the edges of his eyes. "Well, let me just say, that it has been an honor -"

"Whoa, hold up, soft boi. We're not doing this. Bring me my shakes when Bird wants you to, and I'll read her email. I'm not putting up with some crying fool on my doorstep every day." She chugged the gray contents of the shaker bottle. "Guh, that's disgusting. You gon stay on NASA's MC Squared team next year?"

The question made Kevin the intern jumpy. He ticked and twitched as he answered, habitually scratching at the back of his neck. "What? I mean. I'm planning on it. I don't have anywhere else to go. That sounded desperate. I'm not desperate, it's just the only job I've ever really had besides Wendy's, you know? That doesn't sound any better. I was planning...why wouldn't I be on the team?"

"I don't know Kevin, stop freaking out. Have you considered talking to the general about applying for a job at NASA rather than being an R & D intern?"

"Honestly, Captain, I hadn't thought of that. Crap, I just called you Captain. Get it together, Kevin!"

"Okay, hunter. I'm gonna go read that email. I'll see you next shake day."

"Okay Captain - I mean Harla - I mean Gamble - I mean Miss Gamble!"

"Bye, Kevin."

* * *

"Unfortunately, Ms. Gamble, it's just too late in the process for you to jump in like this. But Boston Tech would love to hear from you eight months from now."

Harla hung up and wrung the phone in her hands for a moment.

Her sister walked into the kitchen, or waddled, now that she was nine months pregnant. Without saying a word, she got out some Cherry Garcia and opened the silverware drawer.

"No thanks," Harla said dejectedly.

"Oh, this isn't for you," Nakea said, withdrawing a serving spoon and plunging it into the ice cream. She was on her way out of the big open kitchen and back to the couch when she stopped and said in an uncharacteristically serious tone, "Look. You're too proud to ask, and I would be, too. Hell, I was too proud to ask Mom, but...I'd love to put in a word for you at UC, maybe use my connections."

For an answer, Harla pouted. On the verge of tears, she flexed her jaw while her lip quivered, staring at nothing at all while tears collected in the corners of her eyes. But she never cried, I guess. She fought it. Stubborn Harla. I'd never seen her lose it before when she was hurt, afraid, or even sad to leave a team, but this...she was just feeling sorry for herself.

"Is that who I am? Someone who needs strings pulled to get into a school? Like some rich white kid?"

"Harla. You're trying to get into post-grad a week before classes start. Now either take the help or wait for next semester or year because you know I ain't gon be this nice to you for very long."

Bleary eyed, Harla looked to her sister in total defeat. Her voice broke as she said, "Sure. Thanks, Kee."

Nakea muted Gray's Anatomy, punched a button on her

phone, and scooped ice cream into her mouth.

"Hey, what's up?" some white guy answered over speakerphone.

"Mark, is it too late to slide someone into a post grad program? Math or Sciences? Physics if I can?"

"Dr. Gamble, classes start a week from Monday."

"Mark. She's an exceptional student. Worked at Powers, Limited and NASA. Lots of scholarship offers around."

"Then she should take them. It's too late."

"Alright, if I'm being real? It's my sister. And she was highly recruited by what's-her-face at Roland."

Harla whispered, "Brielle Ward."

"Brielle Ward."

"Then she should go to Roland. I'm sorry, Doc, I can't do anything right now on my end."

"Well, thanks anyway, Mark."

"And tell your sister something's up. There's no Brielle Ward at Roland Admissions. Guy named Hunter recruits for them."

"Kay thanks, Mark."

Nakea hung up. Harla began to speak, and Nakea silenced her by putting one finger up, using the other hand to navigate her phone until it began ringing again.

"Roland College Admissions."

"Hi, this is Nakea Gamble at University of Chicago, to whom am I speaking?"

"This is Greg."

"Hi, Greg, I was hoping you could connect me with Ms. Ward."

"I'm sorry, Ms. who?"

"Ward. Brielle Ward."

"I'm sorry, there's no one that works here by that name."

Harla was about to speak again, but again got stopped by her sister's insistent forefinger. Nakea continued, "I'm sorry, I got that wrong. It's Brielle Ward in Student Aid."

"Ma'am, student aid is right down the hall. There's nobody that works in this building by that name."

"Provost?"

"I'm sorry, ma'am. I work in admissions, can I help with whatever your business was with Ms. Ward?"

"Yes, I'm looking into a prospective student named Harla. Harla Gamble. Was she offered a scholarship to attend Roland?"

"I'm sorry, the name's not ringing a bell…"

Nakea hurriedly said while reaching for the phone," Thank you, have a good day…"

"Didn't you say your name was Gam-"

She hung up. "What the hell's going on, Harla?"

Tight-lipped with her face scrunched, Harla was sobbing again. "He can get to me *anywhere*."

The woman, Brielle Ward, must have been a hologram the entire time. Or maybe Fowler hired an actress. Deep down, maybe I was afraid that Brielle Ward was someone in disguise working for Fowler. Emily could fool anyone, but she said she was finished with Fowler, the game, and the Council. If she was lying to me, I don't know what I'd do.

* * *

The next day, in between watching games on TV, Harla got

a text from Diamonds. She clicked on the link to watch the live press conference. It redirected her to the SuperPowers, Unlimited streaming app she'd already downloaded onto her phone. It also automatically synced with her TV to change to the live network. She was such a good little customer.

Me? I was nervous. I'd spent hours reading and rereading the script the suits had given me, I knew it up and down. But this was live television. Fowler always said to act like you don't care to be cool, but he never did that. And I did care. And I didn't feel cool, despite wearing the most expensive suit I knew existed. Italian. 'Built for me,' whatever that meant. Fowler had paid $8,000 for it. Or was that Euros? Lira?

"What's that corny suit?" Harla spoke at me while watching on her phone.

I thought I looked pretty good in the suit.

"I'm holding this press conference to ensure the dignity of the game. I've been involved in four games, as a captain and as a team member, and I have so much respect for everyone's work here and what everyone is doing. I'm also very thankful for the fans we've cultivated in the short time we've been public. It seems my social media followers are increasing exponentially. But something I've heard, something going around the fan base, is questioning the fairness of the game. Questioning my ethics, being sponsored by SuperPowers, Unlimited. And let me make a few things clear. One, neither Todd Fowler nor SuperPowers, Unlimited own the MC Squared. The game is still a military exercise, sponsored and hosted by a third party. Two, my only sponsor since joining the game has been Powers, Limited. Three, I have not announced my sponsoring team for the new game."

At that, the crowd whispered as camera flashes strobed and

clicked.

"I want to thank everyone at DARPA and my old friends from Powers, Limited, wherever they are now."

That last sentence was a gun barrel aimed through the camera right at Harla, who became vulgar upon realizing it. "You little-"

"And specifically: Todd Fowler, my old teammates, and the competitors out there who made me better. This decision wasn't easy, but after serious consideration and many generous offers from around the game, I've decided to take my talents to Cape Canaveral."

"No," she said.

Yes, Harla.

Not only was she gone from the game, but the door to get back in was now slammed shut. She burned a bridge without knowing it, leaving her spot open like that. The only captain that would be more appealing to a sponsor than an anonymous Harla was a famous Chase.

She thumbed the video off so hard, she about cracked her phone's glass.

Part Two

The Dumps

II

Part Two

The Dumps

Chapter 7

Chapter 7

Of course, I didn't get caught up on all the drama that was Miss Gamble's life until I was in the first of my four weeks training. Only four weeks to train, but I'd been doing press and media for months. My mind was in the game.

My team's? Not so much.

When time to begin training finally came around, none of the scientists or project managers had taken my requests seriously. They all showed up, ready to work, ready to build my equipment and help out like they had with Harla.

That wasn't what I wanted.

No more team members, no more relationships to screw up, no more groups to be embarrassed in front of. No more team.

Kevin, the project manager with brown eyes with light brown skin and darker freckles, got cuter as he got angrier. "So you don't want the engineers to look at your tech, you don't want us taking metrics or running tests, and nobody's allowed to watch your drone sessions?"

"That's right." I didn't look up from my laptop, acting like

I was checking out schematics. I was doing it to get Kevin worked up.

Or was this just how I was with everyone now? Polite and perfect for the cameras, but savage and careless in reality. Why was I like this?

"So what do you expect the rest of your team to be doing for the next four weeks?"

"Shooting B-roll, interviews, and confessionals with the film crew."

"Are you serious? These are the smartest rocket scientists in the world."

"You're right; they'd be terrible doing interviews. We should do a week of on-camera training. The film crew can shoot around for a bit."

"And what about me?"

"Meal prep and coffee runs. And you've got to keep on my caloric stats." That had been in the email, along with the fact I didn't want a support team.

"Are you for real?"

"If it's too much for you, Kevin, pull a rocket scientist off of media and they can do coffee and the meal plan. I'll need the room for the rest of the week. I'll see you every three hours for a meal."

No more teams. It was easier like this. Not getting involved.

CJ had signed a lucrative deal to be team captain for Trillions Solutions under Escondido. Nobody ever stayed. Everybody quit but me. It was easier not getting attached to a team. It was easier to shrug them off now. I'd just disappoint them in the long run.

Besides, Kevin was so cute when he pouted, and he'd probably be pouting for the next month.

I set a timer. Two hours forty minutes. Kevin might be an overachiever and come back early with the next meal.

Once everyone was out of the rocket lab, I got to work.

My adjusted MyPhone disabled all the cameras in the room. If there were recording devices, they were being negated with tones out of range of the human ear.

The hologram buzzed awake. Clear as if he were right next to me, the projection of my boss, my mentor, the man with a firm grasp on most every part of my life, Todd Fowler stood not five feet away.

I uncloaked the suitcase I was hiding from the NASA scientists and Kevin. With a seven digit code, thumbprint, and eye scan, I opened the refrigerated case, withdrawing the ring of plates and circuits. Holding the thing as if it were holy.

It pretty much was holy, as far as Todd Fowler and I were concerned.

Platinum and chrome with copper wiring and white neon tubing formed a loop, punctuated by fiber optic lights, all about half an inch thick, few inches wide, and big around enough to fit on my head. Plus there was a box the size of an original Throne cube sticking out from my forehead.

If it was as effective as I'd hoped, the Crown wouldn't just be our tech for this game, it would be the tech for the rest of my career. The culmination of all of my grandad's designs, Harpreet's engineering, and CJ's assembly: the Crown.

"Figure out how to turn it on yet?" Fowler asked.

"Nope."

And we only had four weeks to figure it out.

* * *

With the rocket lab empty for hours at a time, I did my fair share of looking at the progress of other competitors.

Escondido quickly caught on to piloting his land and air vehicle, though unlike his old stick bug, his new tech had basic shifting capabilities. All tech would be shifting this year.

The General, retired, had another Battlesuit covered in projection plates with basic lightwarp capabilities. He spent his preparation time getting his tired old body into some kind of shape. It was like watching Rocky, but one of the later movies.

Aiden "Captain Awesome" Run was getting older, taller. Pretty soon, he'd be the one with acne and a cracking voice. I was so glad that my voice changed before the game went public. I hated the sound of my voice in media as it was now. I couldn't imagine how cringey it would be if it were still prepubescently high. Aiden played session after session, all day every day, with his shifter tech. He was getting good at flight and was patient enough to hide for hours. Watching him, I often wondered if that's what I looked like when I was that young, training for the game. But thinking about watching my old footage struck me as a little sad. I kept those memories, all that anxiety and uncertainty, but also, the fun and joy and Diamonds-related nerves...I kept all that locked up. That stuff didn't help.

Once the staff left for the day, I would text Mom I'd be late, Kevin's robot (which I swear was just a programmed roomba hauling around a minifridge) would get me my meals, and I'd stay up watching Harla.

* * *

Culturally, our society is at a place now with no specific rites of passage or initiation from childhood into responsibility and maturity. But there is one threshold every child looks forward to that signals adulthood: eating ice cream whenever they want.

Such an epiphany led to Harla's binges. She kept chocolate chip cookie dough ice cream, knowing Nakea wouldn't eat it. But she still kept it hidden in the garage fridge.

And watching games ate Harla's time like Harla ate ice cream. Most games had a 2 hour condensed version, a three episode narrated cut, and hours of uninterrupted multi camera feeds.

Sometimes Harla didn't make it to the guest room and woke up on the couch with some random mid-nineties game still on the television and the baby monitor blasting Andre's wails. Then she realized it was her night and cursed as she got up, rubbing her eyes while shuffling down the hall. Grab Andre, start the bottle, change Andre, feed Andre, burp Andre, and put Andre back down. Sometimes that was followed by a mug of ice cream, sometimes not. But she always went back to watching the game.

In those early games, SteelCut was so young. Still an old man, probably in his late forties, but so much younger than he was at the end, when Harla and Diamonds knew him.

He played more aggressively than anyone, although with tech like his, he didn't have to. When the trend was controllable LED gilly suits, SteelCut had a light-bending box. Then the trend was light-bending, SteelCut had a projection shield. And the trend chased projections while SteelCut was piloting a shapeshifting mech.

And on and on. You could even trace the copycats; the US armed force branches and third party military teams all had crappier versions of SteelCut's tech from three or four games back. And, of course, this led to a long run of terrible Seekers. Copycats of copycats.

SteelCut was stubborn and greedy. He and his sponsor, Todd Fowler, cooperated as little as possible with providing information on their winning tech. Game after game, DARPA built second-rate, clunky tech that often did little more than propel the "mind' of the Seeker around. Whether that mind was a pilot soldier of the early days, or the more recent Seeker programs and hardware.

In the game Harla was watching, a remote control pilot, similar to a drone setup, some soldier in an office on a military base somewhere on a Playstation controller, drove around a 5 million dollar embarrassment.

This particular seeker was the light bending box mounted on a remote-controlled helicopter, bigger than the old Artemis or Apollo units at Powers, Limited. Spray painted a mottled gray and black, the light only bent to its front and rear, leaving the Seeker exposed above, underneath, and in profile. Every time it buzzed along the candlelit castle halls, its spinning blades would extinguish the flames, leaving it to crash in the dark. It happened about ten times the first night, a few times the nights thereafter, then the poor guy piloting the thing back at HQ just gave up and only sought in the daylight.

This game, since it went fourteen days (second-longest game of all time) was a special two-part episode, four hours each.

And, of course, it came down to SteelCut in a t-shirt and jeans, wearing a cowboy's hat and night vision goggles, holding a glowing cube like the Tesseract, and his arch nemesis, Colonel Esau Holter. The Colonel, dripping with machismo, wore two riot-gear-sized shields strapped to each forearm. He could crouch within the two shields to create a tube to hide inside.

It was only day four of this game, and the field of participants was already down to two. These two guys had ten days left together. There was still another four-hour episode to watch. Harla was enthralled, chomping into another handful of caramel popcorn.

From out of a dark cellar, the mini-copter Seeker buzzed up the rounded staircase winding within a corner tower of the castle. As soon as the landing was cleared, moldy stone between suits of armor shifted and separated. The Colonel's shields broke apart, revealing the tall, muscular, young (for him) man, sizing up to the suits of armor surrounding him, though they were on pedestals. The Colonel stretched his legs, his knees and hips popping.

"That don't sound good," said a voice out of nowhere to the Colonel. "Why the hell'd you make the shields so short? If they were over two meters, you'd be able to hide without squatting."

SteelCut. Harla's hand drifted up to cover her open mouth at the sound of his voice. An extreme zoom showed the hairs on her exposed forearms raised. The Colonel sneered, looking about the room before stopping himself and settling to face one of the suits of armor. "How long have you been following me?"

"Long enough to know you're happy the Seeker can't smell."

"The others...*you* eliminated them?"

"They got themselves eliminated. Shoddy tech. Poor decision-making."

"I'll have you know those decisions are being made by war-rooms of some of the most qualified and experienced officers in the United States Armed Forces."

"Then God help us Americans."

"Enough. This isn't some game, SteelCut. This is equipment testing. We're not here to feed your ego, we're here to supply the world with better camouflage in order to keep people safe."

"Then God help us all."

"This is all fun and games for you, isn't it?"

"If you love what you do, you'll never work a day in your life."

"I'm trying to keep soldiers alive."

"I'm playing hide and seek. And I'm beating you."

"It's only a handful of games; you've gotten lucky. And we can adjust the rules to ensure fairer play."

"Are your little soldier boys tired of getting rocked by a civilian, Colonel?"

"You're not rocking anyone."

"If this were basketball, there would be posters of me dunking on them."

Without answering, the Colonel clenched and showed his teeth, emitting a small growl. He then stormed off through the hall of armor, back toward the wine cellar.

But SteelCut wasn't done with him. With the push of a button on his cube, he disappeared, everything but his hand going invisible. Light warp. Then his floating, disembodied hand reached up to the helmet of one of the stationary suits of armor, removed the headpiece, and flung it at the Colonel.

CNG CNG CNG! A crashing tinny sound let out. Instinctively, the Colonel flinched and leapt back, exposing his face. He shot a fiery look, but couldn't locate SteelCut in order to aim anything. "Damn you," he growled through his tight teeth.

Another piece of armor, an arm this time, flew at the Colonel, who raised a shield to block it.

CNG CNG CNG!

The Colonel jogged away, further into the bowels of the castle, the whirring Seeker drone zipping through the hall, following after.

SteelCut, my grandad, laughed to himself in a way nobody could but him. He didn't say half the things he thought, and often the half he didn't say would just crack him up.

On Nakea's couch, a tear escaped Harla's eye. She wiped it away, sniffed it back, but she didn't downplay it. She wasn't hiding her feelings during this moment, alone, watching old footage of a loved one who passed.

Sometimes I forgot that I wasn't in the room with her. I felt the need to reach out, comfort her with a pat on the shoulder, but she was on the other side of a camera thousands of miles away. We were both alone.

"Do you just miss him so much?" Harla's voice startled me.

Who was she talking to? I scrolled through a couple views I had of Nakea's house, but everyone except Harla was asleep.

"I do. I think of him, like, every day. Sometimes, I imagine what he'd say whenever I make a smartass remark or what he would think about me laying around like I am now. I think about him all the time, really. Even during games.

"I think that's what makes me a good captain. I'm literally always thinking of what SteelCut would do. I can't get him out of my head. That's the worst part; he won't shut up. Always pointing out opportunities I missed. When I'm too slow. When I screw up. And recently, since the last game, he ain't stopped. Because I've been screwing up so much. Because nothing I do is right. And whenever I feel like I can't do anything, that I'm trapped by the Council, I hear his voice again — 'Excuses are like buttholes; everybody has them and they stink.'

"Do you hear him, too, Wonderbread? What would he say about you and how you're playing the game? Playing the game *outside* the game now. You know what I think? I think he'd be proud of you. How you're winning. How you're adapting. How you're willing to go as far it takes. I think he'd laugh and scratch his moustache and tousle your hair like some damn TV commercial.

"And it doesn't make me agree with what you're doing. It's showing me that SteelCut wasn't a god, he was just some guy who found what he was good at. That don't make him wise. Don't make him an expert at anything else. Don't even make him an expert on how I'm supposed to play the game."

I always imagined what it would be like if she ever opened up to me. I didn't imagine it like this. It'd been over a year since I left him in the Lack; did Grandad really mean that much to her? But why would she lie?

Breathing to relax my shoulders, I answered aloud, wishing she could hear me. "He'd hate what's happening to the game. And he'd hate that Todd Fowler's in charge." I found myself getting choked up. "And he'd be so disappointed in me...for how I play now...for splitting up the team...for not inventing anything for over a year. He'd tell me-"

Before I finished, Harla left. She gathered herself up, picked up the empty pint and spoon off the floor, and folded the afghan over the back of the couch. After dropping dishes and washing her face, she cut the light.

I never finished the thought, maybe a little embarrassed that for a moment, I pictured her with me, forgetting that I was alone. That we both were.

And why would I say that anyway? That wasn't how I talked to Harla; I wouldn't open up like that to *her*.

In the dark of her sister's house, one foot in the guest room, she said quietly back toward the hallway — to me, "I don't want to fight anymore, Wonderbread. You take the crown."

She didn't know about the Crown...did she?

* * *

A phone call interrupted my viewing. Who was calling me at...wow, it was already eleven pm? Who called on the phone anyway? The MyPhone said it was a producer, out on the West Coast. That meant some decision was recently made over dinner. That's what Fowler told me it meant.

"Hawkins the hero, how are you doing? Sticking to your meal plan?"

It was one of the suits hired for the game, to prep the game for television. There were always more opinions in the room these days. And I was quickly learning what the expectations were of me outside the game. This particular suit had body shape expectations that I already understood were unhealthy to reach.

"I just want to say, I've just had a look at the newest spots, and your voice acting is just getting amazing. Chills. But for real. For real? Honestly, Hawkins, and I'm being completely honest, here — I got chills."

"Well that's great to hear. It was a great experience to work on."

Todd Fowler also told me to always say that.

"Well, it was a resounding success, and everyone is so happy with the finished product. And we are just so appreciative of all of your work, Hawkins. You are so generous with your time."

What was this brown-noser getting at? Maybe a first meeting with executives left me a little light-headed with all of the compliments and fawning, but it wore off quick. Among many other things, I inherited my Grandad's 'crap-ometer." I could smell BS a mile away.

"Again, I'm just grateful for the experience."

"And that's what's so great about you - your work ethic, your generosity, your humility. I tell you, you're a star in the making. Stick to that meal plan, and we'll make you a hero. We were all just saying that, just now. And it's just a shame that we don't have a bad guy to write for you."

"A bad guy?"

"Yeah, I know, you've had it in with Secretary Holter before, and you've got all that beef with Lieutenant Escondido, but nobody's really comfortable demonizing troops. Not testing well right now."

I knew what this was getting at. I knew who he was talking about. And I wasn't hearing it.

"There is really only one player who plays at your level. But really, she's not even at your level; she just plays well on-camera."

This was unbelievable. I was finally rid of her. I was finally going to stretch my legs and throw my weight around the game. I was finally in control.

And then the real people in charge called me to tell me what to do.

"She won't listen to me."

But as far as the suits at SuperPowers, Unlimited were concerned, I could be counted on. I wasn't the kind of employee who talked back. I wouldn't be a problem. I was expected to fall in line and be a good little boy, even doing something I knew wouldn't work, something I desperately didn't want to do.

Why was I like this?

Chapter 8

C hapter 8

The Crown was on...technically. It had power. It just didn't work.

Built to spec, I was pretty pumped that it fit me. But then, it didn't do anything. Maybe that's why Grandad gave up on building it. Maybe it was just a pipe dream.

If I removed the cube from the Crown, the rubix-cube-sized gray block stayed attached to the Throne with a line of pinkish lightning. So the tech was still connected to the Lack, where potential energy and passage of time ran wild.

I tried, every once in a while, to hook it to a computer station, but there was no outlet. I attempted to connect it to an actual Throne cube, but that did nothing. So between watching film on the competitors, my own personal workout routine, and all of the media necessary for the upcoming game, I kept busy. Weeks went by, and I hadn't figured out the Crown, or why the Lack energy came out a pinkish red rather than traditional orange.

I was running out of time. And even with a billionaire and

a team of rocket scientists on my side, I was running out of places to turn, in order to figure this thing out. What was I even thinking? If Grandad and Harpreet couldn't build the thing, why did I think I could?

No. I couldn't think like that. Being moody or mopey, that's talk for losers. Emily kept me focused, she never let me dwell on the negative.

I had too much going for me to get depressed, after all. Success in the game, professional success, financial success, romantic success. So I called her to cheer up.

"Hey Emily."

"Are you just calling because you're still not smart enough to figure out your tech?

"What? No."

"Because I told you I'd take a look."

"I had to teach you how to use WhatsApp."

"And they wound up spying on my info, so thanks for that."

"Do you want to do something tonight?"

"Did you complete all your workouts?"

"You know it."

"Do you think they're hard enough?"

"What? I'm in the best shape of my life."

"Yeah, round." She laughed.

Emily always busted my balls; she was a self-proclaimed ball-buster. But she said it was from a place of love, so I tried to remind myself of that whenever I felt like I was getting fat-shamed.

I wasn't out of shape. I was the fastest and strongest I'd ever been, I just couldn't lose my belly, couldn't fix my BMI. And with me growing and putting on muscle, I was approaching six feet tall and two hundred pounds. But no matter how fast

I got, or how many miles I ran, I kept my chubby cheeks and paunch.

"I just don't want you to let all this reigning champion stuff get to your head. If you're so dead set on cashing in at every turn and not playing the game to have fun, the least you can do is win."

I wasn't cashing in. It's true, I was getting paid a lot, maybe more than my parents, for all the media work I volunteered for. But that wasn't why I was doing it. I was building something with Todd Fowler. Something meaningful. Something even bigger than winning the game two or even fifty times in a row. But that didn't mean I couldn't do both. I'd show Todd Fowler he picked the right person to be by his side through all of this. He'd be so proud of me when I won.

That's what I told myself.

And then I realized something about Emily out loud. "You don't think I can win."

"I know you can win. Why don't you spend some extra time on tech or workouts, and we'll go out this weekend?"

That was how it'd been pretty much since training resumed. At times, Emily seemed to enjoy being the girlfriend of the face of the MC Squared, but she felt far away. Maybe she just missed the game or resented the Council. There was also the year of interrogations with FBI agents, detectives, and a District Attorney squeezing every ounce of information out of her about the Council. She was still in state-mandated therapy, too. Plus, she used to really love playing.

"ESPN was going to do another feature and asked if you'd be interested."

"In an interview?"

"Probably just shooting some candid video of us hanging

out. I don't think Fowler wants me to do any interviews about my personal life. The fans don't really know I'm bi."

The line was quiet for a second. I thought Emily was going to rag on me about calling the network's viewers 'my fans,' but instead she said, "You don't have to keep on with the bisexual thing."

"What?"

"I mean, you're dating a girl. I know you had that talk with your parents...but I guess you can tell them...nevermind."

"I'm still bi, even if I'm dating a girl."

"Whatever. I just don't think you have to push it. I mean, you barely dated Diamonds, and she's probably the one who probably convinced you that you were like this."

I almost didn't say it. Diamonds was no friend of mine anymore, after all. But it irked me. And I think she was saying it to be irksome. The whole subject, the way Emily talked about my being bi, was surprising and aggravating. So maybe I said it to annoy her back.

"They."

"Excuse me?"

"They. Their pronouns are they."

"Whatever you say, silly kitty," she said in her playful sing-song voice. It still unnerved me. She'd spoken like that in the arena, worming her way into my mind through hypnosis. I got queasy when she used that voice. And I think she knew it. "Mr. Popular has so much to do before the big game. And no time for me."

"I told you, we could hang out tonight."

"Take me to the carnival this weekend, Kitty. Throw a ball. Win me a prize."

She said she was tough on me to help me be better. She said

we should confront our flaws. But if I asked her more, or tried to have a serious conversation, she'd go back to the sing-song voice and calling me Kitty.

* * *

Baby Andre was on a "sleep program" which meant when he cried at night, neither sister would come to his aid. Nakea had work the next day, so she turned her baby monitor app off. That meant only Harla could hear the baby as she finished up a term paper on the couch that was pretty much her room now. And as always, the game streamed on the big screen in the background.

This was her third time through the entire series, not counting re-watching particular games Harla held dear. Of course, she never watched *that* game, the one when Grandad fell into the Lack. As far as Harla was concerned, that's how he died.

She clacked a couple keys theatrically and closed her laptop.

"Whew. Another degree down. That's two for me, plus certifications. What are you up to, Wonderbread? Still none?"

She was right. I'd been accepted to Duke, but never replied. I still hadn't finished my high school diploma. Like I said, I got busy.

She watched SteelCut's first game while upstairs, baby Andre cried.

"Poor Dre. Sleep programs suck balls."

She watched the game obsessively, even though she'd seen it before there was even a streaming service. When she was on SteelCut's team, Harla had watched this gameplay footage of her captain. But back then, she toggled manually between wide shots and SteelCut's POV. But now, it was so dramatic. Not only edited, but narrated.

Like I said, they kept me very busy.

"Okay, Mr. Invisible, I'm going to find you." she cued up the game again.

"On day three, the elements begin taking their toll on the civilians. Even SteelCut, who went on to become the winningest player in the whole game, was unprepared for the humid, swampy conditions. As participant after participant began falling ill, getting sick without sacrificing camouflage became another wrinkle in the game. Although the technology is long lost, it was predicted that the gilly suits employed by most participants actually raised the temperature on most bodies by seven to fifteen degrees, often stifling the ability to sweat or the skin to self-regulate temperature. Hawkins' own LED-enhanced gilly suit was an estimated thirty degrees hotter."

And then, in the middle of the swamp, birds and insects as loud as a concert, scum and debris floated on top of gray-brown water. And from that water arose a bubble. A furry bubble that rose until it exposed the top of a head and muddy brown eyes. Eyes opened to shock with fierce dark pupils and clean whiteness. The General, merely a Lieutenant Colonel at the time. The Lieutenant Colonel was not in a Gilly suit. The Lieutenant Colonel was stripped down to underwear. Tighty Whities, long since dyed swamp water brown, his body painted in mud and accented with algae.

"Say what you want, Wonderbread, but the General used to be a BAMF. But then comes this Bugs Bunny fool."

Just as she said it, a rock hit the mud-caked Lieutenant Colonel in the top of the head. His eyes blazed angrily as he turned slowly, searching the undergrowth wildly. Spanish Moss draped over low crooked oak trees, branches running parallel to the water level. No movement beyond rippling water. And all of the wild noise.

Baby Andre cried along to the noises of nature.

Another rock hit the Lieutenant Colonel in the back of the head.

He rose up, revealing his nostrils stuffed with Lord-knew-what and a reed he was breathing through. Standing up to wade, the young alpha male was obviously flexing. It was almost like a nature video, a male appearing fierce or large to scare away rivals. The muddy and jacked young man spun around, splashing the disgusting water.

"Who is that?" he spat out in a whisper, calling out to the treetops around him.

Only the buzz of insects answered.

Harla held her breath. Upstairs, baby Andre had calmed down. She crept off the couch, sitting closer to the TV. She had been watching for weeks, but always came back to this game, always searching for something.

"But even the best trained soldiers can be pushed to their limits."

A few feet above, looking down on the exposed Lieutenant Colonel, a young man covered in fake spanish moss clung to a tree branch. He held his breath as his superior officer spun around. Hugging wood, his breath was stifled and ragged. Sweat poured down his forehead. He blinked hard as it ran down into his eyes. It collected at the tip of his nose and shook. He tried to reach it with his tongue. He tried to wipe it on his shirtsleeve. He tried to blow it onto the tree branch.

He failed.

The droplet on his nose grew and grew from a liquid bowl, gaining mass until it shaped like a drop, its bulk moving down away from the nose tip. The droplet fell. He gasped.

Harla still hadn't breathed.

The drop fell onto the Lieutenant Colonel's forehead, and the officer's focus shot straight into the air.

The spanish-moss-covered soldier let out a microscopic squeal and tightened his hug on the branch.

The Lieutenant Colonel looked up at the soldier.

The soldier looked down at the lieutenant colonel.

A rock flew out of the brush and pegged the tree-bound soldier in the forehead.

"Goddamn-" He fell out of the tree. Onto the Lieutenant Colonel.

SPLASH.

A struggle ensued, one muddy limb clamping onto the arm of another, as they wrestled in the waist-deep mud. It was a jumble of sludge combat, loud with sucking and splashing.

Neither saw or heard the Seeker soldier jog over.

Clothed from head to toe in highly reflective orange, the seeker soldier ran with his paintball gun aimed before his face. He put three paint pellets into the muddy wrestling match.

Three pink circles busted and splashed against the muddied bodies. They froze. Slowly, a figure rose to standing, spanish moss dripping heavy mud, three pink splotches on his back.

The Lieutenant Colonel got away.

A splash and movement in the water beneath him, and the Seeker soldier ran to the water's edge, firing aggressively. A good ten or so paintballs flew into the water, sucked underneath with a quiet splashing noise. And then silence.

The soldier raised both of his hands in surrender.

Over a loudspeaker, a voice crackled, "Army Rangers have been eliminated."

The Ranger in the muddy moss walked out of the water with high knees, searching around him for any sign of the Lieutenant Colonel, but there was none.

The Seeker soldier's gun barrel pointed wildly about the water, seeking movement that wasn't there.

Another rock flew from out of nowhere to a sandy shoal where a cluster of trees met the water. Following his paintball gun barrel, the Seeker jogged off to follow the sound.

Again, the arena stilled. Until a much heavier rock flew and landed in the water with a loud splash.

On Nakea's living room rug, Harla paused the game. Her eyes scoured the screen, almost desperately. She said out loud, "I know you're there."

Was she talking to me? Was this another moment of her opening up to the listening devices?

"There's something up, Wonderbread," she said slowly, thinking aloud. She was talking to me. She went on, "There's something...someone... hidden in these games. Someone we ain't seeing. Maybe we ain't supposed to see."

With a click of her remote, the game continued.

Onscreen, the Lieutenant Colonel jumped to his feet, angrier than before. He charged, limping in the deep water toward where he figured was the source.

"Your soldiers are soft," a voice called out, mockingly. A voice remembered for being lower, raspy, coarse. Grandad's voice, only younger.

"And you're a hardass?"

A pebble knocked at the Lieutenant Colonel's temple. He fumed in anger.

"You're soft, Holter."

"And you're steel cut oats."

With a rustling, the Lieutenant Colonel dropped to his belly, staying low, staying still.

The Seeker soldier returned, taking a few steps, then holding to listen, over and over. A few steps, stop and look. A few steps, stop and look. Headed right for the spot where the Lieutenant Colonel lay. Not ten feet away. Then closer. Closer.

Behind his paintball gun, the seeker soldier swept the area with long, exaggerated arcs, covering everything in front of him and to either side.

A foot away from the Lieutenant Colonel and getting closer.

But the Seeker didn't step on the Lieutenant Colonel. Instead, the scantily clad muddy officer took the Seeker by the boot and pulled. The Seeker went ass over teakettle. By the time he landed on the back of his neck, the Lieutenant Colonel was out of sight again.

It took a second for the Seeker to catch his bearings again, getting to his feet, stretching his head this way and that, blinking hard like he was fighting a concussion. Once he'd checked in with himself, took a breath and a sip of his canteen, he took a step to return to his gunpoint surveying. One step on the muddy patch of ground where the lieutenant colonel had been. A slick muddy step. And the Seeker fell again.

A laugh came from a nearby root cluster. SteelCut's hoarse guffaw, quickly muffled, but it was too late. The Seeker painted the roots.

"Aw, Hell."

The PA system crackled, "Civilian Hawkins has been eliminated."

On her couch, half an hour after baby Andre had gone back to sleep, Harla finally breathed, relaxed, and fell back into the couch. "Heh. Hard as steel cut oats."

I always worry I'm too soft. No, that's not right. I feel like *Emily* worries I'm too soft. *Always.*

Always insisting I confront my weaknesses. Expose my fears. Seek my flaws.

After clicking the remote, she rolled into her afghan, away from the fading television. "There's more going on, Wonderbread. We got to find it. Goodnight, Wonderbread." She laid there for a while, eyes open, looking at nothing but the pattern in the couch cushions. "We can stop them, Wonderbread. You just got to be more like SteelCut. Is your dad like SteelCut? Wonderbread, senior? Mr. Hawkins..." She mumbled something else and drifted off to sleep.

I laughed at the comparison to Dad. I couldn't be less like the guy.

Back in the empty NASA rocket lab, I finally stopped avoiding my boss. Todd Fowler's line rang and rang. Was he sending me to voicemail?

"Who even calls on the phone nowadays?"

I didn't know what was projecting his hologram, but there he was, standing by way of projection in my workspace. He could get to me anywhere.

"Sorry, I didn't want to disturb you."

"No disruption! I prefer to avoid the paper trail of phone records. Honestly, if you said my name out loud, I'm fairly certain I'd get an alert."

Was he being serious? "That's creepy."

"So what can I do for you, champ?"

"The Hollywood suits are nervous."

"Are you being overly gracious?"

"I am. It's not me they're nervous about."

"Chase, there aren't going to be any more surprises like before. We're going to keep the game completely safe from those Council idiots."

"No, they're worried my narrative needs a bad guy."

"Do guys get worse than Esau?"

"They want someone who isn't a soldier. They have someone pretty...specific in mind."

He took a deep breath and fiddled with the strings of his hoodie. "There are other people we need to keep the game safe from."

"Do you think she's a threat to the game?"

"Honestly, Chase, I think she's a threat to you, to making the game too aggressive."

"And she'll be nonstop with the Council theories."

"Chase, I'm not worried about her running her mouth. I'm worried about you."

"Don't. I'm not a fragile little kid."

"Are you in favor of bringing her in?"

"Well, they do have a point. This isn't a singing competition, it's a sport. And a home team needs an away team."

"Rocky needs Apollo, huh?"

"I guess. But I told the suit she's not going to listen to me."

"How do you know if you don't try?"

This wasn't what I'd wanted to hear. I wanted him to say I didn't have to talk to Harla if I didn't want to. I wanted him to say we could pull out the Regalia bots NASA had instead of banging my head on the wall figuring out the Crown. But I didn't say any of that, because I was a good little employee.

"How's the Crown coming along?"

"Still working on it. I may want to dust off the Regalia just in case-"

"No."

Fowlers short, low tone startled me. His eyebrows matched the stern voice, but suddenly it was all smiles again. "Thanks for calling. Never hesitate."

Chapter 9

Chapter 9

As soon as he delicately slid his bare foot back on the rug floor, he nearly fell, doubled over, folded at the hips. Both arms shot out to regain balance, and he straightened to standing again, picking up his right foot and placing it back down under him.

"There! Oh my God! Oh my God! His first step!" Harla pointed and covered her mouth.

Watching through a video call, Nakea was nonplussed. "Nope, doesn't count."

Harla rolled her eyes. "Why are you such a discouraging mother?"

At the word, baby Andre's dimpled face turned to Nakea. They both lit up in a smile. "I am not. But he's just getting his footing; that's not a first step."

"You need to learn to raise this child up instead of knocking the man down."

"'The man?'"

Just then, baby Andre lost his balance again and slowly fell onto his face. Both sisters instinctively gasped and reached out hands to help, but Andre was fine. He rolled off his cheek and pushed back up to sitting, his face concerned, his lip working.

Then he busted out laughing. The sisters joined in, and they let out a well-earned laugh.

Turned out, the university did need Nakea to come in to attend faculty meetings, grading sessions, and department rubric sessions. Basically, she had to go into school all the damn time.

So instead of video conferencing into her job while she was home being a mom, she was video conferencing into being a mom.

"You look so stupid reaching for your baby through the computer."

"Well you look a fool when you can't catch him when you're there. What kind of nanny are you?"

"I ain't no nanny. You don't pay me."

"You pay rent?"

Harla didn't reply.

"Mm-hmm, that's what I thought. You my nanny. I pay you with a dwelling in which you reside."

"I want a raise."

"Girl, you better not be insulting my house. I'm a quarter-million dollars in debt for your palatial surroundings."

The doorbell rang.

"You expecting somebody?" the sisters said to each other.

In her empty plastic and steel office, Nakea pulled out her phone and thumbed around. She pursed her lips and raised an eyebrow at her sister. Her voice rose teasingly. "Girrrrl, it's your 'friend' Diamonds."

"'Friend'? What's that supposed to mean?"

"It means I'll talk to you later, and don't forget about my baby while you're hanging out with your drama teacher."

"'Drama Teacher?' What's that supposed to-"

But the video chat ended.

With a grunt, Harla got up and heaved the big baby boy onto her hip. The doorbell rang again.

"I'm coming!" she called out, stomping barefoot for the front door.

Diamonds looked good. They were in a blue and yellow BTU hoodie (ironically, since neither their undergrad nor post-grad were there) and tight black jeans. They'd filled out a bit, their cheekbones still sharp but now lacking the gaunt drop off from hollow cheeks. And hips now to match their wide shoulders. They wore circular sunglasses and more ear piercings than last time, about four non-matching pieces in each ear, like mismatched scout badges.

"Hey," Harla said awkwardly.

Diamonds faked a smile. "Hey. Oh my God, you're so big!"

Harla's brow pressed down as she opened her mouth to clap back, but stopped when Diamonds made tickle-tickle fingers at the baby on her hip.

"Oh. I forgot he was there."

Diamonds shot her a sharp look.

"I didn't 'forget he was there' like I'm a bad nanny. I know he's there. He's always there. I just think of more like...part of my arm. The adorable, drooly, ticklish little part of my arm."

Harla joined in the tickling, and Andre squealed and squirmed with glee. Diamonds came in, and they all sat on the rug in the living room.

"You look great," Harla said in a dry way. It was polite, and she spoke through a fake smile, her eyes sad.

"Thanks." Diamonds didn't look up from clapping with Andre. "You look terrible."

"Gee, thanks."

"Either you know it's true, or you're in denial. Are you showering? You can be exposing this baby to all kinds of-"

"I'm showering, D, jeez. Back off."

"Well, your hair's shot. And your skin looks terrible."

"Well, isn't this fun? You came over to list out crap wrong with me. Man, it's great catching up, D. We should do this more often."

"Are you okay?"

"Yeah, I'm great. I'm fine."

"Okay. School's good. I'm making lots of friends. I'm up to three."

"That's good, I guess." Harla was pouting.

"I'm going to start volunteering at a school soon. There's an after-school program for disabled kids. Plus they don't have a chess club, so I may start one."

"That's...that's actually pretty cool, D."

"Yeah. I'm super-pumped."

"Would they be flexible if you ever decided to go back to the game?"

"Are you serious?" They stopped playing with the baby and searched Harla's eyes. But that's how Diamonds looked at people. Like they were searching for answers in eyes that mouths wouldn't say.

Harla shrugged, uncertain of what she'd just said. "Well, yeah? Someday, I mean. Definitely not this next game. But down the line..."

"Harla, what are you talking about? I almost died out there. There are no rules. Todd Fowler was manipulating the Council before, and he owns the whole game now. And streaming on global TV? There isn't enough anti-anxiety medicine on the planet that would make me cool with being on TV."

"Okay, okay, stop freaking out, I was just asking."

"Were you?" Diamonds stood. Their voice lowered and clenched up like their fists. "Were you just asking, or are you trying to get the band back together or something?"

"I was just asking. You were the best navigator the game had ever seen, thought you might miss it."

"Miss it? Are you kidding me? I almost died. I met a cute boy there, and a year later, he almost killed me. Harla, if you miss it so much, you go back, but you have got to respect what I went through. I'm never going back."

"Well, me neither." Harla picked up Andre and took him to his high chair in the kitchen. Diamonds didn't follow, so Harla just raised her voice. "I'm perfectly happy here. I love my sister and am glad I can help with this little angel!"

It was an odd thing to yell.

But I was stuck back on Diamonds. After everything that happened, after everything I'd done, they called me cute.

After strapping the baby to his chair, Harla grabbed jars from the fridge, pouches from the cabinet, and slammed an array of baby foods on the counter. She moved manically and talked like she'd burst if she slowed or stopped. "I'm almost up to three bachelors, and I might get my MBA. Then once this nugget is in either preschool or daycare," her voice cracked, "I'll get my post-grad. I'm already postulating theses, and I can practically write a dissertation on the SuperSwarm." She sniffed back tears. "Then I'll get my first doctorate, then—then—"

"Hey." Diamonds appeared at the threshold into the kitchen.

"You're not doing okay. What's going on?" They crossed to her and hugged her gently, almost like they were afraid she would break.

"Nothing's going on." Harla wiped her face and twisted open a pouch. Her voice was thick with spit and snot, like Harla's body was threatening full-out sobs and weeping, but the young woman defiantly held back. "I'm just adjusting."

Andre took the pouch from Harla and hungrily chugged.

"I'm a little stressed from my course load online this semester. I may be pushing myself a little. And he's teething. Plus sleep regression is the absolute worst. And hearing *his* voice just wears on my last nerve."

"Whose voice?"

"You know. On all the game episodes."

"What are you talking about?"

"The shows? On SuperPowers Unlimited?"

"What about them?"

Harla was losing her temper. "His voice. He talks through every show."

"Who does?"

"Chase, okay? Chase does. Haven't you seen a single damn episode?" She slammed a jar on the counter, spilling a bit. As she grabbed and wetted a sponge, Harla muttered to herself, "Jesus. Now old Wonderbread's gon hear us talking about him."

"I haven't seen the shows." Diamonds spoke delicately as Harla spoon-fed Andre. "I don't have SuperPowers Unlimited."

"What? That's ridiculous!" This snapped Harla back to reality, a relaxed, safe space with Diamonds. She snickered. "I thought everybody had it. Want to watch a game while you're here?"

"Sure. I mean, I guess so. If that's what you want to do."

"I'm down for whatever. If you're done with the game, that's fine by me." Harla took over the remote, then filled the silence. "I think it's great that school and everything is working out."

"And I'm glad you're able to help out Nakea with little Andre."

Harla stopped scrolling with the remote abruptly. "What's that supposed to mean?"

"Um...it means exactly what I said?"

"Well I'm also collecting undergrad degrees like you collect broken hearts, so I'm actually up to a lot."

"What's that supposed to mean?"

"That I'm not some sappy depressed girl sitting at home all 'woe is me' while you're out there living your best life."

"I don't get why you're angry."

"Who says I'm angry? Look, Andre's going to chew on these carrots for half an hour, so we can sit on the couch if you want to watch a game."

"Whatever you want, Harla."

Harla sighed and rolled her eyes like she was on the end of her rope with Diamonds. They moved up to sit not too close together on the couch that was Harla's de facto bedroom.

Harla snuck a checking-sniff on her pits when Diamonds wasn't looking. She cued up the game she always watched, SteelCut's first competition. The one in which she insists she sees an extra player.

I've watched that particular game since she started rambling about it. I didn't see anything out of the ordinary. But if someone was there, if there were an extra player, Diamonds would find them.

Chapter 10

Chapter 10

Another of my voice-overs began the 1984 Military Camouflage Challenge (back when it was annually). I'd been in the studio four days a week for a while now. I'd put my senior year indefinitely on hold once I'd turned 16.

"The year the competition first opened up to civilians was also open to newfound controversies. For the first time, since not all competitors were government employees, they were open to all sorts of lawsuits. Precautionary physicals took weeks leading up to competition. Some participants said they felt they were prepping for a moon voyage rather than a technology test drive."

I hated the sound of my voice, to be honest. It was still so high. It changed. It used to be higher, but it was still high. I tried lowering it in the recording booth, but the guys kept stopping and making me speak naturally by telling the story to one of them.

So I had this high voice and my awful accent. It made me sound stupid. I know Harpreet told me that it was bias that made me think that, but I did. And it was worse watching two people who I knew hated my guts listening to my stupid high, twangy voice.

"Still, many third party engineering corporations came out of the woodwork, vying for a lucrative government contract. And among them was fledgling telecommunications company, Powers, Limited, a regional service corporation created out of the Ma Bell antitrust break-up. Simply put, Powers Limited was dwindling, their resources limited. On what appeared to be a dangerous gamble, the small communications business sponsored one of its lead engineers and threw its hat into the ring."

"You're right," Diamonds said flatly. "I really hate his voice."

"Hear that, Wonderbread?"

"What's that?"

"Nothing. I was...it's nothing."

"It's not nothing, Harla. Are you talking to yourself?"

"No, I was talking to Dre. Talking to babies is important for development."

"Do you always call Dre 'Wonderbread'?"

"You heard that, huh? That obvious?"

"What is going on with you?"

"I don't know I'm just...sad, I guess? Lonely? I eat whatever and watch the game all night. I exercise, sleep, and watch Andre all day. Every. Day."

"That sounds really tough."

"It is."

Diamonds muted the TV as close-ups of each of the contestants flashed on screen. "I do think it's really great that you're helping your sister and that you're killing it stacking up your degrees; I honestly wish I'd done that. Plus you're staying active, which is admirable."

"But..."

"But your depression is getting worse, Harla. And you're not getting joy out of these things you're doing. Plus...I miss you. A lot. I think we should see each other once a week."

Without a word, Harla enveloped Diamonds in a hug. This one, aggressive.

"It's ridiculous. We have teleportation technology, for cripes sakes."

Harla freaked out, jumping to standing and pointing at the TV. "There! There! Do you see it?"

"What?"

She grabbed the remote and rewound. "Watch."

"What am I watching for?"

"Just watch."

In the bubble that topped a camo space suit, Lieutenant Colonel Holter's head popped up, then was pegged by a rock.

They both snickered.

Then the second rock, and Holter stood.

"Damn, Holter had abs."

"First, shut up. Second, ew. Third, watch."

"What am I watching for?"

"I don't want to tell you, just watch."

Then the third rock.

Suddenly, Diamonds cocked their head like a parakeet would. They lifted a hand, a finger twitching like they were tapping at a keyboard. "Wait, hold on. Pause."

A smile spread across Harla's face. "Right?"

"Rewind. No. Give me that." They snatched the remote from Harla. They rewound, then paused, then moved the image forward frame by frame.

"I didn't know it could do that."

"Where's the third rock from?"

"Exactly."

"Because someone's submerged in those roots, and they throw the first two."

"That's what I'm telling you!"

"And the third rock is from over... Hold on."

"There's someone else there."

"Yeah, there's someone else there. What year is this game?"

"1984."

"No way."

"It is. Why?"

"Because whoever threw that rock is warping light. And that tech doesn't hit the game until..."

"2001. That's impossible."

"Did the Council have technology before the teams in the game could develop it?"

"Then what's the point of the game?"

"What is the Council even after? Money? Control? Ties to the government?"

"Harla, do you ever think about what Emily the Martian said to Chase when he was hypnotized?"

"All that creepy stuff about playing with people?"

"Yeah. She said something about the game within the game. *There's always a game within the game.* You ever think about that?"

"Not really."

"I do."

They were quiet for a second.

"I talk to Chase all the time. I've convinced myself he's

probably still spying, still has me bugged, so I just kind of started talking out loud to him."

"Could I convince you to see a therapist?"

Sigh. Eye roll. "I guess."

"What do you talk to Chase about? If you don't mind me asking?"

"I don't know. Stuff I would talk to Chase about, I guess."

"Like what?"

"Competition. The game. Trash talking."

Diamonds gave a big nod, flattening their lips, then pursed into a polite smile. "Jock stuff."

"I guess. Do you think you could ever forgive him?"

"No." Their answer was so quick I jumped just listening.

"Do you think you dislike Emily the Martian because of what Chase did?"

"Oh, I don't know. Can't I just never think about either of them ever again?"

"Oh my God, right?"

Sometimes I wished *I* never had to think about me ever again.

An alert went off on Diamonds' phone. The car was here to pick them up. They asked to see Harla's phone. As they tapped away, Harla laughed but seemed nervous about someone else in her open phone.

I wouldn't want anybody to access my browser history.

But Harla made light of it. "You know, I already got like five numbers for you."

Diamonds handed the phone back "It's not me."

They hugged Harla, who closed her eyes when they embraced, then they ran in the evening rain to the black town car waiting.

Apparently, we were all town car people now.

Harla checked her phone and opened a recent app. Maps. A pin was dropped, not three miles away, at the edge of a park.

$$* * *$$

I bit the bullet and did it. During one of the nights of ice cream, bingeing and depression, I consolidated all of the Regalia still in the Gamble household and made a call. I projected myself into their living room.

Harla screamed and fell on her ass when I was suddenly behind her. I couldn't help but chuckle a bit.

"It's nice to see you, too. Have you put on weight? It looks good on you."

"I ain't too big to whoop your ass, fool."

"I miss this. I miss us. I miss Miss."

"What, your little girlfriend isn't doing it for you anymore?"

My holographic projection strolled around Harla's little couch encampment of bedding, snacks, and electronics. I was wearing the expensive suit she didn't like. "Emily? No, Emily's great. That part of my life is great. She's my rock. Keeps me grounded."

"That's funny. Little Miss Martian keeps you grounded."

"You can laugh, but it's true. Mind if I sit down? Don't answer, I'll just sit. But life's been so complicated with all of the moving parts in getting this new game off the ground, so it really is nice knowing I can always call her and she'll make everything better."

"I think I just threw up in my mouth. But I wasn't talking about Emily. Is your little girlfriend Todd Fowler not keeping you interested?"

"That's a gross look on you. A homophobic joke? I'd watch who I said stuff like that around."

"What do you want, Wonderbread?"

"To recruit you. I'm gathering participants. We have eight captains lined up so far, and you'd make a great addition."

"Maybe you should have talked to me before making me a character on y'all's little TV show."

"I knew they would regret that. But what do you expect, all these producer types are so new to the game. Some of them are new to their jobs. It's a new production company, too."

"If you only got eight teams, what other one dropped out?"

"Other one?"

"Yeah, you got eight teams. Powers, Unlimited don't have a team no more. What's the other team that pulled out?"

"Boston Tech University has permanently suspended their camouflage technology projects."

"Well, yeah, they're going to try and stop a time loop. I'm surprised they didn't close up shop earlier."

"But also Shadow Systems and Mayhew, International."

"So who are your eight captains?"

"To be fair, one captain is yet unnamed. But I'm here today on behalf of Useful Plastics and Savant Entertainment."

"You're here on behalf of your competition?" Harla raised an eyebrow.

"I don't know how much you've been following the launch, Harla–"

"Miss," she corrected.

"Sorry. I don't know how much you've been following the launch, Miss Harla, but I've become something of a de facto poster boy. Whenever anyone has a public relations task, I'm usually the one to ask."

"That's funny."

"What, that they'd pick me as a spokesperson? I agree, it's my first-"

"Naw, that's an obvious fit. The best puppets don't have too many thoughts in their head to start with. I think it's funny that you act like you don't know how much I've followed the game. I imagine I'm being videoed, recorded, bugged, droned, and sat-spied every minute. I think you know exactly how closely I'm following."

"Don't flatter yourself. You're not a captain anymore, and I'm a busy man."

"Boy," she corrected.

"It's difficult not to lose my temper when I'm here to grant you an opportunity."

"Harpreet told me how bad you are at hearing no. I'm glad I got to tell you no to your face. Or as Harpreet would probably say, 'Take your opportunity, shine it up real nice, stand that son of a bitch up sideways, and stick it straight up your candy-'"

"I'm not surprised you'd be so rude, I admit. Just disappointed."

"Did you get rid of your accent?"

I had been working on it, tired of hearing my high-pitched drawl all over the streaming network.

"Did you get rid of yours?"

"Wonderbread, you're disappointing. Now leave me alone; the answer is no."

"I'll leave you alone then. I'm sure you've got to get back to your classwork for Roland College."

Her face fell just like it had when she found out Brielle Ward wasn't real. And that had Fowler written all over it.

I lashed out with a direct hit at Harla's feelings, something to rile her up and stick with her. As I left I said, "Tell Diamonds I say hi."

It was mean and immature. And honestly, I felt horrible about what happened to Diamonds. I wasn't even sure why I said it.

I'd disengaged the hologram before she screamed.

III

Part Three

Build

Chapter 11

I'd have done the job myself, but media days, which was what we called any publicity for the network, took up all of my time. That, and I doubted the brothers would listen to a teenager. Thank goodness it wasn't me. I've never been to a jail before.

It was Fowler's idea to recruit them. Why he thought those two could convince her after I couldn't, I hadn't a clue. All I knew was that when I asked Holter to find them, he agreed.

Whatever Fowler had on Holter, it must have been bad because the old retired General didn't give me any guff. And Esau Holter was a guff-fiver. Todd Fowler seemed to have a way of getting what he wanted from everybody.

So when Holter quickly agreed to help, I slipped enough Regalia bots onto his person to keep an eye on things.

I didn't like doing it. Those Regalia bots were tiny and ruthless. When I said 'on his person,' that meant they stayed on him always and hid whenever they risked exposure. Most likely, when the guy showered, they hid...inside.

So General Esau Holter went to the middle of nowhere Canada to find the two brothers that screwed up the General's own plans back in my first game. And he had tiny robots on his body, and up his butt, watching.

The brothers Hubert got drunk and got in fights; it's what they did. Sometimes those fights were with an unlucky third party, but more often than not, the brothers fought each other. And while this happened at a myriad of locations, the placement of such fights were often inappropriate.

And so it was that the brothers Hubert got kicked out of, and subsequently banned from, their local Applebee's. In the parking lot, the conflict didn't get resolved. And as they worked it out, pulling shirts over the others' head and pushing at faces to counter headlocks, the Applebee's manager on duty called the police.

It wasn't their first trip to the drunk tank and definitely not their last. But it was probably the most productive.

They were still arguing over hockey players or sweaters or jerseys or whatever when they were locked up with some unfortunate homeless man who wanted nothing more than a couple hours sleep under the bright florescent lights on a hard plastic bench. Instead of the peace necessary for rest, he got loud shouting.

"By definition, every original six sweater is a throwback." Alex Hubert, formerly known in the game as Captain Spectrum, hung onto the crossbars and yelled.

"Then do more pull-ups than me, and everyone will know you're right," Mark Hubert, formerly Captain Mist, rested at the top of his pull-up a few bars away from his brother, face pressed against the cold metal.

"Wait. You're saying you want *more* throwback jerseys? More merchandise to buy?"

"I'm saying I've done twelve pull-ups, and you have at least eight to do to prove your point."

"Doing more pull-ups don't make you right."

Mark dropped then pulled himself up again, grunting. "Then why'd you agree to it?"

"To shut you up."

"Didn't work," the homeless man on the bench said from underneath his jacket.

"Hubert and Hubert," a skinny rookie cop called out as he pushed a button to open the overnight jail cell.

"Letting us out?" Alex dropped from the bars to his feet.

"Thank God," the homeless man said.

"Not just yet. Someone's here to talk to you."

"Crap." The homeless man rolled over to face away.

"Who's here to talk to us?"

The cop shrugged. "Above my pay grade."

Mark landed on his feet with a bigger thud, the vertical imprint of the bars running up the side of his angry red face. He worked his hands and flexed his shoulders, putting the seams of his flannel plaid to the test. Still squared up with the cell door and the cop, he told his brother, "Don't say anything. Let me do the talking."

Alex batted his eyes. "But what if they don't want to hear incorrect information about hockey sweaters?"

"Damnit, Alex, just stay quiet!"

But that was one thing Alex was terrible at. "Listen, Officer, if this was about that thing with your wife…"

"Alex!"

"Mark!"

"Jesus Christ, Mark, just listen to your brother!" the homeless man called out as the brothers were led into a hallway of locked doors.

The officer escorting the brothers waved at a nearby camera, and with a buzzing sound, the metal door in front of them slid open. He held the door open and gestured to the brothers to enter. He then closed the door behind them.

The room was much darker than the fluorescent halls, and the brothers both rubbed their eyes in the Hubert manner of digging the heels of their hands into their eye sockets.

"The two of you and neither handcuffed, heh? I guess I didn't pay the cops off enough." The voice was amused gravel.

"Who's there?" Mark asked.

"What are you doing here?" asked Alex.

The rough voice let out a chuckle. "Well, I didn't get in a fight in a franchise restaurant, if that's what you're asking."

"We did."

"Mark, he knows that."

"Who?"

Alex slumped into a chair opposite the bolted down table, yawned, and stretched. Mark paced behind him, still blinking hard. "My brother doesn't recognize you without your stupid gundam wing getup on. I hope you didn't pay the cops too much. Bad enough to catch a Hubert beatdown for running your mouth, worse to catch a beatdown and waste your money."

"Well, let's hope I didn't waste my money."

"Yeah, let's hope you don't run your mouth is more like it," Mark grumbled.

"Myself and others involved would like to see the Hubert boys get their hands dirty again."

"I'm about to get my hands bloody right now."

"Mark, take the aggression down a notch."

"Can I offer you gentlemen some water? Aspirin? Gatorade? PediaLyte is supposed to be good for hangovers."

"No, we're fine," Alex said.

"Got a beer?"

"Mark, cool it."

Then the unmistakable crack of a beer can opening came from the table. The general presented a silver can, blue at the edges and dripping cold condensation.

"Oh, hell yes."

"Oh, hell no," said Alex. "Thank you, but no. Now do you mind telling us what this visit is about?"

"I am here on behalf of the United States Federal Government to address several warrants for you two. You can help us out and they'll go away, or the Canadian government will cooperate with me, and I'll haul you back to jail for these outstanding warrants."

"That don't sound outstanding."

"In exchange for what?"

"I'm here to offer you boys a job."

"I could use a job."

"Mark. What job?"

"Oh, it's one you've had before."

"Is this about the game?"

"It is."

"Oh, that ship has sailed."

"Persona non grata."

"As captains," Holter pointed out.

Mark made his move. With a quick step and a lunge, he snatched the can of cold beer and chugged.

Alex rolled his eyes and sighed. "Do we strike you as mission control material?"

Mark belched in agreement, tossing the empty can and pointing a thumb at his brother. "Really, can you imagine this guy behind a desk?"

With his arms folded and mouth pursed, Alex said, "My brother's not exactly a computer guy."

"So, either become computer guys..."

"Fat chance."

"Or face judges for whatever you two did in..." Holter read from the file folder. "Alaska, California, Nevada, New Mexico, and one of you in Texas."

Mark giggled to himself. "Texas was me."

"Not necessary. And, by any chance, are we expected to be good computer men or perhaps are we to abruptly become bad computer men at a particular point in time in the game?"

"Actually, the interests I represent want you to do the best job possible. Personally, I'd prefer you to abruptly stop doing your job well when my neck is on the line out in the new arena."

"New arena?"

"So you're back to playing?"

"You bet your tiny, hairless Hubert balls."

"Cause we shave them."

"And you want us on your team?"

"...not together, obviously."

"Oh, you aren't coming near my team. I want to win. The job is actually recruitment and then team support."

"Recruitment?"

"Bring your own Captain. We have the candidate. You'll have to convince her."

"Why don't you convince her?"

"She doesn't listen to me."

"Why would she listen to us?"

"Oh, she doesn't listen to anybody." Holter chuckled, getting up from his chair with a groan and gathering the

Hubert's file. "You'll have to get creative in convincing her. Good luck."

* * *

"Okay, I'm going for a run!" Harla always took advantage whenever her sister was home. Nakea offered to buy a jogging stroller, but Harla declined. Where she was going, she couldn't have baby Andre getting into things.

The computer system I have is amazing. It took a while to build an algorithm that understood what I wanted from the small amount of time I had to watch film on Harla. But when it did, it was great. All of the film came with filters. The filters were necessary. I was watching Harla as a competitor, not as a friend, or as an ex-friend, or as an ex. And I was thankful for the filters to keep things professional. One, I didn't want to be some peeping tom. Plus, I didn't have the time to watch every second of her runs. So I was relieved when the filter skipped therapy sessions.

It wasn't like a light switch was flipped. Harla wasn't suddenly happier or more open with her emotions. Her skin didn't clear up. She didn't walk out of the therapist's office with wrinkle-free clothes or perfectly sculpted hair.

But she slept that night. Seven hours, which was the most since the last game.

And her running times improved. Her three miles to the park services parking lot actually slowed down, but it was purposeful; Harla didn't shrug her shoulders as she jogged. She kept her head up. She hummed.

In fact, if you weren't surveilling her on the daily and obsessively poring over the filtered video feed, you wouldn't even notice the change in her.

But her sister was noticing changes in Harla.

"You're going for *another* run? Wasn't yesterday the 'big run'?"

"Well, kinda."

Nakea rounded the corner, simultaneously burping Andre while eating the remainder of the orange baby food. "And shouldn't you have a recovery day?"

"I didn't push it that bad," Harla said as she warmed, jogging in place with high knees.

"Oh, to be young and never had a baby."

"Don't say that!"

"Don't tell me what to do in my own house, girl. Are you stretching properly? Looks like you're about to blow out your knees."

Harla switched to jumping jacks. "Just 'cause you some old lady don't mean I am."

"Just 'cause you young right now don't mean you will be forever."

"Oh, I'm sorry, I didn't realize I was living with Mom again."

"Girl, you better not."

Harla stopped jumping. "*You* better not."

Nakea held up a finger in warning, "I'm telling you, you're pushing your body. Hard. And I don't know why."

"You don't get it, 'cause you a bookworm and I'm a athlete." She began to squat into a jump over and again.

"Oh, okay, Miss Mathemagician."

"Don't bring that up." She stopped. "I ain't playing!" Squat jumps resumed.

They both smiled, finally. It was difficult to tell how serious they were with each other. At times, they were in each other's faces, voices raised, hands balled into fists, but then they'd break out laugh or hug or make some childish insult and run away.

"So what are you training for, Harla?"

"I ain't training for nothing. I'm keeping healthy."

"Then what's that notebook you wrote "training" on the cover and fill with your mile times?"

Harla stopped, out of breath but mean mugging once again. "Don't look in my stuff." Harla sprinted out of the house, calling out behind her, "My God, Nakea, you're worse than Momma!"

Nakea whipped her head around to respond with another "Girl, you better not," but Harla had already closed the door behind her.

Of course she didn't stretch. She never did in the off-season.

The pin Diamonds had put into Harla's phone was three miles to the nearby park, up the dirt trail to the wooded hill, then off the trail, through a hole in a chain link fence to the abandoned park systems admin building.

That's where *it* was parked.

Dusty, dented from years of use, the rusty orange and faded red shipping container stood innocuously by the abandoned construction site. Spider webs criss crossed its shadow, and saplings grew on the roof.

Harla walked up, pressed her hand against a painted square, and activated the secret door which slid open. Lights within flickered on as Harla checked around to make sure she was indeed alone before entering the old shipping box for the Throne, now Harla's secret lab.

Chapter 12

C hapter 12

When Harla got home, running back to Nakea's house after dark, she saw someone parked in their driveway. Harla slowed about a half a block back, pulling out her earbuds, getting a hand on her pepper spray. As Harla neared, the figure waited, looking like an old man, silver hair sticking out of a baseball hat, baggie jeans, and puffy brown coat. But it was no old man.

"Captain," came Dr. Bird's terse delivery.

Harla ran the rest of the way and gave the old lady a hug.

"Oh! Go easy on me!"

"How are you, Doc?"

"Fine. I'm well. And you?"

"I'm great, just got back from my big run."

"Yeah, when your sister answered the door, she said you were out for a long run. I hope you don't mind that I waited."

"Not at all. It's so good to see you! Come inside!"

"Thank you. I must warn you, I'm no good at lying. And there's no way you just had a big run."

"What are you talking about, Doc? You just saw me running."

"Oh, I'm sure you put down a quarter mile or so, but you haven't been running for an hour. You'd be much sweatier, and your water bottle would be about empty. Not to mention the fact that I've monitored your complexion under duress and can identify the intensity of your exertion."

"My complexion is black."

"Black that hasn't just run over 10k."

"Okay, fine, Doc, don't lie. I'll make sure it doesn't come up. Have you eaten?"

So they made dinner and caught up. Dr. Bird had gone back to her original career as a medic for extreme sports, but it was obvious she missed the game.

"...but everything is done either on a half-pipe, in the snow, or in a chopper. I miss cots and med stations. I miss teaching, really."

Surprisingly, hearing her say that knocked the breath out of me a bit. I'd hated school. It was boring and easy, but I was no good at it. I might have been lonelier in a school full of kids than I am alone in an empty rocket lab.

I loved school with Dr. Bird. For a year, it was just her and me, and it was great. The year before, it was her and me and Diamonds. And that was just...perfect. And not just because of Diamonds, I realized then. I wish I'd thought of how much I enjoyed being around Dr. Bird back when I was around Dr. Bird. Instead I just pushed her away like I did everybody for reasons I didn't even know.

So it stung when Dr. Bird kept on, "I really loved teaching you guys. Maybe I chose the wrong profession or maybe I just had the three best students I could ask for. But it's nice to catch some of the games on my phone. Have you been watching any? There's some great moments of SteelCut."

"Yeah, I've been watching a little."

Even though she'd been quiet for much of the meal, Nakea let out a laugh. "Girl, you watch non-stop."

Harla shot a look, communicating death threats at her sisters without saying anything.

Dr. Bird laughed, too. "I admit, I have been, too. You're looking pretty good for someone not planning on playing. I believe you're twelve to one to win."

"What?"

"I helmed first aid tents for a poker tournament in Vegas—"

"Poker players need a medic?" Nakea interrupted.

"Yeah, there are some nervous breakdowns, heart attacks. Not at that one. It's a law through Nevada sporting. Anyway, one of my constituents visited the sports betting, and everyone was going nuts over the MC Squared. Of course, everyone thinks more of me now that they know I've worked on a team."

"And my odds of winning the game are twelve to one?"

"Yeah. The board's big, almost every contestant since the game began is up there with their odds to win. Chase is the favorite, followed by Holter, then you, then Escondido."

"Ha! I'm ahead of Escondido! So out of the top four, only one of the favorites to win is actually going to play?"

Dr. Bird cocked her head in confusion. "Don't you watch MC Three?"

"What's that?" Nakea and Harla said simultaneously.

"Evidently not. It's the talk show on Superpowers, Unlimited. They've been announcing competitors over the last few weeks and doing interviews."

"So?"

"Harla...Escondido and General Holter are in this year's game."

She dropped her fork with a clatter.

Nakea was utterly lost, looking back and forth from her sister to the doctor. "What does that mean?"

"Well, General Holter recently stepped down from his position as Secretary of Defense-"

Nakea went wide-eyed. "Oh, *that* General Holter? Girl, you been balling against the real deal General Holter?"

"Of course, *that* General Holter!" Harla shook her head, thinking out loud to Dr. Bird, making sense of the news, "So... Luis? I talked to him last month. He said he was retired."

"Money, I guess? A paycheck can change some minds."

Dr. Bird shrugged. Nakea's voice dropped to ask, "How much money are we talking?"

Harla rolled her eyes. "Sponsor companies get a multi-million dollar government contract."

"There's prize money now, too. And an endorsement deal."

It was Harla's turn to drop her voice, "How much money are we talking?"

"A million bucks."

The Gamble sisters' eyes turned into dollar signs.

Pleased with herself, Dr. Bird smirked a bit, stabbed at her salad, and chewed contentedly while the other two sat aghast.

Nakea addressed her sister with a sudden urgency. "Harla, you got to think about coming out of retirement."

"No shi-"

"Language!" Nakea chided, nodding toward chunky little Andre in his high chair, covered in applesauce.

"Language my butt, we're talking about a million dollars."

"Unfortunately, it's just not that easy." Dr. Bird placed her napkin by her empty plate and took a long, savoring sip of white wine. "You'd need a sponsor, some sort of camouflage tech, a team, and of course, a month away from the game, you'd be way behind on training."

"Well, what about your runs? You've been doing your runs, surely that has to count for something."

Harla looked down at her plate, clammed up.

Her sister folded her arms and raised an eyebrow. "What'd you do, sis?"

"I may have already started building some camouflage tech."

"I knew it!" Bird yelled victoriously. Well, it was yelling for Bird. She barely raised her voice.

"So then all you need is a sponsor."

"It's not that easy. I have one part of the camo tech done, and it took me a month to build."

"Well, how many parts will it take?"

"I'm thinking twelve-hundred."

Nakea broke it down. "So then all you need is a sponsor corporation with access to, what, a 3D printer?"

"That should do it," Harla said flatly.

"And a team."

"The team's easy. I could beat Chase into embarrassment with no one but you three on my team."

Andre let out a noise between a burp, a gargle, and blowing a raspberry.

Nakea cheered enthusiastically, and everyone joined in.

Harla steered it back to serious. "But I'm going nowhere without a sponsor or tech..."

"But didn't that boy Chase want you back in the game? He's got to know some sponsors. Can't you ask him?"

"I wouldn't trust Chase as far as I could throw him. Besides, there is someone I could ask."

Dr. Bird stood. "Well. It's getting late. I should head out."

"Wait, Dr. Bird. Thanks."

They hugged for a while, grunting in that way a long-wanted hug gets.

"You're welcome, Harla. And good luck, whatever you decide to do."

"I think I may have already decided. Maybe I had made up my mind the whole time."

"Well, good luck. Oh, and in case you do put together a team, and you do find yourself in need of a medic, you have my number."

"Nah."

"No?"

"Harla!" her sister chided.

"Nah. I'll hire you right now if you're willing," she said with a smile.

* * *

I honestly wasn't certain where she was going. There weren't a ton of skyscrapers in Portland, and this was one of the tallest. The lobby was dark marble and brass; the kind of building where all the fittings looked old on purpose. One of those places where voices echoed. So did the squeak of Harla's Air Force 1's as she marched up to the front desk. Besides the sneakers, she was in full professional mode: gray and black striped suit, black plastic frame glasses, and her black and blue hair pulled back tight into a poof behind her.

She said in a courteous voice (that didn't fit her at all) to the front desk, "Harla Gamble for Verma Tech."

"Anyone in particular at Verma Tech?" the young lady behind the desk asked before dialing.

"Harpreet Verma."

The young lady furrowed her brow, correcting, "*Doctor* Verma?"

"Just tell him Harla Gamble is here, please."

"So they're expecting you?"

"Just...just tell him Harla Gamble is here. Please."

The young lady dialed incredulously, "There is a person down here insisting I call to say that Harla Gamble is-" The young lady's eyes shot wide open. She stammered, "Yes, I'll send her up immediately, thank you." She hung up, stood, and smiled forcefully. "Miss Gamble, may I show you to the executive elevators?"

Of course, she'd go to Harpreet. There was no way she'd agree to one of the sponsors I suggested. And of course he'd say yes. Thanks to some lawsuits over who owned what tech, no CEO in the world hated Todd Fowler as much as Harpreet Verma.

"Bro! This will piss Fowler off so hard!" Harpreet loved the idea. His corner office was glass and carpet, but instead of a proper desk, Harpreet had a standing workstation. It was right next to a couple arcade games and a Batman Pinball game next to a projector screen Playstation in front of a conspicuous sofa. "But how much is this gonna cost? We're not the most liquid until the next product drops."

Harpreet made millions off remote-controlled robot battles. Players from around the world could challenge each other to fight drones. Players controlled the bots from phone apps but could also access live streams of other fights, including a GameStop-sponsored tournament. They got very popular very fast.

But Harpreet was still in a vintage wrestling tee shirt (this one for a surfer looking guy with pink face paint named Sting) and old jeans. His Call of Duty game was paused.

"The cost should be minimal. I need a medic, a couple mechanics, a navigator, and access to 3D printers."

"I'm flush with those. And obviously lube."

Harla shot him a confused look.

"Quantum lube. For the portal."

"Oh, goopgating? Isn't that owned by Superpower Unlimited or Power Tech or whatever?"

"No, it's my parent's. I was the one who brought it to SteelCut. Just something else Fowler's suing me to control. Do you have a team in mind?"

"I got Dr. Bird. I was kinda wondering if you'd be interested in-"

"No way, brother. Way too busy."

"Well, if I can't find anyone, I'll settle for just Doc. If I've got the printers, I've got tech...I know I'll be able to hang."

"Wow, I dig the vendetta, bro. Shaking the game up Shadow-style."

"What's Shadow Style mean?"

"Something SteelCut would say when somebody broke the norm. Shadow was just a player who never followed the rules. Always ticked off SteelCut and the General."

"Captain Shadow...I saw the games he was in. He became the Shadow Seeker?"

"He became a pain in everyone's butt. Like you. But, you,

know, in a good way."

"Well, maybe he should make the list of potential recruits."

"How long's the list?"

"So far, one. Unless I can have a temp, too. Because I have someone in mind for that job."

The phone rang, and Harpreet had to go. Last thing he told Harla was, "Find someone who can find people for you. And you can have an intern as long as I don't have to pay them."

Then Harpreet Verma, grungy millionaire, took his high-powered executive call. And Harla had her sponsor.

* * *

Shaking a sports bottle to disperse electrolytes, Harla booted up the computers in the shipping container. Luckily, Nakea had a solar box and generator she didn't use (her Army husband, Tyler, insisted), and it wasn't too difficult to haul up to the hidden lab. After checking the power levels of the solar batteries, she plugged in her phone which had died on her run.

It was her own fault; she went to bed, but watched another game on her phone, falling asleep before she could plug it in.

In her lab, she lifted the safety glass of the mini 3D printer (from Tyler's as-of-yet unused workshop, this was much more difficult to haul) and picked up the finished product- a scale, the size of a guitar pick, filled with detailed individual circuitry.

Ever-so-gently, Harla placed the scale to lay flat on the table, circuitry facing up. The computer was on by now, and she clicked on the laboratory journal.

"Test one-ninety-two. Remote battery."

She grabbed a mobile power source, pretty much a battery the size of a pen, and activated the piece of tech. As soon as Harla touched the tip of the power source to the input of the scale, the circuitry lit up. The scale twitched to life as a signal light let out a clear bright green. The scale then lifted from the table and hovered two inches in the air.

A maniacal laugh escaped from Harla. "Sweet Christmas, it works. It works!"

Then the alert went off on her phone. Not a text, email, or call. This was security. Someone was at Nakea's house. And not at the door.

Her family was safe, Nakea and Andre were running errands, but Harla wasn't about to put up with two fools in ski masks trying to open a side window in bright daylight.

Chapter 13

C hapter 13

With a stretch of duct tape, Harla fixed the mobile charger to the single scale and sprinted back to the house. This time, there was no easy pace, no enjoying the scenery, no headphones or playlists, not even a trail. Through the park, the run to the storage container was about three miles. But if she ran off the trail, in a straight line, through woods and ravines and across a creek, it was about a mile. And Harla was SPRINTING.

She had brought her phone along, of course. It was the only way to remote control the scale. However, she had about a 7% charge, and that gave her anywhere between one and five minutes operating the scale.

So she acted quickly.

Behind Mrs. Johnson's picket fence, Harla crouched across the street from Nakea's, at just enough of an angle to see the men dressed in black helping each other into the side window. The smaller of the two, or skinnier, since they were both pretty tall guys, was inside, and they were doing what resembled a comedy routine trying to get the other guy, the big one, up and inside.

I honestly wasn't sure if I even wanted them to be successful. Finally, Harla was out of the game just in time for me to get the fame and fortune. Maybe I wasn't as humble as I could have been when I asked her to come back. But the suits wanted her, and I could tell Fowler wanted to do whatever the suits wanted. And even Emily asked me if I thought my gameplay would be exciting enough without a rival.

So maybe I found myself rooting for Harla this one time as she and her tech of a single, impossibly flimsy nanobot took on these thugs.

Harla worked quickly. She lay the scale flat on a fence post, then opened the phone program to fly the thing. It responded immediately, again floating a couple inches in the air. That wasn't enough to impress her now. With a thumb on her phone, she guided the scale through the air, as it hovered and wavered like a sputtering biplane.

As it crossed the street, a car sped by, the air kicking off its body sending the scale into a flutter. Suddenly, it was a tree leaf in the breeze, blowing this way and that. Harla struggled to gain control, then a gust of wind took over, knocking the scale about, sending the minute electronic piece onto Harla's lawn. It tumbled as it blew across the grass.

"Come on, come on." Harla struggled to regain control in the wind.

The smaller thief had the bigger thief up in the window now, only a few feet away from the fledgling scale on the ground.

With one last heave, both of the men in black fell into the house. With a thud.

"Come on!" Harla mashed at the controls on her phone.

The window to the house began to close.

The scale glowed its bright green and steadied itself in the air before zipping up and into the window just as the glass pane closed behind it. Once it was near enough, Harla could hear the thieves.

The big one was still out of breath, "So what do we look for?"

"Some kind of fulcrum. A means of putting pressure."

"Say what now?"

"A bill, a letter with bad news. Anything. You search the mail, I'll see if I can get into this."

The skinny one lifted Harla's laptop, then strode to the kitchen table.

One step away, he placed his foot on the ground, only the sole of his shoe didn't make it to the tile floor. The scale swooped in underneath his foot, taking his weight, and flying away.

The smaller thief flipped and fell on his head.

The big thief shushed him. "Careful."

"What was that?" said the other, getting off the floor.

"You fell."

Through eyeholes of his ski mask, the small one looked up at the big one aghast. "My God, I hate you so much sometimes."

Meanwhile the scale slid across the floor and rose to the level of the desk by the side door. As the big thief laughed at his cohort, the scale slipped into the stack of papers in his hand.

As the small one booted up the laptop, the big guy returned to the stack, thumbing through bills. "Oh!" the big guy exclaimed, jerking his hand away from the papers and sucking on his thumb."

"What?"

"I don't know. Paper cut. But a bad one," he said, sucking on the print of his thumb.

"Aw, poor baby. Get over it, and keep it down," he said as he tilted the laptop to look at the keys closely.

"What are you doing?"

"Seeing if the keys that spell out her password are especially worn."

"Does that work?"

"I don't know."

"Argh!" The big guy dropped the stack of papers and started sucking on the fingers of his other hand.

"Another papercut?"

"I dunno. I don't like this, Alex. Let's scram."

"Ixnay on the names."

"Okay, I don't like this, Ixnay. Let's scram."

"We just got here, and we haven't found anything."

"Oh, I wouldn't say that." Harla's voice boomed through the house. The thieves instinctively crouched down, half-hiding beneath the kitchen table. Faces suddenly intent, the both stayed quiet and still, breathing slowly through their noses. The big guy squinted to listen for her voice again. "You found trouble."

The small one put up a finger for his brother to hold on for a second, then addressed the homeowner in a fake, nasally voice. "We're armed, and we're desperate. And we're leaving this place with these copper pipes"

"Copper pipes are in the walls, not in the mail, fool. Now take off your masks!"

At the command, the big guy retreated from the kitchen table, duck walking back while looking around, headlined towards the window they came through.

As he reached for the doorjamb only a few feet from the window, the scale slid from the side of his mask over one of his eyes. His hand, reaching for the doorframe missed, and he fell down the step into the next room.

"That's it, run for it!" the small one yelled as he careened past his downed counterpart. His feet slid as he turned up the narrow hardwood hallway. He planted his hands on the bottom of the sill and called after his still-downed partner, "Come on!"

The answer he got was from the window which slid shut after a push with a flying start from the scale. Fast-moving wood crushed the little guy's fingers. He screamed. The scale locked the window shut.

Tears rolled down his pained red face, and he was suddenly sweating, roaring each breath in and out.

The big guy's hand, gloved and raised in surrender, entered the hall first, followed by the rest of him, moving slowly into the living room, a black rectangle of tech pushing at the back of his head. A scowling Harla's black rectangle of tech, out at arm's length, kept the big one's hostage. Over one of Harla's eye sat a prototype scale as a free-standing eyepatch.

"Harla?!" the little guy screeched. "It's me, Alex!"

"Captain Spectrum? Why are you in my house?" She jogged over, unblocked the lock, and raised the window off Alex's fingers.

He fell to his knees in relief.

"You two know each other?" asked the big guy, hands still up. "Wait, is that a phone?"

Harla waved the black rectangle of tech. "Yeah, I held you up with a phone, fool. I know Alex from training with the ScatterSwarm."

The big guy dropped his hands and ripped the mask off his face. He had a huge red indent running up the cheek of his already reddened face. Must've been from when he landed on the floor.

"Am I supposed to know you?" Harla threw a hand on her hip.

"I'm Captain Mist."

"You *were* Captain Mist."

"And frankly, it's pretty insulting that you used the name 'Miss' when you knew 'Mist' was already taken."

"Mark!" Alex quieted his brother before addressing Harla. "We're here with a message."

But Harla wasn't having it. "To hell with your message. Why'd you break into my house?"

"We were hired to."

"Who'd hire you two fools?"

"Hey!"

"We're professionals!"

"Professional what? Who are you? Sherbert, who is this fool?"

"Call me fool again and see what happens!" The big guy puffed up.

"Harla, this is my brother Mark. Mark, shake her hand before she calls the cops on us."

"Harla." He begrudgingly held his hand out for a shake.

"Call me Captain Miss," she said, staring at the hand with hers on her cocked hip.

Mark wasn't going to correct himself. And Harla wasn't going to shake his hand. It was a standoff.

"Cut it out you two. We came to make an offer."

Mark cracked his knuckles. "We are to recruit you by any means necessary."

"What does that mean?"

"Who's the fool now?"

"You. Y'all can leave now."

"Don't you want to hear the offer?"

"No, I want y'all to leave and tell your bosses you failed."

"If we do that, we go to jail."

"Should have thought of that before you broke into my house." She led them to the front door.

"Tell her about the team. We can get anyone on the team you want."

"No."

"They'll build you a new ScatterSwarm."

"No."

"There's going to be sponsors this year. Like ads. You could get a shoe deal."

From within the house, looking down her stoop at the Hubert brothers, Harla gave. Just a little. "Alex, your brother is smarter than you two look. If you can get one person on my team, I'll consider it."

"You name it. Anyone."

Harla smiled.

I was positive it was me.

For a split second, I did wonder if I'd have to sit out a game on Harla's team just to get her back in the game.

But when Harla said someone else's name, I felt a flash of anger. No, not anger. Disappointment. Sure, maybe a little anger, too. And of course Harla added all these stipulations not to break into any more houses or invade privacy. But the unease I saw on her face after the brothers Hubert left...the way she nervously tapped her fingers...she knew she just sicced the dogs on an innocent bystander.

* * *

Diamonds still came over on Sundays. This week, she brought Chinese takeout; setting out boxes of main dishes, rice, and potstickers. Harla was noticeably quiet until they began eating.

"You're an hour early." Harla was sweaty in yoga gear, doing cardio in the living room above and around Andre.

Diamonds came in with the bags of takeout, headed to the living room floor by the baby, shrugging. "I'm terrible at time zones. With the delay in the Verma goopgate, I was worried about getting here on time."

So, Harpreet was supplying Diamonds with teleportation goop, too. And I hadn't realized the Verma family recipe for the purple goop had a time delay.

"Can I ask you for a favor?" Harla asked, shoveling a fork of fried rice in her mouth.

Of course, Diamonds was proficient at using chopsticks. "You know you can ask me anything."

Harla's mouth was full. "I'm putting a team together..."

Diamonds finished their bite and laid utensils across the white takeout box before asking in an overly calm voice, "And what would I have to do with this team?"

"I'm not asking you to come back to the game, I just need help."

"Finding people?"

"Finding a navigator."

"Oh."

"And the rest of the team, too."

"For real?"

"Except the medic. I got Dr. Bird."

"Well, I guess. Um...yeah." Wiping their hands off, they pulled out their myPhone and started a blank page in their notes app. "How big of a team are you thinking?"

"Oh. I don't know. Medic, a couple mechanics, and a navigator. I'm getting used to four person teams."

"But last game, you muted everyone, right? So why do you think you need a navigator?"

"I just...I muted the last team because they were just saying nonsense. No one was... I needed more eyes on the arena."

Diamonds put down their phone and took Harla's hand across the table. "I want to be very clear that I'm not going to come back to the game."

"What? Yeah. Of course. That's not what I'm asking."

"Well, yeah. But you have to realize that the only navigator then that you've liked having on the comms was me, and I want to make sure you should temper your expectation."

"Okay, slow your role, D."

"What?"

"Don't toot your own horn too much there."

"Okay. So you want a navigator and what other necessary personnel?"

"I don't know, that's what I need you for."

"Well, let's think of this. What kind of people do you want on the comms?"

"I already told Bird she was my medic. So her."

"Okay. And do you want a mechanic or an engineer, someone familiar with the tech?"

"Well. I kind of...built the tech."

"Of course you did. Still might help to have a second opinion out there."

"I don't want anyone second-guessing me."

"Okay. So maybe someone who knows about mechanics and the tech but that won't be their primary purpose."

"What do you mean?"

"Maybe somebody who can help with tech but also knows how Esau Holter's tech works."

"Like a practice squad coach. An expert on the enemy."

"Exactly. What about Escondido?"

"Um..." Harla squinted as she said with a mouth full of noodles, "He's in the game."

"Yeah, I know. Should we make sure someone on the team has intel on playing against him?"

"Oh. Yeah. I wouldn't have thought of that. Thanks."

"Now we're getting somewhere. Do we know anyone who played against Escondido and Holter? Are the Herberts still suspended?"

"Huberts. The suspension is just from playing. They can be on teams."

"Great. Spectrum knows physics, Mist knows mechanics. Reach out to them."

"Funny you should say that...they reached out to me," she trailed off.

"To be on your team?"

"To get me on a team."

"Out of the blue? They just contacted you?"

"Someone put them up to it."

"Oh. You're not getting blackmailed into playing, are you?"

"No...not that they didn't try."

"Do you think this is a good idea, then? Going back?"

"What? Yes. Of course. Team building. You're right, I should ask the Huberts."

With a heavy sigh and heavier side eye, Diamonds reluctantly continued, "Okay, do you think they can be trusted?"

"They're not bad guys. I'll keep an eye on them."

Diamonds deliberately put their phone down without looking up. "Do you really need help finding a team?"

"What? Of course I do!"

With a squinted stare that made Harla shift in her seat, Diamonds kept talking in their unnerving, even tone. "Fine. Then ask Ricky Diggs to navigate. There. Done. You got a whole team."

"Okay, great."

They ate for a moment before Diamonds burst with, "Look, it's obvious you were asking me to be your navigator."

"What? No."

"Harly…"

"I wasn't."

"Fine. Then we're done. You have your team."

"Do I want Ricky Diggs on my team?"

"Yes. He's amazing at what he does."

"Can I trust Ricky Diggs?"

"Yes. He worked with SteelCut for decades."

"But should I settle for Rick-"

"Yes," Diamonds interrupted. "The team is complete."

"Yeah." Harla went back to pushing Chinese food around the takeout box before finally shrugging and saying, "I mean, plus the intern."

"But do you need an intern?"

"What do you mean? What's a team without an intern? Who'll get coffee? Who will the team take its anger out on?"

"Hopefully nobody!"

"We'll need one to run errands, or if someone has to leave mission control for some reason."

"But do you need an intern?"

"Stop asking me that! I want one, okay? You were an intern, and I was an intern. It's only fair I get one now that I'm captain."

"You've had an intern for two games and were awful to both of them. Poor Brandi left college and joined a convent. A convent, Harla. She left working for you to go marry God."

Harla tried not to laugh as she shrugged.

"And do you remember torturing poor Kevin? He stopped sleeping, and you gave him gastrointestinal distress!"

"I want an intern!"

"Fine."

"Fine."

They ate in silence.

"Okay, fine, I thought you may miss the game."

"You thought wrong."

"Don't you want to put Chase in his place?"

"I don't want anything to do with Chase! Or the game!"

Their words hit me like a gut shot. But I couldn't blame them. I used Diamonds' weakness against them, triggered a panic attack, restrained them against their will, used them as bait - as an object - to help me win a game. I'd hate me, too. Heck, maybe I did.

"Fine."

"Fine." Diamonds pinched themselves a veggie potsticker. "Ricky Diggs is a great navigator."

"Ricky Diggs is retired. And he already came out of it once to witness his captain burn down the entire arena, so let's not act like he's a sure thing."

"Then think of an alternate."

"What if Ricky's the alternate?"

"Then you still need a navigator."

"Okay, fine. There was one other name I had in mind, but... they'd be too hard to find."

"Don't bait me, just ask."

"Right. Have you ever heard of the Shadow Seeker?"

"No..."

"Had a solid run playing in the early aughts. Came in third for a while. One year, SteelCut was having a fit over his tech being stolen, and that's when he started turning down the contracts. First time he refused to turn over his tech for the prize money. So the Council made him forfeit. And of course, who came in second?"

Diamonds made a rolling gesture with their chopsticks. "The General."

"Yup. But your boy Holter didn't want to be handed a victory, saw no honor or whatever in it, so he forfeited. That left the winner to be..."

Diamonds' chopsticks rolled forward again. "Captain Shadow."

"Even though they had no tech."

Diamonds' chopsticks stopped. They fell loose in her grip, dangling. "No tech?"

"They had a make-up application technique for camouflage. That camo happened to match perfectly with the arena, and they made it to third place."

"Don't tell me they were in black face."

"Hell no."

"So who became the next seeker?"

"The Shadow itself. Captain Shadow. Wore gear and makeup to match the arena. Soldier for a seeker, just like in the early days of the game. Only now, Captain Shadow was against projector shields and LED gillies."

"How'd they do as seeker?"

"Fastest game in history."

"Really?"

"At the time. It's a tough one to watch on the network. The camera couldn't keep up with the seeker. It was in the deep snow. Ended really quick."

"Small arena?"

"Nope. Hundred square kilometers."

Diamonds whistled. "Let me guess, nobody's seen them since."

"Yeah. They're going to be really hard to find. No name, no military service record. I guess we should both work on it."

"Actually, Harly, I think I'm done here for now." Diamonds got up, flicking through their phone, calling the car.

"Oh."

"I mean, I'm curious myself about this Shadow Seeker, so I may take a look in my off time, but it's better if you and your team figure this one out."

"Oh. Well...thank you."

"I'm glad to help. Just because I'm out of the game doesn't mean I don't want you to do well. I just want you to be safe is all."

"Thanks."

"Tell Harpreet and Dr. Bird I say hi. Take it easy on whoever your poor intern winds up being."

They hugged. I found myself scrunching my shoulders, subconsciously imagining the embrace myself.

Their car pulled up, so Diamonds headed off. "Take it to the road, Fury. Go assemble some Avengers."

Chapter 14

Chapter 14

Granted, her parents' old 2008 Buick LaCrosse, an absolute boat of a car, wasn't the most impressive vehicle to drive through the goopgate, but Harla sure managed to look like a badass — black and royal blue suit, whited out sunglasses, and black and blue hair back in a poofy bun.

In a crumpled black suit over a Rowdy Roddy Piper t shirt, her millionaire boss was the first to pick up. He wasn't on the team and wouldn't be showing up regularly, but Harpreet was the one with the portal goop. He probably missed being on a team, too.

The Verma family recipe produced a shiny purple goop, as opposed to the silvery sludge the Powers Team had.

"This smells different." Harla commented as they coated the old boat of a car.

"Yeah, it reminds me of cow tails. Like, caramel instead of cotton candy. Where to first?"

* * *

"Follow with your eyes, not your head," Dr. Bird was getting exasperated with the young athlete. She snapped her finger. "Hey! Young man! Keep your head still. Follow my finger only with your eyes. What's your name, Hunter? Hunter, if you can't follow my finger, you'll be out for three months."

That got the young man's attention.

Dr. Bird was going down the line of BMX bikers, checking everyone for concussions. A loudspeaker echoed through the arena announcing names and events.

Harla yelled to the Doc, "Is this a bad time?"

Dr. Bird, in a wholly different look, was wearing a gray tank top splattered in dried blood, camo cargo pants, and black surgical gloves, revealing an enormous snaking tattoo of black and gray vines chasing up one entire arm. She looked like a badass, but she also looked busy.

"Yeah, I could leave them to the volunteer nurses, but most of them are fanboys and groupies. Text me where we're training, and I'll be there bright and early Monday morning. Good to see you, Harpreet."

"Good to see you, Doc."

"I miss you guys."

Just then, someone limped over, bleeding from the arm.

"Let me know!" Dr. Bird called out before attending to the young woman, calling her a baby as she examined the open wound.

Harla and Harpreet headed back to the parking garage. Harpreet told her, "Um...as your sponsor, I admit I haven't gotten you a training spot, bro."

"I don't even have tech. How am I supposed to train?"

"The printers are running, bro."

"It's not just the printing, boss." Harla opened the car door. "We have to build and troubleshoot the programing for it."

"You've already written the programming?"

They got in.

"I wrote it years ago, Harpreet. With you."

"Does that mean…is your tech that rejected rough draft of the Throne?" he asked.

"He gave me a challenge, that was my answer. The way SteelCut explained it to me was trapping something of infinite size and infinite power within a machine casing finite in size and wattage. It was a puzzle."

"But SteelCut said it couldn't be built."

Harla took off her eyepatch and placed it on the dashboard. She pulled her remote battery out and touched it to the little scale. Immediately, pale blue light shined as the scale hovered an inch up.

Harpreet laughed with glee. "So who do we need to make enough of these to build a suit?"

"An intern and a couple mechanics," Harla said, texting and scrolling through her messages. I thought of the name Harla had given the brothers. And it was them who texted when she said, "Oh, we're in luck. The mechanics are currently with the intern."

"Doing what?"

She put the car in gear and drove blindly through the goopgate. "Intimidating and recruiting him, if they listened to me."

* * *

If two guys drinking by the pool was intimidating, then Kevin was in trouble. But he didn't seem to mind the two rather toned older gentlemen drinking by his pool. Even if it was still technically morning in Arizona.

"Hey, you guys, Harla's here!" Kevin ran out of the back door of his family's house, leaving it wide open behind him. It wasn't an enormous house, but at least something you could call a McMansion.

Coming around the corner and striking her badass pose, Harla cocked her hip to the side and whipped off her sunglasses to reveal the triangular scale bot for an eyepatch.

Kevin collided with her in an awkward hug. He squeezed tight, holding her way too low on the back, while she had no idea where to lay her hands and ended up patting him on the back of one shoulder.

Harpreet suffered the same fate of clumsy hugging, then Kevin bounced on his feet, looking back and forth between his old teammates. "So what's going on, is everything okay? Can I get you guys something to drink? Coconut milk hot chocolate? We don't have any powdered mix, but I can melt some hershey bars and the only coconut milk we have is from the can. Would that work?"

"No, Kevin. We don't want anything to drink."

Harpreet, who was still wearing his gold-rimmed amber-tinted aviators, whipped them off and said dramatically, "We're putting together a team."

Harla put a hand on his chest, pushing him back by the Rowdy Roddy Piper logo and saying quietly, "Whoa, whoa, man. I get to say that. It's my team."

"But I'm the sponsor, bro," he whispered back.

"Fine. You said it this once. It's my turn next time."

Interrupting, Alex called out from a lounge chair, "Yeah, he won't do it!"

Mark was sitting on the edge of the pool, dangling his feet into the water. He'd evidently had a few beers, and his consonants slurred as he said, "Being a rocket scientist is his dream."

"But you're not a rocket scientist. You're Chase's gopher; it just happens to be at NASA."

"I applied for a department transfer," Kevin said.

"We should hear back this afternoon." Alex pointed with the hand holding a beer.

"I had a dream once," Mark muttered to no one in particular, kicking water.

Kevin corrected, "*I* will hear back about my transfer today at earliest."

"And I'm paying you bros to sit here and drink?" Harpreet asked.

"It's an intimidation tactic," Alex said as his brother pounded the rest of a beer.

"I wanted to be a hockey pro!" Mark was now yelling.

"It's annoying is what it is," Kevin whispered out of hearing of the Huberts.

Alex barked at his brother, "Cool it, man. And you *were* a hockey pro."

But Mark was fired up. Or was he on the verge of tears? "Semi-pro. We can't stop him from becoming a rocket scientist. I won't do it."

Harpreet assured them, "Nobody's doing that! Nobody's

stopping little bro from anything."

Regaining her badass pose, Harla raised her voice but took her time, looking each of the three men in the eyes. "Nobody is getting paid until we start work. And in order to win, I will need all three of you clear-minded and present. We need to build the tech, find a navigator, and come up with a plan to both win the game and take down Fowler, along with SuperPowers Unlimited. We only have three weeks. Let's make them count. I'll see everyone at seven am Monday morning."

She about-faced and marched away. Her head was high, and she smiled when no one could see.

Raising a slender finger, Kevin said, "Um....still with team NASA? Chase is my captain. Remember that?"

Good for you, Kevin. I appreciated the loyalty.

Harpreet, still poolside, asked, "What's the workload? How're the hours?"

"Oh, I literally programmed a roomba to do my job. I stopped showing up over a week ago."

I never liked Kevin, I just thought his freckles were cute.

"Well, according to the rules," a smile spread across Harla's face as she said, "no two teams can hire the same team member, and no team can compensate a team member of another team. So we're going to need you to volunteer."

Harpreet added, "To be an intern."

Kevin didn't miss a beat. "If it helps shut up that smug pretty boy, I'm in."

I'd never been called a pretty boy before. It didn't feel like a compliment. I don't think I realized how much Kevin resented the job. No, not the job — me.

Harpreet smiled and waved goodbye, joining Harla who asked him quietly, "You think Chase is a pretty boy?" She obviously didn't.

He shrugged but nodded.

Aww, thanks, Harpreet.

* * *

The Brothers Hubert were even harder to deal with on caffeine.

"You think the US government would let a guy like that walk out after seeing the secrets of the game? A stone cold merc like him? Do you know how much money he could make only talking, not lifting a finger? And if he did lift a finger, think of how many he could kill."

"It's all BS anyhow," Mark scoffed. "There is no Shadow Seeker."

"That's ridiculous. He's the purest player in the history of the game."

"There is no 'he,'" Mark insisted, reddening more crimson than usual. "The Shadow Captain was an operation bankrolled by the Council to regain control of the game once projection panels became widely used."

"That doesn't even make any sense. Everyone had panels in the aughts, even the seekers."

"Then how come nobody saw him at any balls? How come nobody saw him as Seeker?"

"You're just mad you lost to him."

"There is no 'him'! The Shadow Conspiracy was a massive black ops job!"

"He's just some dude, Mark. A dude that got you out in forty minutes flat."

"I told you, I sprained my ankle, Alex!"

Harla barked louder than either brother, "Enough! If he's just some dude, then you can find him. Even though I do love a good Council conspiracy. I noticed something fishy in the '84 game; Council could be behind that one, too. Everybody is encouraged to catch up on tape even when you're not in the lab."

The lab was crowded with so many people inside. Everyone shoved in to get a good look at the monitors as Intern Kevin fast-forwarded into the game in which the Shadow Captain infamously came in third.

"I think I see something." Alex pointed, barely keeping a straight face.

But Mark couldn't move his eyes away from the screen. Almost in awe, he whispered, "No, that's just a breeze in the grass."

"Right there! What's that?"

Mark was getting heated again. "That's just a normal shadow."

"No, can't be. Not with where the sun has to be!"

That's when the shipping container door opened, and Dr. Bird strolled in.

"Hello, everyone. Sorry to be late." Dr. Bird wore a smart, houndstooth gray pantsuit. She set her backpack on the floor and joined the crowd squinting at the monitor. She snapped. "Oh, I remember this one! African wetlands! SteelCut sweated himself nearly into dehydration."

"Do you remember anything about Captain Shadow?"

"The Shadow Captain? In the facepaint? I remember SteelCut wasn't happy about how much they pushed the rules. Abnormal name, no tech, failed to show up at the ball."

Mark raised a fist in victory. "Wasn't present at the ball."

Dr. Bird pulled an apple from her bag, took a bite, and continued, "Yeah, evidently, the Shadow team claimed to the Council that the Shadow Captain was at the ball but was in such good camouflage, they went unnoticed."

"Really?" Harla patted the top of her head, deep in thought.

"That's what they said, but even Ricky Diggs couldn't see him at the ball."

Harla, Kevin, and the Shuberts looked at each other and shrugged. "So?"

"So, Ricky Diggs can see *anything*. Ricky Diggs trained Diamonds."

"Wait." Harla scrunched her eyes like working out a math problem. "Ricky Diggs could see the Shadow Captain in gameplay?"

"Yeah, always." She took another bite of apple.

The room was aghast. Dr. Bird may have just given them the break they needed to find the Shadow Captain.

"Why's everyone looking at me like that?" Dr. Bird asked with her mouth full.

* * *

Ricky Diggs didn't stop raking for Harla and the team's big entrance, not when the enormous black helicopter drone flew to a nearby privacy fence and hosed down the flat surface with portal goop, not when the boat of a car drove through.

"Mr. Diggs."

"Harla Lynne Gamble. You know it costs seventeen thousand

dollars every time you use quantum-dimensional lubricant?"

"I didn't know the exact dollar amount, no."

"And don't you live down in Brookfield?"

"My sister does, sir."

"Child, that's a twenty-minute car ride. If I'm going to be your navigator, you can't waste my time."

"Oh. Sorry, Mr. Diggs, but that's not why we're here."

"Sure it is! You got to have one, lost the last game you had without one. Got caught in a trap a good navigator would have seen."

"What trap?"

"That boy threw his tech at you knowing it would integrate, knowing that you'd react to something flying at you by pulling in your bots to protect yourself. But you just surrendered more of your own tech. Diamonds would have seen it coming. I would have, too. You won't beat Chase Hawkins without another set of eyes. But if you don't think you need a navigator, why'd you drag these knuckleheads to my sidewalk?"

Something in the way Ricky spoke stunned Harla, left her grasping for words, her posture deflating, shrinking by the second.

It was Mark that answered. "Will you tell these knuckleheads there's no such thing as the Shadow Captain?"

"Oh, is that it?" Ricky, walking with a limp, hair now whiter than gray, bobbed along to sit on his concrete stoop. The team was still gathered on the sidewalk past the short chain link fence. "I been in the game, on a team, for three decades. And I've never seen anyone disappear completely. Except the Shadow Captain. Light on their feet doesn't touch it; they were silent. Still as the dead. Blended in perfectly. But I could always see 'em. Until the awards ceremony. After the shortest game ever. One instant; he was there, I blinked, and he was gone.

"Never entered the game again, no record of their identity."

"Definitely no record after the fire," added Kevin.

"You guys are crazy enough to go out looking for the Shadow Captain? Somebody proficient at not being found?"

The question hung heavily in the air as Ricky unscrewed the top of an old thermos to steamy contents and took a sip straight from the big cylinder.

Again, Harla shifted nervously and stammered when she addressed him, "Well, why do you think I'd want you for a navigator?"

"Well, I'm no Diamonds Hunt, but I can keep my head in the eye of a tornado."

"The hell's that supposed to mean?" Mark grumbled.

"So why don't y'all start tomorrow?"

"And when will you join us?"

"Well, let's consider this. You look like you're in shape."

"Thank you."

"There's no need for unhealthy physical expectations," inserted Dr. Bird.

"Judging by that bot you're covering your eye with, you're already an expert on the tech."

"Wait, that's not a real eyepatch?" Mark asked.

"Instantly less cool," Alex said.

"And you know everyone in the game. So all that's really left for training is sparring."

"Sparring? We call them sessions."

"Great. Now they're called sparring. And before you can spar, you need an automated Seeker, which based on the last-minute scramble that all of this reeks of, has yet to be assembled. So why don't you take a week or however long it takes to build a Seeker, either at your personal lab or over at Verma Tech, and call me when you're done."

"What'll you be doing?"

"Well, raking leaves, I suppose."

"Looks like you're all done raking."

"More leaves will fall. Trust me. You guys have a good day and call me when the tech and the seeker's done."

So that's what they did.

Chapter 15

C hapter 15

The next day, Harla left early morning while it was still dark out. After goopgating to pick up Kevin, she stopped by a local coffee shop and sent in the intern. He hated guessing coffee types for the brothers and took Harla's word for what Harpreet wanted.

But Harpreet was too busy to make it in today, according to a text.

And the next text indicated the Huberts were too hungover and would join them tomorrow, probably after lunch.

Harla punched the steering wheel, nostrils flaring. But by the time Kevin came back with the coffees, she'd breathed and was calmer.

A goopgate later, Harla and Kevin were let into an engineering warehouse to grab some 3D printers and cobble together the list of Verma Tech tools and materials the brothers thought they needed...the brothers who never showed up. Which was fine, considering after an 8-hour day of searching the immense silicon-valley construction warehouse, they still were missing all of the electronics the brothers had texted along.

Harla went home tired, frazzled, and frustrated.

The next day, the brothers showed up at 11am. They hadn't goopgated from their home in South Boston but rather pulled up in an Uber.

"Where y'all come from?" Harla asked when they showed up at Nakea's house during their lunch break.

Her lunch break, really. Today, Kevin stayed with baby Andre while Harla scoured the other miscellaneous storage facilities Verma Tech rented. And there were a lot.

In a prop plane hangar in New Mexico, Harla finally found the self-guided drone she'd been looking for. It was in a machine graveyard, row after row of busted up flying machines, steel crinkled up like wrinkled noses, charred, blackened, burned, and bent. Row upon row under the endless blue sky. Harla tossed a rope around the drone, about the same size as her but heavy as all get out, and dragged it back to strap awkwardly on top of her car, then goopgated back in time for another meal of chicken salad.

"Find everything on the list?" Mark was eating a burger.

"Yep."

"The lab here?" Alex focused on picking out the longest fries to eat first.

"Nope, three mile walk."

"Kevin? Can you get Harpreet on the phone and get us a golf cart?"

"Will do, Alex. I'm on it. I'm going to text and email him, and I'll follow up with a call if there's no reply in twenty."

"Don't do that. Harpreet's busy."

"You're right, Captain. I'll hit up his secretary."

"Do I smell coffee?" Alex asked sweetly.

"No."

"Oh," Alex said in mock surprise. "Can you make some?"

"Kevin," Harla said without looking.

"I'm already grinding the beans!"

The Huberts had plans with them, schematics they unfurled on the dining room table. They lifted Harla and Kevin's plates and placed them at the corners to keep the large sheet of paper open.

Harla squinted at the giant paper with such a simple drawing. "It's a stick figure."

Mark ate a carrot stick off Kevin's plate. "It's a skeleton."

"Skeleton? Thing ain't got no ribs, no hips. The joints are all wrong. What are those, ball sockets at the elbows and knees?"

Mark produced another hamburger from somewhere, unwrapped it, and took a bite. "It ain't a human skeleton. It's your seeker's."

"As we mass-produce your new ScatterSwarm," Alex pointed at Harla with a fry, "understand there will be failures. Not every piece comes out of the printer perfect."

"So we're going to build our 'sparring' seeker out of my failed scales?"

"Scales?"

"Yeah. Slightly different than the ScatterSwarm bees. Bigger, but with more capabilities."

"I saw the last game," Alex said. "You're making another hive."

"No. Smaller isn't the way to go. NASA's going smaller and smaller and making replicating units. If there's one of those swarms out there already, plus whatever game Seeker we end up with, add on top of that the beginning of the swarm copycats...it's not sustainable. We need something smart, quick, and versatile."

"Then that's what your sparring seeker will be."

"Dope. So all we gotta do is build that." Harla gestured to the schematic. "How long will that take?"

"The last one took us two months."

"The game's in two and a half weeks."

Kevin walked in with two mugs of steaming coffee in each hand, took one look at the skeleton schematic, lit up, and said, "I love hangman! Eesh, this one looks close to done. Have you guessed 'G?' Sometimes, people don't think of 'G.'"

"Where are we on that golf cart, Kev?" asked Mark.

"Getting delivered tomorrow."

"Great! Then we'll begin constructing tomorrow!" Mark said.

"Tomorrow? Why you acting like we go all the time in the world, James Bond? We have to start today. Right now."

"Right now, we need to discuss gameplay," said Alex, blowing on the hot coffee in his "Best Dr. Mom Ever" mug.

Mark punched his palm. "And how to embarrass Esau Holter."

I loved that she didn't stand up for Holter. If the Huberts needed to hear that the General was the enemy, she would do whatever she had to, in order to secure their help. And the General liked her, too. Probably more than me.

The remainder of the day was spent watching recent games and talking strategy. Mainly, it was just Alex and Mark getting into arguments; Harla didn't say much. I couldn't yet tell how much she wanted it. Was this something to pass the time? Was she still the competitor she once was? How far would she go to beat me?

It was so exciting to wonder. Excitement I hadn't felt since my first game.

* * *

The first day that the brothers drove the golf cart to the lab, hungover and wearing sunglasses, they built a "rig" outside. Or rather, Harla built it while telling the brothers to keep out of the way. The rig would hold the skeleton they designed. They sent Kevin on errands for even more tools, even more materials, and accommodations to help the Brothers "sit and think" (which wound up being camping chairs, an outdoor card table, playing cards, a hammock, poker chips, a coffee maker, a fridge, and ultimately, beer).

Meanwhile, Harla stayed on a ladder, securing the framework that would secure her framework for the seeker. It was like a twelve foot door frame, a rectangle of layered two by fours with shelves to hold laptops, chains and cable coming down to hold the machinery, and a spot for Mark's tablet.

When she wasn't building or checking on the progress of the 3D printers, she was working out. Her running increased, because of course it did. Kevin drove to meet her at certain points in her run with towels and cups of Gatorade. Once she hit ten miles, he started bringing a shovel with him, offering to dig a latrine in the forest preserve floor for her.

The brothers showed up earlier and earlier the rest of that first week, making it in before eleven, then as early as 10:15. Then one day around 6:30am, after Harla had finished feeding baby Andre breakfast, handed him off to Nakea, and got ready for her run, Alex showed up solo with no sunglasses. He wore a US Air Force t-shirt, gray sweatpants, and foggy, bleary eyes.

But Harla didn't see him. As she took a step out of Nakea's house, closing the door behind her, she was ready to start her run. Two steps in, she ran into his chest.

Reacting instantly, she yelled and punched at his throat. Eight years of Tae-Kwon-Do will do that.

Following up, she swung her knee upward, connecting with his crotch.

The noise escaping a barely-awake Alex Hubert was...impressive. Both a low, gravelly, pained grunt, as well as a high-pitched whimper, it reminded me of how high-level monks can sing at multiple octaves.

Alex was red-faced, gasping, and bent over shivering like a car accident survivor.

Harla was mortified, both hands covering her mouth. He leaned into her, planting his face high on her chest, his nose pressed against her shoulder. She instinctively wrapped arms around him and rubbed his back, as she would comfort baby Andre after an owie or a big scare.

It was the first and last time Harla and Alex hugged.

"You scared me!"

"Sorry," he said as dangling drool shook from his lip.

"Why are you here?

"To run."

"Okay. You want to sit this one out and maybe we can start our run tomorrow?"

"No. No." He grunted back to standing straight, took a sharp breath, then jogged past Harla. "Just let me go pee some blood."

In one quick motion, he grabbed the doorknob as he stepped

up, not knowing Harla had locked the door behind her.

He jogged into the cold glass door. Hard.

So when Dr. Bird arrived for her new morning ritual to make coffee with Nakea, instead of a post-run check-in with Harla, she was tending to Alex.

Harla, who'd never got around to her run, was texting with Diamonds, as Sunday was their night to get together. Eventually, it was time, and she told her team members, "Okay, so I guess I'm going to go pick up Kevin."

"Mark, too," Alex said from the couch with bags of ice on his throat, nose, and testicles.

"Where is he?"

"Cozy Inn on 88th."

"Oh."

"What?"

"I thought you guys would have some cooler kind of secret hideout."

"No. Will you get me a coconut milk chai since you attacked me?"

"Fine."

"Dirty. But not Starbucks. I don't like their Chai."

"Enough, you big baby. Stop talking and drink." Dr. Bird gave him water, then addressed Harla. "He shouldn't drink that. Don't get any coffee for him."

"But –"

"Quiet, you big baby!"

So Harla left, and Nakea took Andre to daycare on her way to work, leaving the doctor and her patient alone.

Doctor Bird didn't waste any time. The second Nakea closed the door, her head whipped to Alex and whispered in a low voice (she must have known someone was watching, but spy tech is just superior these days), "Why are you sabotaging her training?"

"Who says we're sabotaging anything?"

She spoke through a pursed mouth, must've been insurance against anyone reading their lips. "I do. And Ricky Diggs agrees with me."

"Well, you're wrong."

"It's been two weeks, and she has no tech and no practice seeker. Ricky Diggs found about the bench warrants in Alaska, and he wants you to know that unless you two quit sandbagging soon, you will be headed back to frozen tundra prison."

"You're wrong."

"Then build the damn thing!"

"What damn thing?"

"All of it. The tech and the seeker."

"The building *is* the training. When I was fourteen and Mark was twelve, we wanted to get bigger for football. Dad said he couldn't afford a gym, so we had to make something. So he brought home some wood and metal from a jobsite. That week, we built a pull-up bar. Next week, he brought more wood home, tires, and chains, and for a whole summer, we built an outdoor gym and obstacle course. We were about twenty pounds of muscle bigger by the time we were finished."

"Harla is competing for a military contract based on cutting-edge technology. She needs focus and discipline, not backyard weight room wisdom."

"She needs to build herself back up. Don't act like you don't know that loss didn't devastate her. She's back in the game just because she don't know what else to do with herself. There's no hunger in her eyes no more; she's just plain angry. We gotta get back the hunger."

"Cut it with the testosterone, buddy. If this is the plan, then fine. But you need to be more straight-forward with her." Dr. Bird changed her tone from her short, hard threatening voice to her short, hard cordial voice. "Alright. I'm done for the day. Ricky Diggs will be coming by fairly soon, and don't think you can fool him. That man sees everything."

As she closed the door behind her, Alex pulled out his phone and texted his brother. "They're onto us. Careful."

* * *

By the time everyone got to the lab, Alex had a different energy about him. As Mark shuffled from the golf cart to his camping chair, his brother made a bee line right for the pile of building materials.

While arranging the tools on a tarp, Alex said to Harla, "I wanted to talk to you about adjustments to the schematics."

"Adjustments? Come on, man. We were finally about to start assembling."

"We will. We're starting today. But we need to talk about what we need in a seeker."

"What *do* we need in a seeker?"

"Fear."

"Excuse me?"]

"The problem with sparring and sessions and practice games is that you hold back. You're not invested. The way you think and react during practice isn't the same as how you'll react in a game. Something is missing."

"Fear."

"Right. So if we can guarantee the seeker is something that creates fear, we can recreate the feel of live gameplay."

"Fool you into thinking you're in the middle of the real thing," Mark said from behind his sunglasses, reclined in his camping chair.

"So how do we do that?" Harla asked.

"By honestly talking about what we fear." Alex stopped arranging the tools and sat on the tarp.

Kevin answered first, "I'm afraid of disappointing my parents. And disappointing Harla. And disappointing the rest of you guys!"

"Okay, that's more sad than helpful," said Alex, "but one of my greatest fears is losing my brother. If something I said or did hurt him or prevented his happiness, I don't know what I'd do."

"I'm afraid of drowning," Mark said flatly.

I laughed out loud watching. Alex had obviously wanted brotherly love reciprocated.

"And I'm afraid if we don't move this training forward, I'm going to show up to the game rusty and dusty."

"So you're afraid of losing. Why?" Alex said flatly, less of a question than a challenge.

"Easy." She shrugged it off. "Harpreet invested a lot in me. He's got a lot at stake. A win would really help his company which in turn will help him fight Fowler in court."

"Cool." Mark was spreading cream cheese on a bagel. "While telling your greatest fear, you managed to spin it into a threat to your enemy. That's pretty metal."

"Calm down, Drowning Ophelia," Harla warned. "He didn't say greatest fear."

Alex pointed out, "But anything you fear, once we analyze,

speak honestly about it, will reveal your greatest fear. Why are you afraid of Fowler?"

"I'm not afraid of Fowler. That fool's shorter than me. He's old. I am literally a professional athlete."

He wasn't shorter than her.

"She's terrified of him," Mark said between bites.

"I know, right?" Alex chuckled.

"Am not!"

"Sure you are."

"Nu-unh!"

"She's regressing right in front of us."

Mark smiled, lips covered in cream cheese. "Textbook Regression."

I could feel her frustration build just watching. I swear to gosh, it was like I was the Emperor, sensing the hate flowing through a nearby Jedi. It was exhilarating to see. My teeth and fists clenched with hers as my body tensed in my seat. Ridicule is the worst type of embarrassment.

"You two gotta stop it!" she bellowed.

"Captain, if we're going to get anywhere with this fear stuff, it's on you."

"Nobody can make us open up. We have to want to do that ourselves." Mark proclaimed it like a mantra or yogi lecture, all zenned out for everyone to hear.

"Ain't that what my therapist is for?"

"I'm glad you brought that up. Kevin here took the initiative and scheduled an extra sesh with your doc this morning."

Harla's glare swept over to Kevin.

His voice cracked as he panicked under pressure, trying to throw it back at Alex. "It wasn't initiative. You told me to." Then Kevin practically bowed his head in apology to Harla,

"They told me to. I would never have done that if I knew this was some sort of emotional trap."

"It's fine. I'd rather talk to her than any of you."

That did it. Everyone clammed up; the only sound was Mark chewing his bagel. Harla attempted to put her attention to a couple of damaged boards they were combining through a series of soldiers, but it didn't hold. "I'm gonna go ahead and leave 'cause I can't concentrate."

* * *

By the time she returned hours later, Alex and Kevin had finished assembling the "brain" of the seeker. Mark was sleeping in the hammock.

The Buick drove out of the far side of the shipping container, which had become the de facto portal. It was Kevin's job to keep the quantum dimensional lubricant wet. He kept the goop goopy.

Harla came striding out of the driver's side door, hair askew, eye makeup smeared and running at the edges, and completely unashamed. The floodgates opened, and she unburdened herself nonstop saying, "When I was younger, I had a recurring nightmare about a man running for office. A white man with blue eyes and black hair. Big and muscley, always in a suit. Good looking, but he was evil. Pure evil. His solution to everything was...cannibalism. He wanted to solve all problems by eating bad people, but nobody knew it except me. But when I told people, nobody believed me. And he would always win.

"He gave out gingerbread cookies as his signature. Sometimes, I'd be in the crowd while he spoke, and everyone chanted his name while I tried screaming to warn everyone. In some nightmares, I'm trying to get to one of his rallies, but the crowds are too big, and I can't push through. Sometimes, I'm just in a regular dream, and then I find a random gingerbread cookie, and I just know he's there."

Mark raised an eyebrow. "And that's your greatest fear?"

"No. I think it's powerlessness when I'm the only one who sees, who knows the truth," she said quietly.

"Wow."

"So how do we use it?" Mark asked from the hammock without opening his eyes.

Alex, eyes still wide from witnessing Harla's emotional breakthrough, cleared his throat and attempted an authoritative voice. "Alright, I think we've got some good things here. An archetype. Maybe the seeker's not exactly some white guy in a suit, but some idea or image. Stand-in, something with the same qualities."

Kevin ruined whatever facade Alex had managed to create. "Like what?"

"Like," Alex thought for a minute before saying, "Holter's vehicle. One of the mech suits, chasing you around. There's the whole power dynamic. Politics."

"It can shoot gingerbread cookies at her!" Mark added, not attempting to be of any help.

"I don't even have that kind of beef with Holter."

"It's not 'Holter.' It's the idea of Holter."

"Why don't we just make it the white guy in a suit then?" Kevin blurted, holding a tray of hot sandwiches. The most help Mark had been was setting up the generator to power the outdoor kitchen Kevin used every day to feed everyone.

"Chasing you for sparring sessions? Normal doofus politician doesn't scream scary."

"Well, it ain't your fear, fool! I don't know how we could get the face right, though. He doesn't exactly exist."

That's when the car pulled up. A little sport Miata, ill-suited for the dirty gravel road cutting through the public park to reach the hidden lab.

Ricky Diggs stepped out, addressing the group and answering Harla's question like he'd been there with them the entire afternoon, "Easy. As we construct the skeletal structure of our drone, we will also sculpt the exterior scales." The short black man, wearing mechanic's coveralls, went around his little sports car and opened the trunk, removing a metal case, letting the heavy thing down with a thud.

Opening it up, he ran his hands through the contents. Within the secure cooler's heavy thick sides, like a chest full of treasure, sat piles of scales. "Hot off Verma Tech presses. This is enough to start on the face."

Chapter 16

C hapter 16

Everyone stared blankly at the old man as he shut the trunk again, headed over to intern Kevin, and grabbed a hot sandwich.

Kevin was the most shocked. "Wait, do you have us under surveillance or something?"

"Welcome to the game," Ricky Diggs said. "You think I'm the only one watching?"

"No," Harla answered the rhetorical question knowingly.

"Good. At least the Captain's not stupid," said Ricky. "Kevin."

"Yes, sir?"

Ricky slapped the side of the metal case, "Put them away overnight and keep this between thirty and sixty degrees, alright?"

"Fahrenheit," Harla added.

"Well, yeah. This is America." Ricky shook his head like he shouldn't have to say what he was saying. "I'm going to start some paperwork."

"What does that mean?" asked Mark, getting out of the hammock for a sandwich.

"Daily reports. Listing ongoing progress, reminder of upcoming deadlines. Any advances in the categories of tech, personnel, strategy, and the Captain's health. I'll write most of it, Dr. Bird can handle the last."

With a mouth full of a pastrami, Mark said, "Good, so I don't have to do anything."

"I'd like everyone to be more diligent about checking their emails."

Mark made a noise somewhere between a squeak and the beginning of the high-pitched phrase, "I don't think so."

"And to make sure, all discussions about your salary will be relegated to replies to the daily reports."

And without another word, Ricky Diggs got back in his Miata and drove away, leaving a cloud of dust, a stainless steel trunk, and a confused team.

"Well that was a lovely visit," Mark said with another bite.

"Boss?" Kevin asked carefully. "I have steamed chicken and brown rice, spinach salad, or mixed nuts. Which would you like?

"Kev, I like it when you call me Boss."

"I know you do."

"Chicken and rice. We got hot sauce?"

"No." Kevin made a note to himself.

He was putting Harla on *my* meal plan.

"Well, jump in the golf cart, my man," she said as she walked to the trunk, took one handle, and dragged it, grating across the gravel and parking lot, into the shipping container.

Alex grabbed a sandwich and sat next to his brother.

"Grab the schematics and get in here, you two," Harla called out from within. Mark stuffed the remains of his sandwich in his mouth and grabbed another half of one, leaving his brother to roll up the schematics.

She was pacing at the front of the shipping container. "I want him big. Towering. I want to feel like a kid next to him."

"You are a kid," Alex said.

"I'm eighteen, fool."

"Ah, to be so young, sweet, and innocent." Mark laughed.

"He should be heavy-set. In better shape than the two of you. A body builder up in this piece. In better shape than either of you."

Mark grumbled, "I'd say 'different' shape, not necessarily 'better.'"

Alex spread the schematics out on the table and started crossing out dimensions, asking his brother, "Okay, if we extend the patella piston to one point one meter at rest, what's that going to do to the weight of the thing?"

"Another kilogram and a half," Mark answered without thinking.

Harla gave a begrudging nod and smile, then turning her swivel chair back to face the trunk of scales.

The work was hard going. Not what the Huberts were doing; they were done in an hour and a half. But even with hot sauce for all of the meals and snacks, manually sculpting the Seeker's head was quite difficult. Hanging scale by scale, layering column over column was delicate and precise.

There was a little metal tree she'd 3D printed. It was the interior of a human head, on which the facade of scales would hang.

Even though Harla would never admit it, the scale design was imperfect. It was downright poor. Each little concave pentagon had amazing maneuverability, like little stealth fighter jets, but fitting them together in three dimensions, across a curved plane, proved to be nearly impossible.

Each time she was past halfway, hanging each scale on the rest, the structure would collapse. The scales would cascade like falling dominoes into a pile. If she was lucky. Usually, the scales scattered all over the lab floor, and she had to start over after searching for each one while letting loose a healthy string of curses. Sometimes she yelled. Sometimes she threw the little metal tree across the interior of the shipping container. One time, she punched the wall. They called in Dr. Bird and handed off the project.

It became like a board game, each team member using a delicate touch to fit everything together. But inevitably, it would crash down.

Alex cussed.

Mark laughed.

The whole set-up made Kevin so jumpy, he couldn't put two scales together.

Even Dr. Bird gave it a shot. Her steady hands did fairly well but could only get as far as the scales that made up a cheek before utter collapse. "Darn it."

Harla, calmer now, gave it another shot, this time shaping each scale before placing it. She got far. Ten scales. She kept it together, gently placing the next one as Mark and Alex shoved at her with elbows, Kevin and Dr. Bird joining in the shouting, cheering, and laughter.

No one noticed when Diamonds walked in.

"Were you going to be a while?" they asked, just inside the door.

Everyone turned but only Harla gasped and stood, sending

the scales crashing down and scattering along the floor. "Diamonds, I'm sorry."

They held it together. "It's after eight. Your sister didn't know when you'd be back."

I couldn't believe they were speaking first in a room full of strangers. Diamonds was more easily embarrassed than I was. What Harla Gamble must have meant to Diamonds Hunt. It filled me with an antsy rage, an anger that prodded and mocked me with my own disappointment in myself. Maybe I could have meant that much to Diamonds. Maybe.

"Oh my God, D, I'm so sorry, we got stuck on this problem. We should call it a day." Everyone awkwardly shuffled out. But the room was still full with just the two of them.

"How'd you find us?"

"Golf cart tire tracks."

"Of course."

"You aren't really hiding here."

"What does that mean?"

"It's half-assed." Diamonds had such a cold way of saying things in the simplest terms. "Leaving tracks up here? Not far back off the road. And a trail cuts through right past the buildings."

"So?"

"I don't think you're all-in."

"Excuse me? What's that supposed to mean?"

"It's hidden, but not really hidden, a lab, but really just a crate in a parking lot, secure, but not really secure. Training, but not really training."

"Not really training?"

"You haven't been sweating. Your hair's intact."

"Maybe it was a study day."

"No, your concentration hanging the tree leaves was too good. No fine motor deterioration after such a long day? You weren't mentally exerting yourself."

"Is this why you came up here?"

"No, I came up here because we were supposed to hang out at seven o'clock. And of course, I was an hour early because of time zones, so I've been waiting a while."

"I'm sorry I got caught up. I don't think that gives you any reason to judge how 'all-in' I am. I'm all-in enough to have forgotten we were supposed to hang out."

"Unless part of you did it on purpose, so I would have to come and see you 'hard at work.'"

"How would I know you would come up here?"

"Because you know me." They said it like an accusation.

"It's a secret lab! It's hidden."

"It's not hidden. Who knows how many eyes are on you? If you were so dedicated, you would have told me we couldn't hang out until after the game. I'm not an idiot, Harla. I've been waiting on the call."

"I'm just keeping things low key. I joined anonymously. I don't want any of this 'Captain Miss' hype."

"BS."

"Damn, D!"

"You're acting like all of this is some game."

"It is a game!"

"Only if you treat it like one. I don't care about first place, but if you approach it the way you're acting now, they will embarrass you on national television, and maybe they'll just unmask you for fun. You're acting like a pawn, Harla. You're not a pawn. This isn't going to be fair. Why don't you have the network on? Why aren't you surveilling other teams? Where's your damn navigator?"

"It's just a game." Harla's voice reached high, desperate notes.

"Stop it, Harla!"

"It is just a game!"

"It killed SteelCut, you think it can't kill you?"

Harla collapsed back in her seat, folding in on herself, defeated. "I want it to be just a game. Not a kid's game — a sport. With the network, and the streaming...I thought... like I could be," she straightened up, wiped her nose and said with reverence, "a professional athlete. Like for life. For a career. And just, you know. Dominate. Face of the league. Endorsements. Maybe name a shoe after me. God, why am I so stupid, Diamonds?"

She fell to the floor, hugging Diamonds' legs, who themselves sank to the chair. They pet her for a moment, maybe minutes.

Harla moved first, sitting up and clearing her throat.

Diamonds said in a pleasant, careful tone. "Want to watch the Network? We missed MC Three."

Harla nodded a yes.

The team had taken the golf cart, so Diamonds and Harla walked the three miles back to Nakea's, silent the whole way.

* * *

"So now it's, what? We're two weeks away, and we're all supposed to wait quietly for Captain Miss to make up her little mind?" the host angrily asked his guest, retired US General

Esau Holter, who looked uncomfortable in his suit.

"Again, I'm uncertain why we're getting mad at Captain Miss when all this goes back to Mr. Fowler and the choices he's made with programming. If she never signed up, why were we seeing her in all the video packages, the commercials, everything on all the time? Why do you ask every guest about it?"

The host, an over muscled and overly tanned white guy, didn't answer Holter but instead pointed to the camera. "Backing down when you're just making it to the big stage is one thing and one thing alone: cowardly. The cowardly lioness is home licking her wounds and her bruised pride for being schooled by our current champion. I don't think she's got what it takes to do this under the bright lights. A live arena? Simulcasting? She'd fall apart."

"Angry Guy hosts this show?" Harla asked, not amused.

"Yep."

As a competitor, Angry Guy depended on overly macho intimidation tactics during the ball. He played under the name Captain "The Warrior," I think.

And he was good at getting himself worked up.

"I say this field of competition is of a higher caliber. Captain Miss won't be missed." In a slick, scumbag way, he looked up to another camera and said, "When we come back, we'll discuss the newest mystery competitor out of Verma Tech Industries, and I'll put Captain Holter in the hot seat and ask him to respond to the recent tweet from Aiden Run."

"SuperPowers owns it all; there are commercials?"

"Not really," Diamonds started.

In super slow motion, Harla's face looked back at her from the screen. It zoomed out, and there she was again, in the sand of the last game, her helmet stripped off as the Regalia dissolved it.

"It's just commercials for the upcoming game. A lot of hype clips of you."

"But why?"

"They're goading you to come back. Because they want to own you. Or the idea of you. Captain Miss. They need characters for their little show."

"And I fooled myself into thinking I was an athlete. I'm so stupid."

"No. No you're not." Harla looked away and Diamonds took her by the chin and stared her down, eye to eye. "No. You're. Not."

They sat silently on the couch, huddled together, Diamonds' arm around Harla, watching the talk show like it was a scary monster movie. Just breathing together.

Sometimes I can be an insanely jealous person.

As the show went on, Harla commented on this or that, calling the host "fool" every now and then, making fun of whatever conclusion was being drawn.

"Like Captain Miss would even fall for that!"

"But *you* are Captain Miss. Why are you talking in the third person like a pro wrestler?"

They both chuckled, but Harla's smile wore away immediately as she spoke with a sudden realization. "Not anymore I'm not. Captain Miss was just some kid. A girl who played just to embarrass these fools, like she was showing out playing streetball."

"For a super genius who graduated college at thirteen."

"You know what I mean."

"Yeah, but I'm not going to *not* stand up for you."

"But that's just it. The game, the tech, the mask, the captain names...it's not us. It's never us. We're more like pro wrestlers than pro athletes."

"Harpreet will be glad to hear that."

"I'm serious, though. It's like we're playing superhero out there. Only my ego..." She trailed off. "It was so important to me that *it was me*. It was important to me that everyone had to know it was me beating them. So important that I had to talk trash the whole time, that I had to let people know they were getting schooled by a kid genius. Meanwhile, that's exactly what they want: to sell their little product and make all the damn money."

"For you to be yourself?"

"For me to be a caricature of myself. Nobody gasped when they saw my black face and braids under that helmet; they heard my voice, knew my style of play. Now they want that sassy black girl back as a character for their little show."

"Is that who you are?"

"If this is going to be my job, if I got a future in this game, then why do I have to be myself? You think Michael Jordan sticks his tongue out when he buys groceries?"

"No I don't," Diamonds said incredulously, like they were unsure where this line of thinking was going.

"Exactly. He had a persona. Made him look more unbeatable. Elevated him."

"So you're going to elevate your persona?"

"I'm gon change the whole damn thing."

"But Chase won't know who's beating him."

"Please, D. He knows. He's listening right now. You hear that, Wonderbread? Your fancy show aint gonna have Captain Miss to make you look good. I ain't giving you a bad guy to push around!"

It was quiet for a second until Diamonds spoke, their voice gentle, hurt. "Do you really think he's spying on you? Even after talking it out with the therapist and everything?"

"D, I know he is."

They cleared their throat, stood up, and shouted, "I hate you, Chase!"

Both of them laughed in their defiant stances, looking up at an invisible adversary in the ceiling, overcome with confidence and solidarity. They both shouted further obscenities at my name. Together.

Andre started crying, and Nakea yelled from upstairs about all of the noise. So they kept it quiet and light, laughing while eating the salads Diamonds had brought over.

And I watched alone, Diamonds' proclaimed hatred of me playing over and over again in my head. It was like they were mocking me by having fun together, as if they knew I was so alone, knew that the only person I could eat and talk with constantly told me what was wrong with me. Why couldn't I have a Diamonds in my life? Not them specifically, I already screwed that up, but where was my buddy who'd always support and forgive me?

* * *

Truth be told, I hadn't noticed that Kevin was no longer showing up for work. That was fine; it allowed me to cover more tape and spend more time figuring out the damn Crown.

I could pull the small cube as far as I wished away from

the rest of the headpiece and the pink lightning would stay connected, crackling lively and sending out sparks. Walking the crackling connective string of energy, I pulled it out the length of the room. The pink light was near blinding, I should have had on tinted goggles, and the room smelled of ozone and burning. The lightning didn't separate, but off shoots crackled away. Nearby computers and copiers hissed sparks, monitors cracked, computer towers busted, and paper caught on fire.

The room's powerful sprinklers kicked on, dumping water rather than spraying. I put the crown away before the fire-fighters arrived.

I texted Emily early on my way home. She couldn't stop laughing. She sent me three videos of her laughing throughout that night.

So the next day, once the room was cleaned up, I tried pulling the cube in different directions and found the pink lightning still followed. In fact, when I pulled the cube to one side, not only did the lightning follow, but fingers of the bolt zapped onto the surface of the Crown, and it began lighting up. So I kept going around, pulling the cube and the pink bolt in a circle, powering up the headband as I went, until I'd walked completely around. Pink light crackled along the outside of the band and the cube slid right back into place, the pink growing brighter and fuzzier. A pink halo.

Then the Crown disappeared. Entirely.

I checked the cameras trained on the prototype. No visible light spectrum. Nothing in UV. I checked thermal, which the Lack always set off, but the screen was blank. I turned up the speakers to the mics recording the process. Silent.

Had the Crown vanished? Portalled away? Did it get sucked into the Lack?

Cautiously, with a safety glove on, I reached to the table that had just held the tech. Leaning away as far as I could, I reached out and poked into nothing. But I hit something.

I reached again and grasped it. The Crown was still there, it was just invisible. It was truly invisible tech.

And I'd just figured out how it worked.

* * *

]

Harla walked into her lab the next day with a set determination, a swagger. Alex came over for their run at 6:30am. Despite his drinking and seemingly careless lifestyle, that boy was in shape. He pushed Harla to her best time yet as they extended a five mile jog into seven, then ten.

She destroyed a couple extra tofu and egg breakfast burritos and floored the accelerator on the golf cart to get to the hidden lab.

"First things first. Kevin, I want you to test the light warp on these scales. I need seven to go up around the perimeter of the lab.

"Whoa whoa, whoa," said Mark, who was still recovering from the night before behind sunglasses. "These things shape-shift and warp light?"

"Basic shape-shifting, but they flatten out to projection, too," said Harla who didn't look up from sorting out scales for the intern to try.

"So you're building another SteelCut Puzzle then?" Anger touched Alex's question. "How are we supposed to power it?"

Mark piled on, "You going to walk around with orange

dimensional flare-ups like the ones killed that dusty old cowboy?"

"You talk about that man with respect," she growled at both of them. "I've been using remote power. The scales don't keep a charge past half an hour, but if I have a remote source..."

Mark laughed. "What? Some magic wand that you have to use to touch every single scale every half hour of the game? What about staying hidden overnight? Resting? Sleeping?"

"If you fools ain't figured it out yet, there ain't going to be any time to rest. There ain't gonna be no overnight. You seen the arena yet?"

"They'll announce the arena after the ball, morning of the game," Alex said, confused.

"Actually," Kevin butted in nervously, "they just announced a permanent arena site. Calling it Energy Arena."

"You two need to keep up on the SuperPowers network."

"I forgot the password," Mark admitted.

"Well, they've built a stadium to throw us in, more or less. An arena filled with moving parts and a million cameras."

"Like a rat maze."

"Pretty much."

"Then why aren't we practicing in a replica?"

"Because you fools wasted my time building up this sparring seeker?"

"Okay then, let's get to it."

"Nuh-uh. You two have to keep up with homework. Sit your butts down in the trailer and catch up on that MC Three talk show. Learn what you can about the arena. Kev, you get our navigator on the phone. I don't care if brother Einstein don't feel like showing up, he can at least help by keeping eyes on the competitors. Start with Captain Kiddo; they're filming his training in public."

"Oman," Kevin pointed out.

Harla chuckled. "That's right."

But the Hubert brothers were lost. "What?"

"Captain Kiddo has changed his title to Oman."

"Oh, I get it...'kid-oh', 'oh-man.'"

"Oh, man."

Harla pointed a stern finger. "I don't want anyone making dad jokes like that around here. Now get to it, everyone's got something to do."

"What're you going to do?"

"I've got to make up my face."

* * *

And so it went for the rest of the day. And the day after that. And so on. The shipping container was now disguised, just a blank spot in the old abandoned parking lot that the team would vanish into. Kevin took a rental car to hang out at Ricky Digs' all day, although often they did yard work rather than spy on anyone. The brothers caught up on all of the original programming on the network and began construction on what they called a "Victim board" but Harla called their "vision board." They laid out each competitor, taping a printed photo of the captain or their tech and sticking it to the surface of the shipping container.

Harla spent day after day constructing the scale head. It fell apart often, but Harla stopped losing her patience with it. When she got too frustrated or her hands began to cramp, she'd shift her focus to the skeleton, which was forming very well, hanging from chains and cables off the wood frame and from nearby trees like an android caught in a robot spider's web. But she made more and more progress, eventually forming everything on the head except the face and holding it in place with about two rolls of plastic cling wrap. The skeleton was pretty much finished as well, it dangled in the air.

Then, staying late one night after Kevin went back to his mom's house and the Huberts went back to their hotel, she began talking out loud again. To herself, but not to herself.

"I wonder what they got on you, Wonderbread. How they convinced you to volunteer to be some corporate puppet?"

I wondered the same thing sometimes. It couldn't just my being afraid to say no. Maybe it was saying no to *the* Todd Fowler.

She held a screwdriver in her teeth as she bent a scale's hinge, all delicate work. She spat the screwdriver out onto the tabletop.

"I see the strings they're trying to put on me. All kinds of strings. A web. They're catching us and using us. Well, I'm going to use them. I'm going to turn their web against them. I'm going to expose the whole bunch of those dirty cheaters, Wonderbread. I'll expose you, too."

"You ever heard the sentence, 'you can't deconstruct the master's house with the master's tools'?" Ricky Diggs appeared in the doorway.

"Yeah, ain't that some militant stuff?"

"It was, but it's a kind of universal truth. Besides, I ain't as militant as I used to be. The truth is, if you follow the rules the game gives you, you can only defeat other players. You can't defeat the game itself."

The wind picked up hard and fast in that way it only does in Chicago. I felt cold just looking at them. Diggs' white afro blew with the air, and they both huddled into their puffy coats a little more.

"SteelCut wasn't the first to die in this military exercise for the expressed purpose of furthering camouflage technology," he said the last part as memorized rote but with disdain. "But as soon as word got around that there was a high-risk military exercise within the Department of Defense, the game had more volunteers from each branch of the armed services. Soon enough, third party companies, manufacturers of weapons and jets, wanted in. And they paid Uncle Sam just for the chance to compete.

"So the game opened up to civilians. But it was still a military exercise, so deaths weren't investigated by the local authorities, they were reviewed by superior officers. It wasn't murder, just an abundance of paperwork. But now..." His voice trailed off as wind whistled into the shipping container, blowing all the papers around.

Harla finished his thought, speaking reluctantly, afraid of the words she was saying. "They'll be on live TV now and won't be afraid to kill anyone." But the thought went deeper and Harla's face contorted, nostrils flared, mouth in a nauseated grimace, "And it'll all be legal. People dying for a cause, to keep our soldiers safe. And everyone watching..."

"Will eat it up with a spoon. An entertainment company has monetized death. Selling real-life violence in the name of science and patriotism. That's right. That's the plan. That's the newest plan. But I'm wondering, Miss Gamble, when was the last time you turned on CNN and saw our soldiers fighting in MC Squared tech?"

She collapsed back in her chair. "Well, it's stealth. You wouldn't see it."

"You wouldn't see old tech then? Why aren't projection shields standard issue by now? SteelCut was playing with those in the nineties for cripe's sakes!"

"So what are we building all this tech for?"

"More like 'who.' That's the question that's got its hooks in me. That's the question that drove me to join up with SteelCut, the question that drove me off the team, and the question that brings me back now. Who is this tech for? Steel Cut stopped asking. But you ain't the kind to hush up for the good of the ship, are you, girl?"

"No sir."

With booming authority, Ricky Diggs pushed his voice to fill the shipping container, "Don't you dare address me as sir. You are my captain, girl!"

She sprang onto her feet, got within inches of his face, and matched his intensity. "Then don't call me girl!"

"You're damned right, Captain!" He shook with intensity. "I'll see you bright and early tomorrow morning! We'll start your training then."

"I've been training for two weeks."

"You been playing grabass for two weeks, and you know it, Captain. We start training tomorrow."

"Alright then."

He nodded and disappeared out of the doorframe. Harla practically fell down with the sigh of relief after he'd gone.

Chapter 17

C hapter 17

Watching Harla was now my solace, my vacation from work. And there was so much work. The Chase Hawkins brand, the Captain Oman brand, the MC Squared, the network, SuperPowers, Unlimited... Sometimes I didn't think I could keep it up. Other times, I doubted others will keep it up while I'm in the arena competing.

She didn't know how lucky she was, only having to focus on the game, on winning. I envied the simplicity of her task. Yet she got so much more support.

What was it that pulled people to her? What about her convinced folks to lower their defenses, to do their damnedest, to give of themselves whatever it takes? Was it her bullying? The way she made fun of any and everybody that ensured such resolute loyalty to her? Maybe the way she constantly refused help, stubbornly insisting on going at it alone.

I simply didn't get it, and the fact I didn't get it wound up being the source of most of the confusion and angst in my life. How could someone who treats people so poorly, thought so little of them and even less of what they think, gain such dedication?

The only thing that ever mattered to me was what others thought. How I looked, whether I was offending anyone, how whatever-it-was would affect my brand. And yet, compared to her, no one liked me. Sure, I had Emily, but she was sick of me. All she did was make suggestions. Deep suggestions, about me, not pointers on how to shake hands or pronounce "y'all.' She wanted to change the kind of person I was. Sometimes, it was like she didn't know me at all.

In a weird way, the only time I was myself, relaxed, felt understood, was watching Harla. She couldn't even hear me. Yeah, she talked out loud too, but she was really talking to herself. Still. It was nice. For those few hours of footage I sat through every week, I wasn't so alone. And, I liked to think, neither was she.

My phone buzzed. Emily. The thought of her raised my shoulders a couple inches, and suddenly my shirt was itchy, the neck of it too tight, and I was uncomfortable all over.

She texted to tell me she was video calling. But she only wanted to video chat to see what kind of mood I was in. Emily didn't want to be around me if I was in what she called "a Chase mood," whatever that meant. But I did find myself smiling extra hard and lying if it was a tough day. Maybe it was even helping a little. Faking it if I couldn't make it.

"Hello, boy of mine!" she said excitedly as she tossed her shoulder-length black hair around.

"Hi, Emily!" I smiled, and my voice went up, trying to keep things light, not looking like I was in any kind of Chase mood. "Did you want to get together tonight?"

She'd been meeting me sometimes right after work. Mom

knew I'd be out late training, so it's not like I had a curfew.

"Yeah, I can head over to meet you. How'd today go? How are you feeling?"

Such a loaded question. Sometimes Emily was just poking to see how I was doing, check my Chase mood; but also, she always thought that I wasn't working hard enough, not taking strategy seriously enough, or not having enough fun.

"I feel cautiously optimistic? It's going to be extra hard with all of the added pressure and distractions."

"Ugh." She rolled her eyes. "Cheer up, you'll be fine Mr. Mopes. You sure you even want to hang out tonight? I don't want to break up your pity party."

"It's not like that. I don't know how much we'll get to see each other with the game coming up. And honestly, it could be a really long one."

"Okay, but I'm not headed over if you're just going to be sad all night. Cheer up."

"Okay," I said with my best fake smile. "I'll see you soon."

When the call ended, I couldn't help but feel worse. Emily used to be so happy, so joyful. She didn't care if she appeared too much like a kid or immature; she just wanted to have fun. Didn't she?

But there was a loose thread to that idea. Something about Emily that made me wonder if she was ever happy or fun, or if I had just imagined that. When I thought about meeting her, seeing her at my first ball, saving her in my first game, hiding in the dark house, my memory blurred. Like I could think about Emily, and she was in focus just fine, but when I thought about her in that game, my thoughts got fuzzy.

She had been playful then, right? Sure, she was controlling, but that was just her strategy to win. Right?

I honestly couldn't remember.

I should have been packing it up for the day, since it wouldn't take Emily long to get here. But that loose thread, that doubt that maybe I'd misremembered Emily, how she played in that game I met her...I had to pull on the thread. I had to know.

So I fired up the network and clicked over to my first game, which felt like forever ago but was just a couple years. Fast-forwarding through, I didn't take the time to relish how young I looked, how small out there, how vulnerable. I never wanted to be that small and vulnerable again. I never wanted to be that out of my depth, or out of control in any situation for the rest of my life.

Then the brawl — Alex and Mark Hubert vs. General Holter and his co-conspirators. The giant RoboBug Seeker rushed in, and I rushed away with Emily before the robot could get to her.

Once we were in that dark house together, watching it, I realized I'd forgotten it. How creepy she was. She wasn't thankful for being saved or even worried about the Seeker who'd been going berserk on players. Her only focus was me, getting in my head, freaking me out.

And that *voice*. Her sing-song lilt taunted me, toyed with me, and tortured me. At the sound, I was queasy. Then light-headed. And suddenly tired. She began the phrase that always made me sick, and I could barely keep my eyes open.

"Silly Little Mr. Kitty-"

I woke up on the floor of the rocket lab. My phone was ringing. Had I fallen asleep? That was weird. I'd never taken a nap in the lab before.

My mind was cloudy as I figured out what I was doing on the floor. The phone. I checked it; it was still that evening. I'd just put the game on a few minutes ago. Emily was calling me. I answered.

"Chase? What are you doing? You invited me over, and now you're stuck in the lab."

"I'm sorry." My thoughts were confused as I attempted to assemble them. "I was just watching an old game."

"Why? You were supposed to hang out with me. Come out now!" And she hung up.

Outside, it was raining heavily. A heavy spring Floridian rain that reminded me of how close the ocean is. I stood under an awning outside of the mostly dark building: the visitor's entrance to NASA's Cape Canaveral base. Just far enough away from the awning that I'd get soaked if I ran for it was Emily's car. Dry, warm, probably full of my favorite music and a girl who wanted to make out all night.

What was wrong with me? Why was that car the last place on Earth I wanted to be?

I stepped out, not to the car, but out from the awning, heavy cool rain thumping my head and shoulders. But I didn't walk one more step.

Emily lowered the passenger-side window. "What are you doing?"

But instead of answering, I asked the question. A question that had been on my mind for years but had been stuffed away with hurt, anger, and embarrassment. But it all came flooding back like the streams of water now soaking my shoes. "What did you hypnotize me to do?"

"What?"

"In the game, in my first game, when we were in the house together, after I saved you. What did you do to me?"

She laughed, "You never saved me, Chase. You were a scared little boy, who could you save?"

"You did something to me."

"Chase, you're talking crazy. Get in the car." And she closed the window.

"No. NO!" I didn't know where the anger in my shouting voice came from, but I wasn't in control of it, and I didn't want to control it. "Tell me! You've been messing with my mind since day one!"

She got out of the car, rolling her eyes underneath her black hooded raincoat. "What are you talking about, Chase? Let's just go get some food and talk."

"Tell me what you've done to me!"

"I fell in love with you, alright? I'm crazy about you, Chase. And it hurts me to see you unhappy and going off the deep end like this."

"No, don't do that! I'm not crazy. You did something, and you know it!"

"Chase, please."

"Stop. You don't love me. You don't even like me. Why are you doing this? You don't want to be around me."

"Not right now I don't. Not with you acting like this. What has gotten into you?"

"I watched the game. I know you hypnotized me. What did you make me do? Did you make me go into the Lack? Did you make me save the chameleon? Did you make me betray Harla? And what I did to Diamonds?"

"She betrayed you, Chase." Emily walked around the car as her tone softened.

"You betrayed me!" I backed away from her.

"Listen to me, Chase." With every word, she inched closer to me, her voice quieting but going up and down. Her sing-song voice. "You're under a lot of pressure right now, and I understand you're upset. Let's just go inside and talk."

Her hand went to my elbow, but I ripped it away.

Her eyes narrowed. Beneath her dripping hood, she sang, "Silly Little..."

My stomach turned. I stepped back, but my footing was uncertain.

"...Mr. Kitty..."

My eyes, hot with threatening tears, were now overcome with heavy eyelids. The back of my brain reached for me, reached for control. My angry thoughts screamed at me to hold on, but there was such sweet calm in surrendering. If I surrendered, it would all be easier.

No.

"No!" I ran. I dashed through the entrance doors and flung them open. The second set of doors took my keycard. Once inside, I was safe. The glass doors behind me locked, leaving Emily slapping the glass. I could see her trying to reach me, trying to talk, but the doors cut off her sound. I read her lips, though. She went from yelling to pleading to begging to threatening, all while saying one phrase. "Silly Little Mr. Kitty Cat."

But I didn't listen. I didn't answer my phone when she called thirty times that night. I went back to work and did my best to keep that ex-girlfriend out of my way.

* * *

"I think the biggest mistake," Ricky Diggs paced back and forth in front of the shipping container, "is thinking that we need to know the Council in order to take power from the Council."

At the edge of her rolling office chair, Harla sat in the middle, elbows on knees, chin on fists, taking in every word with a grim, determined look on her face like a boxer about to fight. The Huberts, each barely awake, slumped in camping chairs behind their sunglasses. Whether they were both hung over, or just pouting about the old man taking over, I didn't know. Kevin bounced in his folding chair, the closest seat to Diggs.

"At this point, anything that hurts the game, its legitimacy, undermines the ratings grab, will hurt the Council. Slow gameplay, like the old days, would kill ratings. I don't know who's watching the old games, but I'm sure they're not as popular as the new stuff, and that's the three hour version. A game lasting one week could kill the fan base and popularity of the game."

"Or a game ending at an off-peak time, like during business hours, or early in the morning."

"Good! What else? And keep in mind there are ears on us, so if you got a foolproof plan, don't blurt it out."

"An incredibly short game. Something less than an hour would take away their ability to promote the rest of the network."

"Easy," Mark said like he straight up didn't care. "Cheat to win. Be obvious about it."

"But that gives them a scapegoat. Cut the cheater out, save the purity of the game. We need to take away the reputation of the game itself. So, right now, here's what we have."

He turned to a whiteboard that had appeared this morning and wrote 'longer/shorter game' and 'off-peak.'

"Keep these in mind. But if you think you have a specific idea, do not say it out loud. Do not write it down. Only generic, vague things get said aloud or written. Does everybody understand that? So let's all work on plotting a strategy as we make the most out of the rest of our time. Alright, Captain, what do we need to work on?'

Everyone turned to Harla, who shrank under the focus. "Um okay. I'd love to see a video package put together on the arena. Why don't you work on that, Ricky, with Kevin? Cover all the bases you think I should know."

Ricky wrote the assignments on the whiteboard as she doled them out. Harla gained confidence and volume as she spoke and his marker squeaked.

"Huberts, go collect what we have from Verma Tech as far as printed scales. I'll continue assembling, and we'll see everyone for lunch!"

So they set about it. The lunch break served as an opportunity for Harla to see that the brothers had finished, come back, and were napping, while she, Ricky, and Kevin needed more time. Always more time assembling the scale face.

So she set to work on the skeleton and put the brothers on the scale face. Kevin edited footage and prepared stills for slides while Diggs made notes to present.

At the end of the day, the Seeker skeleton was complete, a presentation on the new MC Squared arena was ready for the morning, but the team was nowhere closer to assembling the scale face.

The team gathered together before heading into the various vehicles, though Harla would run home.

Ricky Diggs took the lead. "Instead of the normal daily reports which I know nobody is reading, I'd like to cover some notes. We should talk about what we're focusing our time on. We're days away, and we've got too much to work on."

"Crap, days away? Time flies," Mark said, yawning.

"Can't wait." Alex cracked a beer.

"What are y'all talking about? We still got way too much to do! I haven't even sparred once."

Alex shrugged. "Well, yeah, you never finished your Seeker."

Mark agreed, "He got no face."

"*My* seeker? It's your design. I been running all over creation to put together your plans for the dang thing!"

Mark laid the sarcasm on thick. "And you did *so well* putting the thing together too."

"Well if it's so easy, why don't you do it?"

"Because you haven't asked," Mark said simply.

His brother perked up. "Oh, is our great captain actually asking for help?"

"What's that supposed to mean?"

"It's my design," Mark said. "My schematics. My list of materials. And then I watched you flounder with building the damn thing for a month."

Harla was stunned. "You could have helped this whole time?"

"Of course."

"Even the remote power source?"

"Easy as pie."

"Why didn't you say anything earlier?"

"You didn't ask."

"Well let me go ahead and ask. Is there anything anyone thinks they can fix?"

A wrinkly black hand went up.

Harla's eyes got bigger. "Ricky?"

"Yeah, I can probably fix the conundrum with the scale face."

Kevin added, "And I've been compiling a list of weaknesses

of prospective participants, but that was really just for me. Like I have a daydream where I get interviewed for a job as an analyst, so I've been keeping notes."

"Why ain't y'all tell me any of this?"

"You were busy telling us other things to do," Mark said.

"Okay. Well, starting tomorrow, all y'all gon do this stuff you're good at, and we gon finish strong."

That was obviously meant as the closing sentiment of the day's work, but Ricky Diggs stepped up. "Before we move on, I was thinking there may be something else that the brothers may want to share?"

A frustrated grumble roared out of Harla. "You know, we don't have to save all the surprises for the last minute, we been here for about a dang month!"

Getting into the golf cart, Mark said, "No we're good."

"Nothing to share." Alex joined his brother.

"What is it?" Harla pressed Ricky Diggs.

"Well, if I found out about outstanding bench warrants, you know damn well somebody with better clearance knows about it."

Mark looked Ricky dead in the eye and spoke while cracking a beer. "No idea what you're talking about."

Alex's sincerity was much more fake. "We're just happy to be here."

She reeled around on the two of them. "You two want to tell me what he's talking about, or y'all want Ricky to tell me?"

"It's not even that big of a deal." Alex looked to Mark.

Mark pointed back and forth between his brother and himself. "We never even wanted to be on a team."

"We never would have!"

"He practically made us!"

"Who's he?" Ricky asked.

I feel bad..."

"I don't, he's a jerk. Holter."

Harla's jaw about hit the floor. "Holter is..."

"...on the Council?" Ricky clearly couldn't believe it either.

"He ain't that bad," Mark explained. "We might still be locked up without him."

"You were in prison?" Harla asked.

"I knew it," Kevin said to no one in particular.

"Jail. We were in jail. We've never been to prison."

Mark shrugged. "I have."

"I haven't," his brother insisted.

"So what did y'all do?"

"Nothing!" Alex said.

Mark admitted, "We joined the team when we didn't want to."

Ricky asked, "You didn't want to join the team?"

"We were pretty straightforward about that."

"But y'all joined."

"We wouldn't have, though."

Ricky pressed them, "And what were you supposed to do?"

"Nothing!" Alex insisted. "He just said we'd be asked to join a team, and we could be reluctant, but we had to say yes."

"Then he gave us a crap ton of money," Mark said.

Ricky asked, "And he hasn't been in contact with you since?"

"He left, and we haven't heard from him since."

"Like how much money?" Harla asked.

"Oh, it's all gone," Mark assured them, "We drank it."

"How much?" asked Ricky.

"A couple thousand."

Kevin gasped.

Mark defended himself, "We had to drink it so he couldn't take it back. Especially if we refused orders."

"What orders?" Ricky asked.

"Listen, we're not idiots," said Alex. "We were expecting instructions to sabotage..."

"And if the payment was gone," continued Mark, "he couldn't threaten to take it away..."

Alex finished the thought, "When we refused."

"Refused?"

Mark stood from the golf cart. "I ain't no snake. I said I'd join the team, and I did. We're not here to double-cross anyone."

"How do we know we can trust you?" Harla folded her arms.

"I don't care if you trust me or not. I'm the team mechanic and the best one you know."

"Oh yeah? Then how come you haven't solved our remote power source problem?"

"Because you ain't asked." Mark belched. "You try a static field with a one-touch charge?"

The idea hit Harla so hard, she fell back into her chair. Ricky began chuckling to himself. Alex struggled to keep up. "Like, just a field of static electricity? Wouldn't that be just a single shock? Don't you need steady current? Don't you risk a surge?"

In a numb voice, Harla said barely audibly, out loud to no one in particular, "Each scale has a built in ac/dc adapter. You just have to adjust the flow at the source."

Alex asked, "What source?"

She explained, "The power will move throughout all of the scales that are touching, so you just need to 'shock' one scale."

"What about when they're scattered?" Ricky asked.

Mark shrugged, cracking another beer. "It's a static field. The field will expand to hold them."

Harla added, "And when they can't, the scales will be individually charged for half an hour."

Ricky folded his arms and ran a hand over his face in thought. "OK. What downsides do we watch out for?"

Mark said, "None."

His brother disagreed. "Gathering static electricity won't be an exact science. She can't lug around equipment to measure the charge, so..."

Mark conceded, "So if you have to restart it in the game, you'll be out of luck."

"Yep."

Ricky kept on. "Okay, what other downsides?"

Mark answered, "If we don't get the charge pretty exact, we run the risk of surging."

Alex didn't follow. "And what would that do?"

"EMP," said Mark before making an explosion sound.

Harla explained, "An electro-magnetic pulse. Chances are, it'd fry nearby electronics, but it could get too big."

"Nearby electronics including the scales?" Alex asked.

"Not if they're off," Mark pointed out, "Material's hardened."

Ricky interrupted, "So we take precautions against surging. What else?"

Kevin asked "Won't Captain Miss be charged up herself?"

"We can do rubber shoes for grounding," said Alex.

"Sorry, I prefer to play in Jordans."

"Okay, I'll have to spray them with rubber," Alex said.

Harla hung her head in defeat.

"Okay then, it's getting late. Keep these problems, these

solutions in mind, see what else you can think up for a fresh start. Think about how we can turn these weaknesses into strengths. Then, bright and early tomorrow, everybody knows their jobs. Tighten up, let's get this stuff done, and get Captain Miss game ready."

"Hold up, that's another thing." Harla stopped everyone. "Enough with the Captain Miss stuff. Captain Miss is retired. Captain Miss is dead. Thanks to you all, we rebuilt my gaming persona. I got rebuilt. From now on, I'm Captain Gingerbread."

Chapter 18

Chapter 18

Ricky Diggs was obviously trying to get Harla away from the lab. "Morning, Captain. Kevin and I are profiling other players. The brothers will work on static field application with the sparring Seeker skeleton. Why don't you spend the morning visiting Dr. Bird?" The smile on his face told Harla and me that something was up. Diggs never smiled. It was creepy to see.

She took the hint and directions and drove off. The address Ricky Diggs gave her was a random plaza in a suburb of Tempe, Arizona. Between a dollar town and a pet store was a sign that read 'Western Medic.' There were no hours of operation on the door. Inside, there was no one at the front desk. But there was music. Something faint. A fast, pulsing baseline. Harla followed the music past the waiting room, down a hallway lined in doors. It was rock. Heavy, growling guitars and drums.

Past the normal knobbed doors was a pair of industrial double doors with little windows. Diagonal black and yellow warning stripes bordered. Looking through the wire-enforced windows, Harla saw Dr. Bird, typing at a computer set up next to what looked like a futuristic coffin, a big white tube with several button-covered control panels. But the big white tube belonged there, obviously medical equipment, like a CAT scan or an MRI. What didn't fit in was porta potty in the corner. A regular, run-of-the-mill porta potty, like for fairs or outdoor concerts.

Harla pushed open the door, and angry sounds of hardcore 80's punk music escaped. It was too loud for Dr. Bird to notice someone else in the room. Instead, she bobbed her head along with the raging guitars and continued typing at her work station. "Doc? Doc!"

"Captain!" Dr. Bird had a bubbly lightness, bouncing over to the speaker to turn it down. "It's great to see you! You look well. You ran this morning!"

Almost out of habit, Dr. Bird began poking and prodding her patient, as easy small talk led to an investigation of Harla's ears, eyes, and mouth, stethoscope moving over her collarbone, chest, and back as the two spoke.

"I run every morning."

"Yeah, but you're pushing yourself now. How many miles?"

"Seven?"

"And how're your times?"

"About fifty minutes. I broke one six minute mile."

"I don't care about numbers. How's your time compared to how you normally run it?"

"Fastest yet."

"That's good. Captain. Really good. Did Ricky Diggs tell you why you're here today?"

"A physical?"

"No, y'all have enough security cameras and body sensors

that I can pretty much run those any time of day. You're here because of this bad boy." Dr. Bird went over to the control panel of the big machine and went back to typing. Lights along the white tube came to life blinking and chasing.

"Are you going to look at my brain or something?"

"Oh, no, we're not going to use this on you. It disturbs electrics. First, the magnetizing will screw with any electronics or signal coming off of you, but it also lets out an electrical interference that will fuzz up any signal."

"For what? Bugs?"

"Well, yeah. Surely you know you've been bugged, Captain."

"I do. But I didn't know anyone else knew. I thought I was going crazy."

"Don't...Captain." Dr. Bird paused her work and came over to Harla, taking her by both shoulders and carefully looking her in the eyes. "You're a mentally sound young lady. Don't let anyone else convince you not to trust your own thoughts."

The goop around the porta potty began to flare up, pulsating and glowing bright.

It shocked Dr. Bird a bit, who checked her watch, then scurried back to the control pad. The big machine whirred to life. Bird had to yell to be heard, "We just wanted to ensure you two some privacy when you talked strategy."

The machine was deafeningly loud now, drowning out the punk guitars. The signal from her jaw mic went spotty. I checked through her myPhone but wasn't getting any audio. The porta potty door pushed open. End transmission.

I couldn't figure out who met with Harla. No one from the team, I figured out that much. Must have been Harpreet. But what did they talk about?

* * *

By the time Harla returned to the secret lab, everyone was busy, nose down in work. Only Diggs looked up to address her as she closed the Buick door behind her.

"You found Dr. Bird?"

"Yep."

"Take care of what you needed to?"

"We got a strategy."

"Good. We don't have to talk about it then. I mean it, too. I never want to hear what was said or whatever the plan is."

"Plausible deniability?"

"Cockamamie aversion. Chances are I'll think you're being too reckless, but my job isn't to understand or condone the captain's actions. My plan is just to navigate."

"Alright then. How's it coming with the face?"

"Now don't get mad..." Kevin began.

"Why would I get... Oh no, what did y'all do?"

Ricky said simply, "We finished it."

"Finished what?"

"The scale face. We still need you to program the details, but..."

"For real?"

Kevn couldn't contain his excitement. "For real, for real."

Harla approached the table the two were working on. On it, the silver tree housed most of a head, but missing half of a face. The thing looked like the terminator, a blank, nondescript, white guy half-face, and then you could see into the mechanical workings, the tree and the underside of the scales where the head was incomplete. And laid out next to the head were a series of scales, fit together like a puzzle piece, all upside down, concave bowls with their electronics facing up to Harla. Her happy-go-lucky smile melted when she realized what they'd done.

They had put together the face on the table. On a flat surface. Because obviously, trying to hang the scales made it much more complicated.

"God, I'm so stupid."

"No!" Kevin protested.

"Sometimes when you're working on a problem," said Ricky, "you just need another set of eyes to see things a bit differently."

"How long did it take to assemble the thing on a flat surface?"

"Promise not to be mad?"

"I guess."

"It took like ten minutes for the whole thing."

"Yeah, we ran out and got chicken sandwiches."

"Y'all already had lunch?"

"You didn't? Well, sit down and eat while we finish this."

"Okay. Kevin, the rest of the scales are in the trunk; could you get them out?" Harla sat to enjoy a cold fast-food chicken sandwich.

At first, she didn't hear the footsteps. Arrhythmic pounding and dragging. Hard crunch and scraping on cement coming up behind her. Shambling behind up behind her, the Seeker skeleton was a walking three dimensional stick figure with a camera flanked by motherboards for a head.

"The hell?" Harla was sufficiently creeped out by the delicate-looking sentient robot.

Laughter broke out from the camping chairs where Alex and

Mark were already celebrating with beers. "Captain, meet Broteas!"

The android stood at rigid attention, clicked its heels and gave a salute. Like something out of the Star Wars prequels.

"Looks good, but will the field hold the scales?"

Mark held up a joystick in his hand, like the kind that operated old video games. "Clear out, Kevin!" he yelled at the intern who'd dragged the heavy trunk-sized metal case over. The boy stood back.

Mark mashed the red button at the tip of the joystick, and the metal case shifted and rumbled, like a shoebox with a cat inside. "Well, open it first, then clear out, Kevin!"

Visibly scared, Kevin neared the case while crouching, then flicked the lock to the lid open, retreating quickly to safety behind Diggs' white board. The Huberts let out a laugh at the kid, but it didn't last.

One scale zipped through the air from the case to the skeleton like it was shot out of a slingshot. It stuck to the arm of the seeker, magnetized in place.

Alex's tablet, still on the wooden frame that once housed the skeleton, lit up. A progress bar appeared, the only clue as to what the tablet was doing was the word "synchronizing." The progress bar filled, and the rest of the scales leapt to life.

A cloud of them, bigger pieces than the ScatterSwarm, moved like a spikey, angular cloud through the air - direct, quick, precise, and looking very, very, deadly. The spikey cloud pounced on the skeleton, seemingly devouring the thing. The spikes shifted, jutting and darting until the cloud of bots settled into a humanoid form. They rippled with color, changing shape and texture, settling into blue, red, or white with the appearance of cloth. It was a suit. A business suit, taut, as if someone were wearing it. A big someone, a headless businessman.

A tomato fell out of Harla's chicken sandwich as she stared at the thing. The ends of her agape mouth curled up into a maniacal smile. She whispered in wonder, in triumph, like Victor Frankenstein seeing the monster move beneath the sheet. But instead of proclaiming life, she whispered in joy, "The gingerbread man!"

"I was thinking the same thing," Ricky said. He lifted the complete white guy face off the metallic tree. In a grotesque, unnatural way, the empty head skin fell limp in his hands. "I know the plan was for this to be the face of the sparring robot..."

As he approached her, she put the sandwich off to the side, preparing.

Harla nodded to herself, understanding something unspoken. "Something tells me that was never the plan."

"Do you mind?" Ricky asked as he raised the limp face.

"Let's do this."

He lowered the skin over her head. The neck and chin bulged as she fit in. Suddenly her body — tall, curvy, and powerful - seemed small. Her head, now a white guy's, was one and a half times too big.

The features of the white man she'd become stretched and morphed. When the eyes opened, they were not hers, but cold blue. But the man's lips moved perfectly in sync with Harla's surprised voice, "This ish is amazing!" Her new face looked around, smiled, sniffed, and winked. "How do I look?"

"Like a white dude with a black girl's voice," Mark laughed.

"I think we can actually adjust that." Ricky nodded at Kevin, who went ham on his laptop.

"Okay. Try now!"

"Ain't no black girl," a gruff, low voice said with Harla's African American accent. "I'm a white guy played by a black woman."

"Well, excuse me. Still doesn't sound right."

Harla shifted her accent, speaking in the cadence of a news anchor. The lowered voice sounded like any cheesy old white dude talking. "All I have to do is talk like I have a stick up my butt. Film at eleven."

Everyone busted out laughing. Harla chuckled in her low old white guy voice. Ricky snickered to himself while the brothers howled, and Kevin theatrically guffawed, trying too hard, as per usual.

"I think we've got our Captain Gingerbread." said Ricky. "Tomorrow, Mark and I will put the finishing touches on her scale armor while Harla - you, Kevin, and Alex get the Seeker up and running. Plan for the thing to be self-driving, but I'd like Alex to have the option of remote controlling."

"Really?" Mark asked with an eyebrow raise before looking around to see if the rest of the team was thinking along the same lines as him, "Two days out, and we have to still build the practice Seeker?"

"Sparring partner."

"I don't care what you call it, it's a waste of time. We've got our tech. We should spend these days practicing- oh, I'm sorry, Rocky Balboa, sparring. There's nothing that Alex and I can't do with some basic stealth suits that the sparring partner can."

"It wasn't my idea to spend all of our training time building a dang robot, you two. If it were up to me, we'd have been running sims all month. But you two had the big plan to make an analogy of our captain. Well, the analogy is almost done. And this team finishes things, no matter how hard or misguided. This captain finishes things. She fights 'til the end. She wins. That's why I agreed to join the team, and that's how we're going to support her. She isn't going to quit out there in the arena, so I'll be damned if we're going to quit days before."

For such a rousing speech, Diggs didn't garner much of a reaction. Everyone sort of shrugged and grumbled as the night ended. No one really spoke or looked at one another as the weight of the game, which was a distant impossibility, suddenly loomed very real and quite heavy. Kevin and Diggs got in the Buick for Harla to drive home while the brothers took the golf cart back to Nakea's to Uber back to their hotel.

After Kevin was home, Harla took the fifteen minutes from Nakea's to drop Diggs off at his little home on the south side. They hadn't spoken the whole way, but when Diggs did say something as he opened the door, Harla knew exactly who he was talking about.

"We can trust them, right?"

Harla shrugged and answered without putting too much thought to it. "Like we got a choice? See you tomorrow, Ricky."

"See you tomorrow, Captain."

* * *

The next day went as Ricky had said — Mark and Ricky worked in silence, forming the best scales printed by Verma Tech into a Captain's suit, while Harla, Kevin, and Alex finished programming the sparring partner, now a hulking man with electronics instead of a head. Broteas.

But as each team finished up their task and everybody sat down to lunch, Diggs dropped a bomb on everyone. "If it's alright with the Captain, I'd like to show her something. Maybe the rest of you can take the day off."

Alex's voice jumped high. "Are you serious? The ball's tomorrow! This is our only chance to spar."

"We can spar tomorrow."

"This doesn't make any sense!"

Ricky shrugged. "It's up to the Captain. I just wanted to present the intel Kevin and I put together, maybe take a field trip to the Energy Arena."

"A field trip implies a class going. Like all of us. Unless you two are looking for something more like a romantic rendezvous?"

"Ew." Just then, Harla's phone went off, vibrating in her pants.

"It's up to the Captain."

But Harla was checking her phone, her lock screen telling her she had a text from Diamonds.

"Captain?" Diggs repeated himself.

Harla pocketed the phone, cleared her throat, and regained her focus. "Why don't you guys spend two hours talking through possible hiding spots in the Arena. Need some sniper angles, too. Diggs and I are going on a field trip."

"Field Trip?" Mark asked.

Harla winked, "Top-secret plan stuff."

Alex and Mark were getting out of shape, Mark huffing and Alex pacing in anger.

Harla offered, "Beers on Harpreet. Just for tonight."

Immediately, it was obvious the gesture worked on Mark; a

smile now smeared on his face. But Alex didn't seem as sure, giving Diggs the stink eye.

As she and Diggs got into the Buick, Harla managed to sneak a look at her texts.

"Nervous about tomorrow?" Diamonds asked.

Harla quickly shoved the phone back in her pocket as she buckled up and started the car.

Diggs said, "You can answer that."

"You're not going to get mad or lecture me about kids today?"

"Nah, my grandkids got me a Droid. I'm all over TikTok. Go ahead."

"We have a plan," Harla texted back.

"So where to?" she asked the old man.

"Swing by my place."

Fifteen minutes later, they pulled up. "This will only be a second. Unless you need to run in."

"I'm good." Harla's hand went down to her pocket, grasping her phone.

"Okay, be right back. You want a water or Gatorade or anything?"

"Sure." She slid the phone out of her pocket without Diggs being able to see.

"Well, which? Gatorade or water?"

"Gatorade." She was losing her patience.

"What flavor?"

She just pulled her phone out at this point and thumbed it to unlock. "Don't care."

Diamonds had texted back immediately. "U didn't answer. Nervous?"

Harla responded, "Yeah nervous. I think a good nervous."

Immediately, Diamonds answered, "Go to therapy this week?"

"Yep."

"Need anything?"

"Good actually. Team's got my back."

"Good to hear," Diamonds texted, then paused. "I've been watching some of the network."

"You gon watch me play?"

"You know it. Noticed something odd about the Shadow Captain."

The idea must have taken Harla by surprise, as the smile melted from her face and she gave a double take to the phone.

"What?"

The text conversation turned to three dots. Ellipses showing Harla that Diamonds was responding, but taking their sweet time. Finally, a picture came through.

It was a photo of a tv screen, an old interview on the Super-Powers, Unlimited network. It was somebody in facepaint-alternating greens, just classic camouflage. A graphic at the bottom identified "Captain Shadow."

Another photo hit Harla's phone. This was a close-up of the desk behind the Shadow Seeker, stacks of files and pages.

Diamonds sent a third photo, blurrier than the others of the stack of pages, file folders, and notebook. A blue notebook.

"The Council's big target."

"What?"

"H — That's the notebook from the files the Council kept. From the Documents Room."

I truly believed that Diamonds always has Harla's best interests in mind, but feeding into more of these Council delusions was dangerous. I squinted and enlarged the photo.

It was just a notebook.

But of course, since Harla believed it, her eyes were as wide as her open mouth by the time Ricky Diggs climbed back in.

"You alright?" Ricky raised an eyebrow.

Harla laughed it off. "Are *you* okay? Thought maybe you fell in..." She put the car in gear. "Where to now?"

"Verma Tech HQ."

* * *

Harpreet was expecting them, so the Buick goopgated right into his large top-floor office, San Diego and San Francisco in the distance out of different windows. The car dripped purple sludge, sitting in the middle of the penthouse.

"Good driving. I know I've got a big office, but brother, I was nervous about parking."

"Big office? It's bigger than my house," Ricky Diggs said, looking around at the clean, minimalist shiny black and white surfaces that made up the matching ceiling and floors.

"Yeah, I don't really use it. It's mostly for business deals to intimidate people. I work mostly down in development on the third floor."

"Y'all take up the whole building?!"

"Whoa, no. Just the top floor and the third. We're not that big."

Ricky asked, "It's a multi-million dollar corporation?"

"Well, yeah, bro."

Ricky continued, "Number one selling app in the world?"

"For now."

"Then we have different definitions of 'big,' bro."

Harpreet laughed and grabbed a case from a nearby glass table. Or was it just an empty desk? The sleek emptiness didn't fit Harpreet, so it made sense that he was never there.

"Here's what you came for. I could have sent it over, bro." Harpreet handed over a case about the size of a briefcase, all chrome and black. It looked important.

Harla entered a code and flipped the latches open.

"Should I..." Ricky gestured, offering to leave or avert his eyes.

Harla shook her head no, opening the case to reveal what looked like antique video game controllers. A bunch of joysticks, each topped with a red button, mounted in foam. Harla nodded in approval at the contents, and closed the case back up.

Ricky picked it up, "We're keeping a tight lid on this one, sir. Mystique is important.

"Ricky Diggs, we were in too many mission controls for too many days for you to call me sir, bro. I'm so glad you're on this team."

Ricky's lip curled up in an earnest smile. "I'm very happy to be here. I think the Captain is set up well. And I can't wait to see whatever this is." He lifted the case he held.

"Oh, you don't even know?"

Harla got back into her old Buick, Ricky following. "It's a need-to-know basis. Thank you sir."

"I won't be at the ball," Harpreet said, shrugging and pocketing his hands. He really did act like a big kid. Not in the cruel way Emily did but as someone so excited about everything. So full of wonder. "So I guess I'll see you on the other side, Captain?"

Harla left her door open and ran to hug Harpreet.

"I'll miss you out there, big bro," she said into his Stone Cold Steve Austin shirt. "Thank you so much for everything."

I stopped watching because I was caught up. Tomorrow was the ball, then the game. I wouldn't have time to catch Harla's one day of sparring. I wouldn't get to see her in action until the MC Squared was live.

I was genuinely excited to see Captain Gingerbread.

But I had one day to figure out how to disappear with the Crown.

* * *

Angry Guy's suit was too tight, just like his skin was too tan and his teeth too white. "It's the eve of the first ever televised MC Squared ball and one question remains — Where is Captain Miss? With the Gingerbread Man joining on behalf of hot app developer Verma Tech, all but one slot is taken. But to be clear, Colonel Veil, do the rules require ten competitors?"

The old naval officer had been forced into retirement after his ties to the Council, but that was hardly punishment. And it wasn't soon after that he got rehired by SuperPowers to run the game's rules.

"They do."

Angry Guy leaned in expecting more, but he got none. "You heard it here first, folks. As we near the famed MC Squared ball, the event that will introduce each individual captain and force them and their teams to mingle, the mystery remains. Will Captain Miss fill the final spot in the competition? You'll have to tune in to the network special, primetime, 8/7 central on the eve of the MC Squared."

After the break with Emily, I threw myself into the game even more, if that were possible. I opened the door to my house way after Mom would have gone to sleep. But that was normal since I started working for SuperPowers. Only tonight, the TV was on, playing the end of MC Three.

And instead of running into Mom, Dad was in the living room.

The image made me bristle. Dad was something that didn't belong here anymore, a picture of home with him in it didn't make any sense in my brain.

"Hey, Kiddo," he said in a raspy, tired voice.

My face flamed hot like fire while my armpits sweated ice cubes. "What are you doing here?"

"Sorry. I talked to your mother, and she said it was okay if I stuck around and talked to you after you were done with work."

It felt like a betrayal, but I wasn't sure why. His presence, but also his sad face, his hoarse, calm voice...all of this was wrong. It sat in my gut like a bowling ball. I had no problem with the guy, he was my Dad and I loved him, but we hadn't really been close since he moved out.

"You mother said it'd be late, but wow. They sure do keep you long hours, huh?"

"It's a big job."

"It is. I've seen. And man, Kiddo, I am impressed, so proud of you."

"Nobody calls me Kiddo anymore," I said coldly, stabbing at his feelings with an icicle. I wasn't even sure how this got adversarial. Just a gut feeling something was wrong; it wasn't right that Dad was here, and I had to push back. But why? Why was I like this?

"Well, Chase, it's very impressive to see what you've done. You should be proud."

"Thanks," I said, dropping my bag and heading to the kitchen. "I'm supposed to have a shake before bed, you want anything?"

"No, ki-" He stopped himself, "No thanks, Chase."

So I walked past him as he stood there. I don't know if he was expecting a hug or a handshake, but he awkwardly rubbed his hands on his jeans like he didn't know what to do with them. "I'd, uh, like to talk to you about something."

What was this? Something was wrong. Dad hadn't talked to me about anything for a year other than fishing trips, birthday, and Christmas presents.

"Fine, I guess." I wanted to get this over with, cracking the green shake and chugging it.

"Well, this is tough. I just wanted to apologize for things I've said before. Maybe I wasn't supportive of you, when... when you came out, and I could have been. And before that, I may have said some things that made it harder on you to tell me and your mother...for you to be comfortable enough to talk to us."

I had no idea where this was going. Dad was admittedly always "old school," and pretty toxic about what he thought it meant to be a man. I'd always knew I was never going to be this idea he had of what I should have been.

But this was different. This was the opposite. He was nervous, his posture submissive, and he couldn't keep eye contact.

"I'm just so sorry, Chase. I had no idea what you were going through. Heh, maybe I did know but couldn't admit it. You're just...you're so brave, Chase."

Brave? Me? It actually made me laugh out loud. I wasn't in the same neighborhood as brave, I just was pretending. Reminded me of Dad's own words. "Fake it 'til I make it, huh?"

His drooping, sad eyes flared, suddenly angry. "No. No, I was wrong to say that. I was wrong to tell you that. Don't fake being something you're not, Chase. If you're just faking, you never get a chance to be the real you."

"Well, the real me is tired from a long day, so..."

"Chase, I'm gay."

The words didn't make sense. I understood them, but in the context of my dad saying them, the concept hurt my brain. Like I felt the idea as I tried to grasp it spin in my head, a literal twisting. And then the room spun. I had to put effort to keep my eyes from crossing or rolling back. I thought I should say something, but I couldn't even form words.

However my reaction looked, Dad felt the need to fill the silence. "Or bi, maybe. Because I was in love with your mother."

Mom. I immediately wondered how awful this made her feel. A burning started at my ears and spread to my cheeks, embarrassed for her.

"I want you to know that. That I was in the marriage before we drifted apart. But maybe, I'm just gonna be gay for a while. With men, that is."

How long had he been lying to us? To me? How much of his life was a lie? Did I even really know my dad? Was I being selfish for just thinking of myself?

"I love you, Chase. And I'm so proud to be your dad, and that's always going to be what's most important. I haven't been very good at it, but I'm trying to be better for you. Because your being my son makes me a better person."

A lump in my throat, a monster choking me I hadn't felt since I was a little boy, stole my attempt to say something. To tell him not to use me as some excuse. To say I couldn't trust anything he said now. To say I was different and special, and he couldn't stand that. That now I was just some kid who's bi because his dad was.

But I couldn't talk. I couldn't form a single word.

So I hugged him.

I'd never seen Dad like this, so...little. I couldn't trash him. I didn't want to be like that. I didn't want to feel the need to be like that anymore. I just wanted to be with him, to hold him like I had always wanted to hold him.

In that moment, crying together while hugging so tight before either of us said anything stupid to screw it up, it was perfect. He was finally the dad I secretly wished he was — not gay, but honest and soft with me; proud. And I really wanted to be that Chase he described that he was so proud of.

IV

Part Four

The Ball, Game

Chapter 19

C hapter 19

Okay, I cheated a bit. I was so nervous about the game and doing well, and maybe a bit emotionally drained from the talk with Dad, I spent my time preparing for the ball looking in on Team Verma Tech. And maybe Diamonds, too.

* * *

On the drive there, everyone was bustling. Kevin couldn't shut up complimenting everyone on how they looked, Diggs and Dr. Bird were singing some song together, Harla laughing at them while Mark bitched and moaned although he couldn't stop from smiling a little. Only Alex was quiet, staring out the window, checking his phone every now and again. He was evidently less impressed with riding in a limousine.

"Why the long face?"

Alex didn't hear Ricky Diggs talking to him at first.

"Thinking about all the times you struck out at prom?" Mark ribbed his brother.

"'All the times?' How many times did you go?" Harla asked.

"Are you kidding? Sexy Lexi was so popular, he went as a freshman, sophomore, junior, senior-"

"Sexy Lexi? I think I'm gonna be sick." Harla clamped a hand on her mouth.

"And then again in college as a freshman, sophomore, junior..."

Everyone but Alex had a good laugh.

"I never went to prom," Harla said, shrugging.

From the front passenger seat, Dr. Bird agreed, "The burden of the homeschooled child genius."

But Kevin was concerned. "That's awful."

Harla obviously didn't think it was that big of a deal. "It's not so bad. I doubt Prom could have been that great."

"Ask Alex," laughed Mark.

"Sexy Lexi," corrected Ricky Diggs with a wry smile.

Alex burst, yelling out something he'd been holding back, "They contacted me."

"What? Who?" Harla asked.

"The Council." Alex looked to his brother. "They finally reached out again, before you picked us up."

Mark stared lasers back into his brother's eyes. "You didn't say anything."

"Of course they did," she grumbled.

"What do they want?" Ricky asked, looking through his rearview mirror.

Alex didn't look at anyone but his brother. "I'm supposed to get something and hand it over."

"What?" Dr. Bird asked.

He fished in his jacket pockets before withdrawing a flash-drive.

"What's that?" Mark asked slowly.

"Proof that Verma Tech was spying on Powers, Limited and its subsidiaries."

"What are you going to do?" Mark was so quiet and serious, acting like he gave a crap about something for the first time since joining the team.

"I don't know, but I'm not turning on you guys no matter what."

Mark flared up. "What do you mean, 'no matter what?'"

Alex said, "They've got enough evidence that if we can't pin this on Harpreet or Verma Tech, they're going to pin it on me."

"Evidence of what?" Kevin asked.

"Spying."

Ricky protested, "But spying is part of the game!"

Harla understood though, saying slowly, "Not when spon-soring companies are in the middle of corporate espionage lawsuits."

"So, what, you're gonna take the fall as some nefarious third party?" Mark said, his voice shaking a tiny bit.

Alex couldn't even look at his brother, much less say any-thing.

I didn't get it. Alex was willing to go to jail, for what? To keep Harla in the game? To keep Verma Tech in business?

"Aren't you on probation, bro?" Harpreet asked gently. 'They'll put you away for as long as they want."

"I think that's the idea." Alex's voice was full of dry regret. I could practically hear him craving a beer.

Bird asked, "So what's on the flash drive?"

"Just ISP addresses so they can trace any breaches to the

Verma Tech offices."

Kevin was panicking. "So what do we do?"

Ricky set his jaw and said, matter-of-factly, "We do what this team always does. Takes a weakness and makes it a strength. Alex isn't vulnerable; he's got the upper hand."

"How you figure?"

Ricky explained it like he was bored. "He's got a rendezvous with someone on the Council, so we got them right where we want them."

Harla didn't buy it. "There's no way they'd risk it."

"Risk what?" Ricky laughed it off. "Tonight is the most important event in the history of the Council. The ball has to go off without a hitch. This is how they plan on introducing all of the players to their audience. The way I see it, I don't think the Council can afford not to attend, they have to make sure *everything* goes right."

"Okay, so we know they'll be there," Harla said. "Will they risk meeting Alex in person?"

"No, they'll use a proxy."

"Captain's right," said Alex. "Somebody is going to come up to me and ask me if I have something for them."

"Great. When that happens, you need to plant this on them." Ricky handed something to Dr. Bird, who handed it back to Harpreet, who handed it to Alex.

"What's that?" Mark asked.

"Is that a Regalia bug?" Harla immediately whispered like she was afraid of being recorded. "Are you crazy?"

Ricky assured them, "It's reprogrammed and synced to our computers."

"So what's the plan?" Kevin was still lost and panicking.

"Bug *them*," Harla said. "I know a district attorney who

could take the Council down with a little more evidence."

Pulling into their goop portal destination in the back of an abandoned industrial complex, Ricky came to some conclusions of his own, putting the car in park and telling the team, "We draw a line between Chase's spying, blackmailing the Huberts, SuperPowers, Unlimited, and the Council."

This was all news to Dr. Bird. "Wait, so the plan is to take down everyone? The entire game? What are you playing for, then? Why'd we train if you never wanted to play?"

Harla answered quietly, "Ever since I joined up with SteelCut, I saw how things just aren't fair and there's nothing to be done about it. How everyone knows there's cheating, everyone knows it's a stacked deck, but that's just the way it is. Since I've been in this game as an intern, I've wondered what it would look like if this game was fair, if it was just a competition to help make tech to keep soldiers safe. What if this game was used for what it was made for? This isn't a circus, this is people's lives we could be saving. And I know I can be the best to ever play. Not just at some game, but science, engineering, keeping people safe, all of that. Conspirators have manipulated this game long before any of us even heard about it. It's about time to see it played fair."

Everyone looked around at each other, realizing that this was now more a game, that this ball was more than the debut of Captain Gingerbread. The ball now had an objective. This was a mission, and they were agents. Eventually, all eyes went to Alex who was no longer lead team engineer but the bait. He was nervous, sweating and shifting uncomfortably under everyone's stares.

His brother said gently, "What do you think?"

The question hung in the air. Alex wasn't a long-time

friend or someone who volunteered for his job. The Huberts were hired hands, they didn't owe Harla anything. They were being pulled into the game again after getting dumped unceremoniously to the side.

The Huberts looked at one another, tight-lipped, nodding. Finally, Alex said, "Let's go fishing."

* * *

Meanwhile, on the West Coast, Diamonds was back to their old obsessions. Maybe it was the amazing streaming capabilities of their brand new myPhone X Zeta they assumed their Dad had sent. Maybe it was nerves on Harla's behalf. Maybe it was what they found.

The notebook. A blue notebook with a black border. All of the photos of it were burned in the fires of that fateful game. The game where I went out of control and assaulted Diamonds.

They'd found a filing cabinet full of pictures from different decades, all containing the same black notebook. But they all burned.

In their old room back at their dad's house, Diamonds hid something. Something none of their school friends could know about. It wasn't right for a psychiatrist to have an obsession after all. Each and every wall was covered with page after page of pencil sketches, marker drawings, and crayon renderings of the blue notebook. They were dated over the last year. And every representation of the notebook had the same logo on the cover. The new Superpowers, Unlimited logo.

And that logo was going to debut tonight.

Of course Diamonds didn't know that. In their obsession room, they were combing over the same three interviews again and again, watching each still frame from the network's extras.

Their phone alerted them. Someone on the MC Squared Reddit (I couldn't believe that existed) replied to Diamonds, rather CptMissWanna-B's, post asking for more shots of the Shadow Captain.

From an anonymous throwaway account, it read simply, "He's in the SteelCut tribute."

Of course. I wasn't surprised, but I couldn't bring myself to watch it. And according to their streaming history, neither had Diamonds or Harla.

And the week had been emotional enough already.

But I watched it with Diamonds — the grainy old photographs of a young, skinny SteelCut, the interviews with competitors, the tear-jerking harmonies of Boyz II Men playing beneath.

And then, there: the Shadow Captain.

Diamonds hit pause and gasped.

His face was still in blotchy camo makeup. Still at the same wooden desk covered in files and papers. But the blue with black-border spiral notebook was missing. Instead, on top of the stack of files, a spiral-bound notebook sat open.

Diamonds whispered to themselves, "That's my handwriting. How?"

My hand was literally covering my mouth in disbelief when there was a knock at my door. They'd given me a dressing room outside of the Ballroom, which everyone called the "Con Floor."

I put my phone and the footage of Diamonds in my suit pocket and followed the guy with the clipboard through a series of doors. I had to stop watching. I was out of time. I had a job to do.

Cameras everywhere. And lights. God, the lights. The high ceiling of the SuperPowers Con floor was brimming with hot theatrical lights. The new facility, looking fancy with galaxy carpeting, was filled with exhibits, players, media, and fans.

Honestly, I hadn't even thought about having fans, but there they were. Teenage girls, all white with shoulder-length brown hair, all screeching and squealing, descended upon me in a pack.

Wearing the old Regalia tech, I was in a simple black suit with a skinny black tie, my helmet forming the head of an American lion — an extinct species of enormous mane-less big cats. And I got rushed.

They all wanted autographs, and I made my helmet snarl for dozens of selfies.

Suddenly, a TV camera was in my face. Angry guy was pushing a mic on me. Instinctively, my helmet growled.

"Are you ready to battle against Captain Miss again? Do you have any words for her before the game?"

I was confused. Harla was playing as Captain Gingerbread. There was no Captain Miss.

"No comment," I grunted. I wasn't supposed to say things like that, though.

Angry Guy railroaded me and kept right on, "How prepared are you for tomorrow?"

This time, I stuck to the script. "I was born for this game."

Angry Guy nodded and cued me some more. "Bold words from a young competitor."

"If you think of me like that," I looked to the camera and finished the line through my talking cat helmet, "then you've already lost."

And I marched off. It was my exit line, but I'd used it too early. Still, it was a great walkaway, and I doubted any suits would be mad at that performance.

More selfies. I signed a kid's leg cast. One family that didn't speak English insisted we take a photo in front of my old tech... Grandad's old tech, the Throne.

It sat on a little stage, lit from above, like much of the old tech. An antique chair, high-backed and wooden with intricate arms and red cushions, all scratched up, corners melted, splotches of orange tagging solvent dried on. In my head, I heard Boyz II Men for an instant and got teary eyed. Thank goodness for a lion mask. I snarled, we took the pic, and I looked down on the big con floor.

On a nearby wall, gooped up in purple with a platform of its own jutting out, lights flashed and electricity crackled. Suddenly, all of the ball attendees looked around confusedly, most checking their phones, listening in, mashing buttons and getting confused or angry. Metallica laid down a driving beat with a guitar screaming over it. The music was coming out of everyone's phones.

Impressive.

Then the purple goop did its goopy thing and out came the van. The timing was perfect. The building intro had just opened up into the driving beat of the song. Vocals led up to the chorus, and as James Hetfield asked, "Where's your Crown, King Nothing?" Captain Gingerbread stepped out, chin jutting, chest puffed, brilliant smile flashing.

All fans recorded it on their phones. The team paid no attention to the fanfare, it was a very expensive production that SuperPowers Unlimited was putting on to impress their audience. Alex attempted to look relaxed but couldn't, so he walked to the bar and pounded beers. This induced eye rolls and sighing from the team, but everyone seemed happy to keep easy tabs on him. They were all in matching suits and rubber masks of Superman faces. A team of dark haired, blue eyed white dudes in suits.

Not to brag, but Harla — Captain Gingerbread — had decidedly less fans looking for selfies. She – or, he, rather – stood patiently with each of them, throwing a corny thumbs up with each photo. The rest of the team spread out on the con floor, each of them obviously keeping eyes on Alex.

As soon as the Captain was done with her line of fans, I approached behind them, cleared my throat, and said, "I figured from your handle, you'd be red-headed."

"Sorry to disappoint." Gingerbread seemed to take pleasure towering over me, slowly looking down and grinning. I'd be lying if I said it wasn't intimidating, being this close to them on a stage next to an old gilly suit.

I could feel every camera in the room on us as we stood toe to toe. This was all a part of the spectacle, the storylines that would get played out tomorrow. But I was so sick and tired of playing...or maybe getting played.

So I gave the Regalia the command and warped light. Once we were invisible to everyone in the room, I said another command, wrapping us in a crackling field of magnetism to stop anyone from listening in.

"You look great," I said without thinking, then stumbled over my words to play it cool, "Not like that. I mean all of this, the captain, the persona. Picking a white guy, hiding in plain sight. Genius move."

Now, without the scrutiny of the other guests, Harla relaxed and the big bulk of Captain Gingerbread did too, shifting weight to one leg, cocking out a hip, and folding the big robot suit's arms. "What do you want?"

Her wording threw me and a laugh escaped my mouth. "Ha. Good question. The last two years erased?" I cleared my throat and took a breath. "Look, I wanted to say, Harla, that-"

"Captain Gingerbread," she corrected.

"Sorry. Captain Gingerbread. So that means...he/him pronouns?"

Sassy hip still jutting out, Captain Gingerbread deflated a little. "Uh...yeah. I hadn't put a lot of thought into it."

"Well, sir, Captain Gingerbread," I said so carefully. It wasn't easy being serious and polite with Harla...or the captain. But I had to. It was time to be the Chase that Dad looked up to.

I took a deep breath.

"I wanted to say..."

My lion helmet yawned open. I wanted my face visible.

"...I am..."

Another big breath. Man, opening up like this was awful.

"...sorry."

Captain Gingerbread practically flinched at the apology.

I took another deep breath, waiting for an answer. But I realized the answer didn't matter. I felt better already. Taller, standing straighter, able to take deeper breaths. Opening up like this was awesome.

"Sorry?" Captain Gingerbread's unreadable face asked back in a white, Midwestern accent.

"For everything. You were right. We should have split the Captain. You were right about going into the Lack and getting suspended. Heck, you were right that I should never have been Captain in the first place. It wasn't just your turn in line, you had earned the Captain's seat. The Throne. The Puzzle."

Captain Gingerbread stared blankly at me.

But I was riding a rush. It was an incredible high, letting something that weighed so much off my chest. I honestly didn't know how much I'd been carrying around. I couldn't stop.

"And I've been so petty this last year, moving over to NASA and bringing you up in interviews. The best part of my last six months has been seeing you. Watching you. I should apologize for that, too, but...I just wanted to tell you good luck tomorrow. I mean that. And I wanted to let you know I'm not cheating or being part of any conspiracy. I've just been...listening in, but you already know that."

"Anything else?" Captain Gingerbread was unimpressed.

So that's how it was going to be. No begrudging respect. Just grudges. Fine. I hadn't been treating her any better.

"Yeah, I did want to say thanks. For talking to me. I know you know how lonely it can get and how scared? Not scared. Vulnerable? Not vulnerable." My words failed me.

"Isolated."

"Yeah. Isolated. And hearing you talk to me, even though I couldn't talk back, made me feel less isolated."

"Me too."

"I'm just...so sorry. I really am." My emotions caught in my throat, and my face flushed hot while tears burned my eyes threateningly.

"Stop." The Gingerbread Man said without looking at me. "I'll be alright. Nothing you ever did to hurt me couldn't be outdone by me, but...but you did Diamonds wrong, and they're my best friend. It's just the way it has to be."

Of course, she was right. Harla was always right; it was one of the most annoying things about her. "I know."

And we sat there, quietly, and I wished it would have lasted forever. "Well, I just wanted to say good luck and that I'm not cheating."

"Is the Council?"

"I don't know. I'm probably being naive if I say no. But I don't think they're as bad as you say. They're not innocent, they're not in this to protect soldiers; all they want is money and power. It's not sinister, though, it's just life. It is what it is."

"It needs to be better."

"Sure it does, but...what are you gonna do, you know?"

"I'm going to make it better."

She said it like it was a simple thing. Like it wasn't a collection of the richest, most powerful people in America colluding for years and their long investment finally paying off. But she meant it. And I wasn't doubting Harla Gamble anymore.

"I'm sure you will. Just be careful. You're going to cross all kinds of lines going after them. I can see that. Because I used to be willing to cross all kinds of lines to win. Be careful, or you'll lose sight of what's important."

"Listen, I have interviews and fans to get to. Say hi to your girlfriend for me." And Captain Gingerbread turned to leave the bubble.

"I dumped her," I said. "Turns out she doesn't just mind-control for the game or the Council."

"You ain't the first guy to get duped by a girl."

"Yeah, well, I got duped into being a pretty terrible guy. And I know I was just awful to you and Diamonds."

Captain Gingerbread turned, arcing a sharp black eyebrow.

"*She* made you do that?"

"I don't know. I'll never know. But I did them, not her. And I'm the one who has to live with that."

Gingerbread was quiet for a moment, then said, "Oman is such a lame name. Should have gone with Captain King. Fits the brand. Talk to your puppeteer; maybe it ain't too late to change."

And then the big guy stood up at attention, clicking patent black leather dress shoes together, straightened his tie, and marched out of the protective fields.

I lowered the bubble just in time to see a purple goop-covered Diamonds tangling with two security guards.

Chapter 20

Chapter 20

Seeing Diamonds seized my heart. They were in sweats and yoga pants, coated in Verma portal goop. That made them difficult for Security to hold onto them.

The scuffle got everyone's attention, and soon all cameras and eyes went to Diamonds as they broke free from Security's grasp.

I don't know if it was the gut reaction of seeing Diamonds after finally admitting to myself how badly I'd screwed up or maybe it was seeing Diamonds in danger or maybe I just still had feelings for them. Whatever the reason, I gathered and tossed a ball of Regalia at them. On impact, it coated them, covered their body and accompanying goop, and blipped out of sight. More light warp.

Of course, each step they took left purple footprints, but luckily, the final contestant entrance stole the focus.

Balls of fire exploded from an empty platform. Pyrotechnics. Fountains of sparks. Spotlights. And there, appearing in the middle of it all, to rising orchestral music, was Captain Miss.

Only, Harla, Diamonds, and I knew that wasn't Captain Miss. But it was her slender, pointy helmet, her matte-black bodysuit showing her curves. Somebody had a great Captain Miss disguise.

And a pretty good impersonation, too. With cocky swagger, the contestant stepped down from the platform and sauntered across the room, ignoring Angry Guy's questions, teenager's selfies, and throngs of guests in her way. Calm and badass, she walked right up to the bar, ordered a water, then leaned over to the nearest bar patron.

I commanded my helmet to listen in just in time to hear Captain Miss whisper, "Do you have something for me?" to Alex Hubert.

* * *

I heard a couple gasps throughout the room. That must've been Team Verma Tech, listening in on Alex. As much as I wanted to follow the intel Alex was about to hand off to the Council's new and improved Captain Miss, I was listening in on something else.

The Regalia bots were transmitting a conversation between Diamonds and Harla.

"You didn't answer my texts... It's the Shadow Captain..." Diamonds was out of breath.

"What about him?" Captain Gingerbread didn't move his mouth as Harla whispered. The captain was looking at a nearby exhibit, the three time-travel pyramids on their own platform.

"He had the notebook. Back then. It's full of dates and times, in my handwriting, including tonight at 6pm. We only have an hour."

"Tonight at six?" Panic rose in Gingerbread's voice.

Suddenly, Angry Guy was in Captain Gingerbread's face, camera and light pouring over his shoulder. The intrusion was abrupt, and Gingerbread instinctively stepped back and shielded his face. Diamonds backed up onto the platform, staying invisible and out of the way.

"What do you have to say about Captain Miss and her entrance?"

Instead of answering his question, Gingerbread simply, "But it *is* six pm."

Confusion flashed across Angry Guy's face. Confusion and strobing light. And not from camera flashes.

Electricity crackled on the nearby exhibit platform where Diamonds hid.

The pressure of the room changed suddenly, hair and table-cloths all shifting in unison.

I'd felt this before.

My gut clenched, my brain turned off, and my instincts took over. Leaping in the air, I commanded the Regalia into rocket boots. Flying across the screaming heads of the crowd, I commanded Diamonds' light warp off.

Fingers of lightning chased up from the three small pyramids surrounding Diamonds. It crackled and leapt up to touch their face, their hair standing on end, the sweatshirt covered in goop.

My rocket boots blasted me as fast as they could.

Bolts of electricity suddenly connected the pieces of the time machine, the artifacts surrounding Diamonds.

Wind whipped their hair, bluish light illuminating their pale face. They looked absolutely beautiful.

I cut the rockets and threw my arms out, colliding with Diamonds.

I pushed them away.

They landed feet away on the floor with a thud. But they were okay.

'They were okay' was the last thing I thought before I was ripped through time.

I landed with a thud on the cold slick floor. But the con floor was carpeted. Where was I?

Either I was going to be sick or pass out. My limbs shaky and empty. Drool stringing down from my lip.

Oh wait. The time machines. I should be asking 'when was I?'

Then I saw *him* staring at me. Expecting me. Of course it was him.

But that was a different story.

* * *

I eventually did see what happened to Harla: the ball, the game, and what came after. It was one of the only things I was allowed to watch, the games up to that one. My keepers worried about exposing me to too much. It's fine. I couldn't wait to see what happened next.

* * *

Meanwhile, the SuperPowers con floor was in chaos. Security pushing through, myPhones in the air recording everything. The deafening sound of screaming and cheering.

Everyone thought it was part of the show. This was a spectacle of the highest rate.

Diamonds collapsed to their knees and joined the rest of the ball in watching me disappear. A woman in an expensive gown and long silk gloves helped Diamonds to their feet, but they pushed her away.

As Diamonds got to their feet made for an exit, the other guests parted like they were contagious. Harla, or rather Captain Gingerbread, ran after them, waving Diggs off from the door Diamonds burst through to leave.

Gingerbread caught up in the empty lobby. "Are you okay?"

Diamonds was in a chair, their dried-goop hair in t/heir hands. "Oh my God, Harla, I am so sorry. I was too late."

"You always sucked at time zones. You're okay, though?"

"Why...why'd Chase do that?"

"Believe it or not, D...Wonderbread had a change of heart."

Ricky Diggs rushed up. Instead of his white guy mask, he was covered in new SuperPowers Unlimited swag. hat, sunglasses and tote.

"Are you okay?" he asked Diamonds.

"Yes."

"Anything bruised?"

"No."

Gingerbread was on the comms. "Dr. Bird, we need you in the lobby."

But security for the ball was already on them, medkits open, checking Diamonds' eyes with flashlights. One of the guards ushered Ricky and Captain Gingerbread away, who were arguing to see their friend when Kevin came in over the comms.

"I need backup in the ballroom, guys."

Ricky headed back in to help Kevin when Security rushed through doors and let out a cacophony and flashes of light, like they'd opened the doors to a concert.

Security pushed back at Gingerbread, who eventually moved when a cart zipped up. Ricky kept a hand on the Captain's chest as venue medics put Diamonds in an oxygen mask on the back of a golf cart.

Even through the Gingerbread suit, I could tell Captain was a wreck of nerves, his big shoulders rising and dropping, giving away a raised breathing rate within. I got it: Diamond just *had* to be okay. They'd been through too much and been too smart of staying out of danger just to...I couldn't think about it. I wouldn't.

"This must be yours." One of the medics handed Diamonds Ricky's swag bag. Driving off with more medical attention than they wanted, they sat with the tote bag in their lap, eyes suddenly going wide.

Ricky and Gingerbread looked after them as they zipped away, probably wondering like me about what had spooked Diamonds.

Just before the cart turned a corner, Diamonds withdrew and held up a spiral blue notebook with the new Superpowers, Un-limited logo; the notebook the Council wanted, the notebook that would travel through time.

* * *

Meanwhile, back on the con floor, Security was desperately separating Mark Hubert and the doppelganger Captain Miss amidst punches, kicks, and bites. Miss was no good up close, so she switched to rockets and pinned Mark to the wall. Gingerbread, Angry Guy, and loads of security broke them up.

But Miss already got the flash drive from Alex. Whether Mark meant to punish the fake Miss with a whooping or get the drive back, he failed. He also failed at planting a Regalia bug, he'd been too angry. Which meant he was way too angry now.

Using the power of the suit and a surprisingly strong Angry Guy, Gingerbread managed to hold Mark back by the arms.

Another of the venue medics ran up to usher away Captain Miss. They would be protecting her identity; they couldn't take the disguise off now and show it's wasn't Harla underneath.

In fact, it wasn't a medic at all helping the pretender Miss escape. But pretty soon Gingerbread saw what I saw. As he repeated to Mark to calm down and let it go, his head snapped to look after the medics as they pulled Miss out of the room. "Formal gloves?"

Sure enough, one of the medics, in a bright orange jacket with the SuperPowers logo, had on blue rubber medical gloves. But under those gloves were another pair — formal elbow-length gloves. Like the ones worn by the woman who checked on Diamonds after they fell.

But Gingerbread didn't have a chance to mention this to his team. Security descended. How many guards were at this event? Everyone was separated and walked off the con floor.

Again, the fans and media thought it was just extraordinary production. All a part of the circus. Step right up and see all these clowns fight.

* * *

He sat in the small, tight room and waited for police or security. Although he looked unfazed in his giant white guy skin, within, Harla was chewing gum nervously, tapping her feet and sweating. Comms didn't work, and her phone had no signal. She waited, most likely watching downloaded movies on the interior projection within the Gingerbread man skin.

Hours and hours passed.

Was there going to be an interrogation? Did running out of the con floor make anyone suspect Gingerbread's involvement in the time travel trap intended for Diamonds?

And then there was a knock at the door.

Some young guy in a headset wearing an Energy Arena polo shirt with MC Squared credentials handed Gingerbread a breakfast burrito, saying, "Lactose free. You can eat it on the way. Follow me please."

The Gingerbread Man arched an eyebrow on his otherwise blank face, then got up, burrito in hand, and followed.

The halls were like the guts of a sports stadium- wide concrete halls, white up top with a silver strip about chest-high and deep gray below. Industrial blue carpet with light blue triangles covered the floor. Cables were taped along the floor while bundles of cables ran along the ceiling. And people in headsets and lanyards of MC Squared credentials and security passes and clipboards dashed this way and that. Everybody was in a hurry, nobody looking up from their work or where they were going.

The Gingerbread Man took the opportunity to put the burrito within his suit jacket, seemingly in his breast pocket, but actually in Harla's face.

Further down the hall, being ushered into a room by another person with a clipboard, were the labcoats of BTU.

Captain Gingerbread was taken into a different room. As the clipboard dude pressed his credentials to a pad by the door, it opened itself to a woman's voice screaming.

"You can take your experimental treatments and shove them you know where!"

Within the room, the Hubert brothers, Kevin the intern, and Ricky Diggs huddled close to the wall, absolutely terrified by what was at the other side of the room.

Ricky pleaded, "Laura, control yourself!"

Gingerbread came all the way into the room to a surprising sight — Dr. Bird was getting in the face of three with a clipboard, knocking things out of their hands, pushing at their clipboards, and just generally losing it.

"Ma'am, please!"

"Get out of here! Don't ma'am me!" She chased them out, then immediately rushed to Gingerbread, opening an arm panel to access Harla's person and checking her vitals by hand. "Are you alright? You're burning up. Have you slept at all?"

"No. How are you Dr. Bird?"

"What? I'm fine. Why would you even ask?"

Ricky was the first to break the silence, giggling louder and louder to a laugh, audible even through his hand clamped over his mouth.

Harla stifled her own laugh until Dr. Bird joined in. Then everyone laughed.

"Well, they want to put you in some ridiculous forced-sleep state before the game."

"Why not just give us sleep breaks?"

"Captain—"

Everyone looked at her like she was about to get some bad news.

"It's six am. The game starts in two hours."

"Damn."

"An hour, fifty six minutes," added Ricky Diggs.

"Do you *want* to lay down, Captain?" asked Dr. Bird.

"No. How's Diamonds? Where's Diamonds?"

All eyes went to Mark. "I saw him. I was resisting a little when they were moving us. The guys were very handsy, and I may have drawn some blood when I bumped my head."

"Against a security guards' head," Alex added.

The Captain's shiny black dress shoe tapped impatiently.

"So they took me to the infirmary. Don't worry, I'm fine-"

"Blood wasn't his."

"And I saw your friend Diamonds in the infirmary. Looked fine, sitting up, a bit pale, but I think that's just how they are."

Gingerbread asked Mark, "And how are you?"

"Honestly, never felt better. It's been too long since I was in any kind of action."

"So, everybody's good?"

"Everyone is fine."

"And what do we do about Diamonds?"

"We're good, champ," Ricky said in his soothing voice. "We just got to stick with the plan."

Alex, who may have been hungover, asked, "Care to share that plan with the rest of us?"

"Nope," said Gingerbread.

Mark grumbled, "Don't trust us?"

"I don't trust who could be listening."

Ricky calmed everyone. "I don't know the plan, either, but

if the Captain is confident, then so am I."

Alex pushed the issue. "Can I at least ask what our overall strategy for the game is? So I can be of some use on the comms?"

"Would you prefer the team muted?" Ricky asked.

"No." Gingerbread's voice boomed definitively. "Everyone stays on the comms. But I'm planning on a short game. We need a plan to find Diamonds."

Mark smiled, showing he'd lost a tooth the night before. "How short?"

"Short enough. I don't want y'all worrying about me out there. The objective of mission control should be finding Diamonds."

"I understand your concern, Captain," Ricky explained, "but for the sake of safety, Dr. Bird will be monitoring your health throughout the game, Mark will keep an eye out for tech, and I may glance occasionally."

He smiled at Gingerbread who stared blankly back, wearing just his permanent smug look. Ricky continued, "We'll figure something out, okay? We won't give up on them. Or Chase."

That quieted the room quick. Then, without a facial expression, Gingerbread replied, "Chase is gone. He made his peace. We have to deal with the controllables now."

Both Dr. Bird and Ricky looked like they were about to say something, to stand up for me, or voice some concern, but they didn't. The silence in the room was the nicest thing they'd said about me since Harla and I had our falling out. And not being openly hated was a welcome change of pace.

Again, Gingerbread was unreadable, but didn't mention me any further. Ricky went to work on his phone, evidently the only one in the room with service.

Dr. Bird broke the silence, telling the Captain, "You need something in your stomach."

"Coffee," Gingerbread said with urgency.

Kevin lit up, literally pointing one finger in the air as if to politely ask a question in class. He knew the Captain's favorite by heart. "Almond milk hot chocolate with miniature marshmallows, extra hot."

But Dr. Bird declined. "Need something with caffeine."

"Can I just get like a tall cup of just espresso?" the Captain asked.

"That'll have caffeine."

Kevin darted off.

Dr. Bird yelled after him, "And some fruit, like a banana!"

Alex asked, "Okay, so should she start stretching or any-thing?"

"I'll start an hour-fifteen out. You think I don't got this?" There was an edge to the Captain's question.

Dr. Bird had moved onto breathing exercises. "Calm. Captain. Breathe."

But the Captain wasn't having it, growling, "Yeah, I'll be calm and breathe once I know Diamonds is okay."

"Look-" Mark's eyes locked with the Gingerbread Man's. "I'm sorry. They. Are. Fine. Get your head out of your ass."

Gingerbread stepped to Mark, a few inches taller. "This is how you talk to your captain?"

"No." Then Mark stooped to talk directly into the Ginger-bread man's chest, like he was talking to a tie clip. "This is how I talk to my captain. Don't be a hothead. Focus on the game. You haven't slept. Chill out. I am not your enemy."

"There they are!" Ricky looked up from his phone. He flipped it to show the team. "There's a livestream of the arena, or level, I guess. And from this angle, you can see the box seats. So if you look up here— there they are."

It was dark and zoomed in so much, it was a little fuzzy, but there they were. Diamonds laying back on a cot, half-sitting up, but unconscious. Fresh-faced now, no make-up, dark circles under their eyes.

Surrounded by four dark figures.

"That's them, that's Diamonds. At the arena still?" Captain wondered out loud.

"And do you suppose those people around her are keeping them there?"

"Yeah, but they're not the muscle. They're all too relaxed," said Mark.

"There's plenty of security here," pointed out Alex. "In the orange jackets."

"So D is being held against their will?"

Mark said, "Or maybe drugged."

"Any chance those others are also being held?"

"Most likely not."

"Not a chance," said Alex.

"Who are they?" she asked.

"Wait." Ricky said, then rewound the video before playing again.

The most slender of the shadowy figures shifted, light rising up momentarily. A tight black woman's suit, a dark gray top with a high neckline, a necklace, then her chin, nose, high cheek-bones appeared. Then the light subsided.

Ricky went back and paused. The figure pursed lips over a strong, sharp chin.

Within the Gingerbread Man, Harla's eyebrows scrunched as she squinted, mouth open.

Ricky pointed out, "That's the woman who picked Diamonds up off the floor at the ball."

She'd been the one in the formal gloves.

Gingerbread said, "It's also the same person who pulled the new Captain Miss off the con floor. I imagine she's the one who got the flash drive."

Ricky looked closely at his phone's screen. "It looks like… Diamonds."

Mark took the phone and gave a look himself. "Yeah, but older."

Standing tall, Gingerbread commanded, "We have to get them out of there."

"Is that part of the secret plan?"

"Mark."

"Alex."

"No," Gingerbread broke up their squabbling. "I'll finish the game off as fast as I can, but I need someone here to try and get into that box and find out how to get D out of there."

Mark didn't buy it, pacing angrily. "Are you kidding me? Security knows everyone on your team. We'd need someone to just accidentally stumble in there, say 'Whoopsie me,' then report back here without being suspected of anything? Someone who is believably that aloof?"

Just then, Kevin backed into the room, tray of coffees in his hands. "'Scuzi," he said, nudging past security at the door. Then the coffees on his tray wobbled and tipped over. He stooped and grabbed at them, flailing and knocking them all off into a puddle of coffee on the floor.

Alex looked to Kevin and said to himself, "My God, he's perfect."

Chapter 21

Chapter 21

The Level, as the playing field within Energy Arena was called, looked like the set of a gameshow. Lights pouring down hot from the dark rafters, cameras and seating on one side, high walls on the other. And in between, a ninja Warrior obstacle course on steroids. Where the floor didn't drop off to twenty feet below, it was tilted or moving, striped with conveyor belts. Large sections had rope running across, vertical beams for stepping stones, or rings dangling from the ceiling. Bursts of water, smoke, steam, and fire shot out periodically from nowhere in particular. And in the center of the football-field-sized course, a circle with ten points marked around it — the starting ring.

It looked like a nightmarish circus.

Ricky's mouth hadn't closed in the five minutes since he'd seen it, "This place is crazy. There's no…"

Alex and Mark guessed, since so much was missing from previous arenas.

"Foliage?"

"Cover?"

"Water sources?"

"High ground?"

"Hiding spots," said Ricky, fear creeping into his voice. "What do they expect is going to happen?"

Just then, the motion on the level slowed to a stop. The doors opened, and the PA system blasted an overly calm, feminine voice, "Players to the starting ring."

Harla stiffened. "I know that voice. That's Diamonds."

Lights moved and aligned, pooling on a direct path from the Level's doors to the starting ring.

Dr. Bird, red-faced and with tears in her eyes, managed, "Well, Captain, I guess this is it."

"Go get 'em champ," said Ricky. "Stick to the plan, but be ready to throw the damn plan out the window if you have to."

Alex fist-bumped Gingerbread. "Go kick some ass, Captain, I know you will."

Mark's low gravelly voice lightened. "Be safe out there, Captain. And remember to double check your voltage and ground."

Kevin was already out on his task. He'd miss the whole game, never making it back to mission control.

* * *

So big Captain Gingerbread strode out to his place, chest puffed out. He was positioned between two soldiers in all black with swat helmets, covered in scaly bots rippling and moving. Across the circle was Aiden Run, this year in an even bigger mech, making him at at least 15 feet, the tallest competitor by over half.

Beside him on one side was Holter in another tight, austere mech suit, nothing more than panels running along the outside of his torso, arms, and legs. He wore a busy gray-white and orange camouflage coverall, some newly computer-generated camo pattern closer to light spraypaint blotches rather than pixels or puzzle pieces.

And next to him sat a pilot in an invisible cockpit a few feet off the ground.

"Does Escondido have an invisible jet?" Alex asked over comms.

"It's very Wonder Woman." said his brother.

Standing still, hands at both sides with clenched fists, stood the fake Captain Miss.

Taking my spot in the starting ring was a last-minute entrance from BTU, a Saint Bernard-sized tarantula in a tight cage.

Diamonds' voice filled the arena again. "The Level will set for the beginning of the game. It will shift every hour for the first three hours, then every thirty minutes thereafter."

All of the parts of the obstacle course floor plan went into motion, like set pieces sitting on top of clock-work machinery, spinning and rotating while everything settled into a dull, mottled blue.

"Shift?" Alex asked through the comms.

"They're going to constantly flush everybody out," said Ricky Diggs.

"It'll all be done with by then," Harla whispered to her comms.

All of the contestants adjusted their color and texture to the dull blue.

"Players release in sixty seconds. Seeker release in one hundred twenty," Diamonds' voice echoed.

"That's quick," said Alex.

"Good," whispered Harla.

A shield-wielding soldier next to Captain Gingerbread growled at him. "Don't block my camera lines or my light."

"Doesn't this guy know it's a camouflage challenge?" Mark laughed.

The Gingerbread Man, eyes open with a smile frozen to his face, slowly turned to the soldier. Without moving his mouth, his voice emanated in an excited whisper, "Run, run, as fast as you can, you can't catch me, I'm the Gingerbread Man."

The soldier shrank back, made a face, then powered up his shield, disappearing into a blip of warped light.

"That's so cool! Why didn't I think of a catchphrase!" Aiden Run seemed seriously in pain from jealousy. "Mine's going to be something like 'now you see me, now I'm invisible' or, 'You just got invisibled!' Eh, I'll think of something!"

"Thirty seconds," said Diamonds.

The Captain repeated, this time staring blankly at the new Captain Miss. "Run, Run, as fast as you can, you can't catch me, I'm the Gingerbread Man."

"Are you going to keep saying that? Because it's pretty annoying," asked Alex.

Across the circle in the dull blue arena, Esau Holter growled, "Shut up," giving Captain Gingerbread the stink eye.

By then, all of the eyes of the contestants, where visible, were on Captain Gingerbread. Still in a dark blue suit, red tie, and perfectly oiled black hair, the oversized white guy, raised his hand in front of himself, and gave the thumbs up.

Only it wasn't the thumb's up. In the curl of his forefinger, sticking out of his flesh, was a red button. Like the captain was holding a gameshow buzzer or a small joystick.

"The hell's that?" Esau Holter asked.

"Fifteen seconds."

Dr. Bird whispered, "Stick to the plan, Captain."

"Run, run..."

"We heard you the first time, pal." Esau said.

"Enough!" Fake Captain Miss's distorted voice roared.

"Yeah!" Aiden Run said. "Prepare to get invisibled!"

"..as fast as you can..."

"Ten seconds."

"...you can't catch me.."

Gingerbread pressed his button.

The suit's remote power source, a static field generated from a battery pack on Harla's hip, surged. Fingers of lightning darted over the big guy's body. At the same time, the suit powered down, going from a cartoonish white guy in a suit to a collection of gray scales, a bumpy shell. The electricity built and built and built. It was going to blow.

What was the plan?

"Five seconds."

The giant tarantula scrambled within the tiny cage. Nearby contestants leaned away. Others ducked from the electricity coming off the powered-down Captain Gingerbread.

POP!

The EMP wave expanded instantaneously.

All of the mech suits fell to a lifeless stealth black. Escondido's jet revealed itself as a big trapezoid covered in jet engines. Bots poured off the fake Captain Miss, revealing Emily underneath. She shrieked in bratty anguish.

The overhead lighting within the arena shut down section by section. Emergency red lights gave off an eerie glow.

It was a localized electromagnetic pulse. An EMP.

The scales that made up Captain Gingerbread scales collapsed, falling in on themselves to reveal Harla Gamble with no mask, short near-bald blond hair, and a black jumpsuit.

Diamonds' yelled out now from the press box, "Three... Two...One."

Harla smiled. "I'm the Gingerbread Man."

"The game is live!" they yelled in the reddish darkness.

With a flick of her fingerless-gloved hand, Harla released the old powerpack on her hip, fried from the EMP, and loaded up another one. It let out a soft, high-pitched whine. Then Harla held out her hand and the scales on the ground leapt to life, stirring from piled on the ground and connecting scale to scale to make little baby turtle shells, then connecting shell to shell into a long string, building upward to reach Harla's hand.

The other players groaned and grunted, trying to reboot their tech. But all their hardware was fried. They threw their shields to the floor or shook against their mech cockpits.

Escondido pulled his ejection seat and fired into the sky, detaching midair to make it to a higher foam platform above them.

Harla swung the rope of scales up at Escondido, and it reached a clean two stories up and wrapped perfectly around his ankle.

She tugged him down.

He tumbled, gaining speed as he fell, arms windmilling.

What appeared a loose falling chain still wrapped around his leg suddenly halted, its form hardened. Escondido fell a bit more until the big circular curl of chain, frozen in the air, held him upside down by the ankle, his face a couple feet from the floor.

"Thirty seconds until Seeker's released."

Two other soldiers who abandoned their projection shields, ran off in opposite directions. Harla shot two lengths of scale chain, one at either of them, to grab each by the arm.

In a gruff voice, Harla yelled, "Get over here!"

She pulled the soldiers back to starting then shot chains to secure each of the other contestants by the arm, with the exception of the chain holding the giant spider's door shut.

And then Harla took her time walking to connect each chain of scales, making a web, like a pie chart splitting up the starting ring.

"You can't do this!" one player cried out.

Screaming and flailing, Emily pulled at her chain, which had solidified, freezing in place, not letting her move from where it had her arm. "This has to be against the rules!"

"Hi, I remember you, you're the other lady! I 'miss'ed you! Get it?!" Aiden shouted happily, waving in his idle powered-down mech suit.

Just then, a circle in the center of the starter ring appeared. An aperture door that opened. The material had protected whatever's inside just like the hardened outside of Regalia bots protected my camera view of the chaos.

Out from the door flew a swarm of bots. The game's attempt at recreating the Regalia? Another nanocloud Seeker?

"Fifteen seconds until Seeker is released!"

The cloud of bots solidified as the aperture door closed. The buzzing fly-sized bots formed a humanoid figure, short for a man. Hands on his hips in a superman pose, intersections of scale-chain running between his wide standing legs. In a flash, color filled in.

"Ten seconds."

It was a replica of a young white boy with brown hair and blue-green eyes, taller than Harla, maybe a little tubby. I sucked in a breath when I recognized him. It was a replica of me.

"Wonderbread?" Harla asked.

The Chase Seeker smiled, then lost his balance from the chains wrapped around his calves.

"Five."

Harla shrugged and brought her hand in front of her again in a thumbs up, revealing another red button.

"Four."

Recognizing the EMP button, the Chase Seeker slouched in disappointment. In a metallic voice, it said dejectedly, "Crapadoodles."

"Three."

She pressed the button. Another EMP, this one small, localized.

The newly-formed Chase Seeker fell to pieces.

"Two."

The scale chain fell to piles of scales once again.

Escondido ran off. Esau Holter detached and ran, as did a couple other soldiers.

Diamonds sounded confused. "One."

Harla flicked another switch on her hip, locking in another power pack, lighting up the static field and holding out her hand as an oversized machine gun formed out of the scales into her grip.

Diamonds shouted, almost with a sense of triumph, "The

Seeker is live."

Harla scooped a handful of shiny black Chase Seeker nanobots and pressed them into an open slide in her cartoonish AK-47, then fired at an escaping player. The little bots burst on contact, leaving a mark that shone bright white.

She fired again and again, hitting player after player, scooping more bots into the gun, firing on more players.

When she was out of ammo, and no one was left to shoot, her screaming along with the massacre was the only noise left.

She dropped the cartoon gun at her feet. And put her hands on her knees, catching her breath.

"Captains Darkness, Silence, Awesome, Arachno, Battler, Miss, Holter, and War are out."

Scooping a handful of Chase Seeker bots into her gloved hand, Harla walked to the other side of the starting ring, now dotted with bots and eliminated players.

"You want to drop the bubble, Luis? I can shoot you in the prosthetic. Otherwise, I'll just start firing at you, and hit whatever I hit."

"How'd you know I was bubbled?"

"I can smell the ozone."

Escondido unbubbled, appearing out of thin air, hands up in his full blue flight suit, helmet, visor, and oxygen mask. He unclasped his mask and chinstrap, showing off his sweaty, smiling face.

"How'd you get so good at this game, Captain Miss?"

"I was always this good; I just wasn't playing as myself."

In a fierce pitching motion, she chunked the handful of Seekerbots at her old mentor's prosthetic leg. The bright white bots splattered.

"And I ain't Captain Miss anymore. It's Captain Gingerbread."

"Captain Pilot is out. Game over. Captain Gingerbread has won." For some reason, Diamonds sounded disappointed.

Harla's comms fizzled back to life, a backup she had in her other ear anticipating the EMP. Ricky Diggs said, "We've got eyes on Diamonds, Champ."

Chapter 22

The press box was luxurious- heated plush seats, mini-fridges for each guest, and everyone's water had lime, mint, and cucumber. But with all of the luxury, all of the accoutrements, the guests in the press box were not happy.

"It's over," the Japanese woman said in a thick accent.

Todd Fowler was pacing and pulling on his hoodie strings. "I'm having them cut the game up with snippets from the ESPN-produced stuff."

"What 'stuff'?" she growled.

"Hype videos," Fowler answered. "Dramatic music over action-packed video packages."

"Great!" Retired Colonel Veil was seething. "Where will that put us? Half an hour?"

"With commercials, I can stretch it to forty-five."

"We failed." The woman didn't seem to be paying attention to anyone.

The scruffy white guy I couldn't identify was younger than the other Council members and not as certain of their doom. "We could schedule another game in the spring?"

"Restart the game," Veil said. "Disqualify Captain Gingerbread."

"I think I agree." said Fowler.

"I am failing," the woman said.

"It's not too late," Veil insisted. "Let's reset, get the crowd going with the warm-up guys, and restart without her."

Before the lady could respond, she leapt to her feet in a quick motion, reversing to point at the press box entrance. "Wait. Who is that?"

Standing at the entrance to the room, next to the cot housing Diamonds, stood a quiet young man, hugging the walls, trying not to be noticed.

Kevin the Intern's voice shook as he spoke, "Where did you want the fresh fruit platter?"

The eyes in the room slowly turned to him. Diamonds' pale brown eyes flared instinctively while the four others in the room looked him over carefully. The woman Harla had recognized - tall, pale skin, incredulous eyes, seemed the leader, and a young bearded white man, Colonel Veil, and Todd Fowler all stared down a sweaty jittery Kevin.

"Who are you working for?" the woman asked him.

"I know." Fowler broke from his pacing, wagging a finger at Kevin.

The intern shook under the pressure, attempting to begin a sentence but mostly just shaking his head, smiling,and forcing a chuckle.

Fowler grimaced with disgust as he got in the boy's face, finger on his chest. "You're the valet who spilled something wet in my Tesla last night after the ball."

The boy's eyes got bigger than was naturally inclined as did his mouth. Then, after a quick exchange of looks with Diamonds, he shot his focus to the ground and began groveling. "I am so sorry about that, sir."

Kevin was a bad liar. Picking him for a covert operation was a poor choice.

"What did you spill? It wasn't lime, it was..."

"Fresca?" His voice cracked.

Veil asked, "They still make Fresca?"

"Yeah," Fowler admitted, "it relaunched. I own a piece."

"Enough!" the woman hissed. "The boy is lying. He is here for the Wayfinder Emeritus."

"Yep," the scruffy guy said before adding, "The what now?"

"The retired navigator."

"Oh, Diamonds?" Fowler chuckled a bit, walking back with his arm up and out until it floated down to land comfortably on the arm of a reclined Diamonds. "Diamonds can leave whenever they like. Isn't that right, Hon?"

"You should get out of here...young man." Diamonds spoke carefully but sternly.

Veil growled, "He can't leave now. He knows too much."

At the same time Diamonds said, "No he doesn't," Todd the intern said, "No, I don't."

And then Diamonds whispered to him, "Run."

Todd the intern, closest to the door, took one step, twisting his body away from the Council and toward the safety of his team.

But then they were all hit with the lights and the sound.

That sound.

High pitched and gut-shakingly baritone all at once. A sound that felt like your ears would bleed and you'd poop your pants. It shook the floor and vibrated the fancy drinks in the pressbox.

The bright light, a blinding blue, subsided. But the sound rumbled and squealed on.

And everyone in the booth, Kevin, the Council, and Diamonds, turned to see where that awful sound was coming from.

Above the level by about twenty five feet spun a disk of floating...junk. All chrome bits of varying size and shape, spinning, everything in orbit of more junk at the center. The disc was expanding, more chrome junk coming in from somewhere and pushing out from the middle. Causing the sound.

And then it appeared, curled in a fetal position. Naked, slick, gray. Almost human but limbs too long, head too big.

The noise stopped.

Hands went to mouths. People gasped. A tear ran down Todd the intern's face.

The junk continued orbiting about the figure, not like electrons of an atom, but like rings of Saturn. The figure stretched and opened up its all-black eyes and sexless gray body. The being opened up its hands, palms facing each other at about hip width.

A bubble formed between its hands, purple and fuzzy, like it was full of smoke, but different. Lighter, whispier. Like a ghost. The ghost bubble expanded as the figure spread its hands wider and wider, enveloping the figure itself, then widening more, until the bubble encased the starting ring with all the contestants, the entire level, then out past the Level's walls, overtaking the Council's booth.

Fowler shut his eyes and held his breath. Kevin the intern flinched behind his hands. The woman grabbed Diamonds and slid underneath the table.

But there was no difference within the ghost bubble. They could see the gray figure again.

When the thing spoke, it was high, raspy, but with an utterly human quality to it. Amused. It was amused. The alien said, "I should like to watch you play. And then we could talk. About keeping Earth safe."

Even I gasped when I watched from about fifty years into the future.

It's not THE END...Chase, Diamonds, and Harla will return!

Please take the time to REVIEW Gamble.

And if you did like the book, tell friends who might also like it.

Special Thanks

My wife and daughter
    Jess Clapton
    Taylor Anderson
    Liz DiNorma
    Michael Chandler
    Evan Engle
    Kim Garvey
    Carol Beth Anderson
    Margaret Casner
    Robyn Lustbader
    The Muppets...not *The* Muppets, though shout out to them, too
    Mikki Noble
    Charlie Knight
    Edgy Writer's Workshop
    My parents and family

Sneak Preview

The following is a sneak preview first chapter

Gamble: Two Lives Away
Book Four of the Hide & Seek Chronicles

Time traveling was nothing like walking through a door into the Lack. Behind the door is just light. Energy I was impervious to and bright orange light everywhere. Being pulled through time feels like imploding, like pushing your skin into your lower intestine, then expanding back out again through your butthole.

Of course, I immediately fell to my hands and knees and started retching. Snot and tears poured out of my face onto a textured gray floor. Once I was sure I wasn't going to spew anymore, I pulled off my jacket and wiped my face, getting to my feet. And when I dropped the snotty jacket, I saw *him*. He's older by about twenty or thirty years but still instantly familiar. Todd Fowler, flanked by two younger teenagers in weird clothes, didn't look surprised to see me, just pissed off.

We both said at the same time, "You."

One of the kids - hair shaved short, glasses opaque and oddly oval, in a long-coated suit, spoke excitedly with a lisp, "Chase Hawkins, age sixteen! You're reigning champion heading into the first televised MC Squared!"

I honestly didn't know how to react. Why was this guy so excited? "What?"

"I'm a real big fan of your earlier gameplay, so wild and raw. You played like you were on fire and just straight didn't give a-"

"Thanks, great."

"We're big fans," the other kid, with long straight black hair and light brown complexion, added.

"We represent the Einstein Society. This is Dr. Telly," the shaved head kid said, gesturing to the kid with long black-and-white checkerboard hair back in a ponytail. A doctor? But these were kids...children younger than me.

The taller one with the shaved head said, "I am Izz."

I nodded back to *him*, to Todd Fowler, "And of course this guy is..."

"The Gatherer," he said, his voice gruff and gravel with age or fatigue. "Everyone calls me Gatherer."

"Is it *the* Gatherer or just Gatherer?"

Fowler rolled his eyes over to Izz. "I told you."

"What'd he tell you?" I asked.

Izz answered, "That you would be a smartass. In particular, to him."

Wait. I thought I'd saved Diamonds from being sucked through time. "So you were expecting me? Not Diamonds?"

"I know what happened, Chase. I can remember."

"Then why am I here, Gatherer?"

"*They* brought you here," the old man nodded to the kids as he turned and headed off. "I had to. I always have, I always will."

Finally, once the door out had slid shut with a hiss, Izz answered me. "It's 2069, the one hundredth game in the MC Squared, and Chase Hawkins, you're our entrant."

* * *

She snuck along thin ledges. She hugged walls and peeked around corners before leaping to safety. Under the hot lights, edging a dusty shoe along concrete overhangs, Harla Gamble kept the entire world enthralled.

The US government had already cut off the Energy Arena feed several times in the past week, but the MC Squared had already proven itself to be leaky. Just because the videos were now property of a giant corporation didn't make the leaks stop.

Everybody watched.

The game, officially called the MC Squared, the way the US military developed camouflage technology, was under siege, bubbled up and occupied by an alien intruder. And the game participants needed water.

Harla slid one of her Air Force Ones to the lip of the ledge. Beneath her, concrete blocks made for a sheer dropoff a good hundred feet to a concrete floor. Above her, hovering and watching, the big grayish blue alien sat silently as if weighing judgment of all below. The alien who'd encased the Council and contestants in a violet force field dome floated above the arena near the ceiling.

Nobody had seen the Seeker for hours.

She stayed out of sight of them both. Sweat dangled from her nose as her eyes darted to measure the distance to the next ledge. Then she leapt.

The Air Force Ones, sprayed down with rubber, soared across the gap between the concrete cliffs, fingers of falling dust trailing behind.

I held my breath watching. I imagine the rest of the world did, too.

With a crunch, the sole of her shoe met the next ledge, the force of Harla's body flying forward. The rubber sole scraped and slid, the inertia carrying her to the ledge and farther. She flew over to the corner precipice, falling past it and down toward the hard floor.

With a slap, her hand landed on the corner of concrete. Her arm slowed her slide, and she grunted. In a crouch, she caught herself on the next ledge before slipping off the side and falling down, down, down.

But there was no time to celebrate. No enjoyment of little victories. Up she climbed for the only current water source on the level.

For the game, the levels shifted, changed, and advanced. I imagine it was some suit's idea to add tension, maybe rope in the online video game audience? It was no longer a gimmick but an obstacle, the level shifting each hour as it had for days. And the players needed to get water while they knew where it was.

Harla used her bare hands to climb. She had her cloak on, covering everything on her except her face, hands, shoes, and dangling canteens.

The rest of her was camouflaged against the sandy concrete, still covered in her Gingerbread suit. She used a couple of the scales that made up the suit to chip into the concrete, essentially chiseling a ladder of handholds. Breathing heavy with fatigue from each step up, Harla grew sweaty within her suit. The television lighting blared down onto the surface of the level.

From here, she saw the tops of each column, staggered terracing up and down like a still picture of a concrete sea.

But this column had the basin of water.

Her eyes didn't look away from the field of lights above. Squinting, sweating, but constantly searching.

Within the middle of the big arena, thirty or so feet higher than the water column, was the alien. But Harla paid no attention to her captor. Her head was on a swivel for the Seeker, the murmuring of nanobots that formed a fake me. The game had a Chase after all.

"Who the hell uses canteens, anyway?" First Harla filled the camelback pack she had on, taking in a good gallon. Dipping each of the two canteens from the former soldiers in her survival party, she flicked her eyes to her task only for a second, then back up to the lights.

Once the canteens were full, she knelt and tightened the caps. With a command, she shed a sleeve-full of scales that made up her suit. They formed a vertical tube with a cone on the end, about the size of the cardboard tube inside paper towels. The scales flexed and interconnected to make the shape and automatically attached themselves to the canteen straps. Then with another command, it took off, launching like a rocket, canteens dangling, blipping out of sight with light warping technology. Through Harla's display, I could track the arc of the missile.

But Harla didn't stick around to see the missile hit its target.

It was a distraction, hopefully keeping the Seeker off her tail. With her backpack full of water, Harla ran a couple steps and leapt off the column into the space between them, the deep, wide gaps.

Falling down, down, down, practically a skyscraper's height, she commanded the suit. Glider wings popped out as she plummeted faster. The concrete rushed up to her display like a fast zoom-in. Then she soared, arcing upward to sail parallel to the concrete floor. It was darker and cooler down near the floor.

With all of her scales forming the wings on her back, Harla was in the open, vulnerable. Like some techno archangel.

Darkness suddenly fluttered across the floor of the arena. Something was above her. Immediately, she took evasive maneuvers, concentrating her tech's exhaust out the end of her wings, impersonating engines. At each opportunity, she turned to lose anyone or anything following, right then left, then five rights in a row, a path of jumbled nonsense, with no reason in her flight course.

Until she saw him.

With her fake engines, she rocketed up thirty feet to a figure clinging to the sheer concrete wall. The metal clawed hands of Esau Holter's streamlined mech made their own holds in the side of the huge block.

She floated up to ten or so feet behind him. She kept her voice low. "This wasn't the plan."

The old man startled and about lost his grip.

"Sh!!!" he commanded in an angry whisper. They both switched to comms. "I just got him off my tail."

"This wasn't the plan, Esau!"

"The Seeker was going to intercept the canteens!"

"Good. Better he finds the canteens than me!"

"Waste of good water!"

"We had a plan, Esau. Don't get in the way," she said before speeding away.

He engaged the rockets on his forearms and calves, making a face and saying to himself sarcastically, "Thanks for saving the water, Esau. Couldn't have done it without you, Esau."

A hundred feet away, Harla sipped at the camelback dispenser as she flew through the air. Her display no longer showed the missile.

"Good. Nobody wants no fool canteens," Harla whispered through cracked, dry lips. A green circle on her display led her back to camp, a wide ledge four stories up toward the north corner of the level. Harla's impromptu rocket pack flew her up through the jungle of concrete columns.

White sneakers sprayed black in rubber landed in a simultaneous thud. Harla unshouldered the water camel back and said, "Coast is clear."

"We almost lost two canteens!" Luis Escondido chided. Then he whipped his focus away and whisper-shouted, "Coming in hot!"

While the old man didn't crash-land, Esau did slide on his belly and into the concrete wall. In a quick, procedural way, he stood, checked his body, specifically joints, as he approached them. Then, acting as if nothing had happened, pulled circular discs from the forearm of his mech and one by one, flicked them open — small telescopic cups. "We can't afford to lose two days' worth of water."

Aiden Run kept a look out as he had so far. "Seeker's so badass."

"Language!" Esau barked as he opened capsules into each

cup and handed them out.

"I needed a diversion." Harla shrugged and chugged her water.

"Drink slower," Esau commanded.

"Either of us could have been a diversion," Luis said, taking a water from Esau.

"The mission target was water," Esau growled. "You don't make the target the diversion."

"They could just fly right through someone without stopping," Aiden Run whispered in awe, still searching the air above for the Seeker. "Like a school of piranha cleaning a cow skeleton."

Esau jeered, "You've never seen that."

"How old do you think I am?" Aiden shot an angry look over his shoulder. I wasn't sure how much longer he would tolerate an overprotective Esau Holter. Aiden huffed, "I'm fourteen; I'm not a child."

"So I'll get water again in a couple days. If we even need it."

Luis pointed a finger. "Next time, you're not going by yourself."

Collapsing the cup and handing it back to Holter, Harla checked the battery pack for her suit: a little under fifty percent. It'd been a couple days, but Harla hadn't pushed the suit, hadn't played aggressively or gotten into any dogfights. She knew her power source was her tech's weakness. The rest of her surviving party didn't know, though. "So are we doing this next shift?"

Luis took a deep breath. "If it is visible, we should take our shot. We have an idea of its capabilities. The alien is too much of a wildcard to attack first."

Esau flung his hands up and raised his voice. "Are you kid–"

Everyone hushed him.

"-kidding me?" he whisper-yelled. "We have no idea what we're up against. We don't know what he or it can do!"

"So, we just wait around and let the flock of Chase bots kill us off one by one?"

"Hey!" Esau hushed him and poked a thumb toward the kid, saying, "We don't *know* if he died."

One soldier had gone missing since the game went feral. All the other contestants were still out there somewhere, but one soldier vanished after being chased by the Seeker into a corner. Nobody was talking about it, but the kid knew what was up. Aiden was no idiot. "And where's the giant spider, huh?"

"It's going to kill us all," Harla said simply, ignoring Aiden. The idea sunk in silently on everyone, each of the party relaxing their shoulders a bit, lowering their chin a tad.

Luis nodded and repeated, "If it's visible, we should take a shot."

"We have our orders. Play the game."

Harla's voice dropped. "I don't take orders from *it*."

Aiden asked, "Is the Seeker the it and the alien thing the him?"

"No, the opposite," Harla said. "Agreed. Starting with the Bizarro Chase Seeker, we take them down one at a time."

"We should name him," Aiden decided.

Esau had about enough. "Why are you two so set on attacking?"

"I'm naming the alien."

"If that makes you feel better, Aiden, go ahead and do it." Esau switched his tone to something softer. "We should explore the sub-basement, try to get out by tunnels."

Luis played neutral between Harla and Esau. "Whatever we

do, we have to make our move with the next level shift-"

"No," Esau said sternly. "We wait out the next shift. We shouldn't make a move until we know what we're up against. Get some intel. Then we should escape from this blasted dome."

"Neil. We're calling him Neil."

Harla whisper-yelled, "I'm not going to sit here and wait to find out what happens when we get caught."

"It's like 'Alien' backwards. Like his secret name to prevent anyone from knowing he's an alien is Neil A."

But the two retired soldiers were less interested in naming the alien than negotiating with Harla.

"Fine," she said, agreeing with Luis. "After the next shift, I'll draw the Seeker away from Neil and into an ambush."

"I think we should name the Seeker, too."

"Why are you two so excited to start fights without any intel? We should go test the dome again. Find a way out."

"Anti-Chase? Proto-Chase?"

Harla said, "And we're not leaving Diamonds."

Luis was exasperated. "We all got burned testing the force-field, and we didn't learn anything."

"Ace-Chay?"

Harla agreed and added, "We've been here for almost a week, and we have no intel."

Everyone's eyebrows furrowed at once.

Luis whispered, overly nice, "Harla, the game only ended forty hours ago."

"Really?"

"Hide!" Aiden said suddenly.

Everyone ducked, warped light, and cloaked. Three of the best players in the Military Camouflage Challenge did what they did best and disappeared.

Aiden stood alone, uncloaked, still looking out at the arena to keep watch under their concrete overhang. He continued, "We'll call him 'Hide.' Get it?"

Everyone groaned and uncloaked.

Esau dismissed him. "We're not calling the evil version of someone's personality 'Hide.'"

"Why not?"

"It's a reference you'll get when you're older."

Harla refocused. "So I'll get Hide to chase me and draw him into an ambush."

"Oh God, we're really calling him that, aren't we?" Esau rubbed his temples. "And we're really going to attack the damned nano-matter seeker."

"Hide," everyone corrected him.

"I'm not calling-"

The crackling of the PA system coming to life interrupted Esau.

Diamonds' voice spoke steadily, informing everyone trapped in the arena as well as anyone watching at home, or in my case, in the future, "Next Level."

With a BOOM, the ledge began to shift.

But it was no surprise to the players by now, who commanded their tech to lock down, helmets snapping into place, and suits made of bots forming around each of the figures. Then the concrete ledge fell out from underneath them.

They fell, screaming, hands flailing above their heads, sliding as their column turned and angled. Holter and Aiden Run fell off the column to the dark below. Harla formed and lit up rocket boots to slow her descent as Escondido continued sliding off to the side. As he fell past the edge of the column, a concrete wall slid into place, locking him within or underneath or some other place out of Harla's grasp. Once all of the concrete locked into place, Harla was alone. The only reminder of her party of survivors was a streak of water on the dusty, dry concrete as the splatter of the camelback squeezed and burst between shifting walls like a zit.

* * *

Diamonds Hunt isn't exactly an open book. For real, it would take a crowbar for that kid to open up. I wish I could say that eventually, they did. I wished that way long after all of this mess was over with, they gave me permission to watch the footage, to listen in on their conversations with the Council. And then maybe we talked about what it felt like to have the weight of the world dropped like it did on them.

I wish I could say that Diamonds forgave me. I wish I could say I earned it. But things don't always work out clean. In fact, as far as I've seen, they never do.

I had to know, had to see what happened while I was off in the future. I had to witness the journey Diamonds went on that got everybody where they ended up.

Where they started was a cot, coming in and out of consciousness. They mouthed off to the Council. They told Kevin to run. They told Todd Fowler to go to Hell. But outside of that, they were out cold.

While Harla was making water runs, Diamonds was actually waking up, shaking the drugs off. They were alone, at least within the partial privacy of standing curtained screens, hooked up to an IV and wired to a machine taking their pulse, breathing, and heart rate, all on wheels, just like the standing cabinet. But the room was obviously not normally an infirmary. There was carpet, wood trim, and under a display sconce, there was a framed photo of SteelCut.

"Thank God you are okay," a feminine voice with a heavy Asian accent said.

Diamonds almost jumped. I'd never seen anyone sneak up on Diamonds like that. Since when could they miss a person not five feet away?

"We were worrying." The woman's laser-focused gaze was picking Diamonds apart, her angled eyes methodically and efficiently judging Diamonds' state. Her face was a creamy pale with high cheekbones and black hair dark enough to suck up light, chopped short at her sharp chin with a heavy turquoise streak from her temple back.

"Who are you?' Diamonds asked like an accusation.

"You can call me Mrs. Cacciatora."

They looked alike, but not exactly. Cacciatora skin was a near alabaster white, juxtaposing a pasty Diamonds with their pink tones. Her cheeks were higher than theirs, and her mouth more severe, but in the eyes, the two looked alike. Diamonds' were lighter, but both sets of eyes sat up high on cheeks, looking down, condescending in their searching and judgement.

Diamonds' eyes swept right back over this lady. But if Diamonds learned anything about their captor, they kept it silent. "Who was worried?"

"The Council."

"You're on the Council?

"I am with the Council."

"With or on?"

"One may say on. I was joining the Council two years ago, but I am not making any decisions."

Between the odd verb tenses and the woman's accent, I could tell English wasn't her first language.

"You don't strike me as a Mrs. Cacciatora."

"And how is a Mrs. Cacciatora striking you?"

"Not a middle-aged woman from rural Japan."

The woman almost betrayed a smile. "And you are no diamond. If you are feeling okay, would you like to begin meeting the rest of the Council?"

"Do I have a choice?"

"We are not keeping you here; we are just watching your health. You are free to be leaving, but you must know about him."

"About who?"

The woman's eyes went wide, her mouth sliding back into a cheshire smile.

"An alien!" someone shouted from beyond the privacy screens. *That voice.* That overly enthusiastic voice, trained to sound excited without being eager, educated to command people's hope, ingrained into the minds of every budding scientist and entrepreneur on the planet. A voice brighter and smoother than the gravelly Gatherer of 2069.

Todd Fowler.

"A life form from another planet, Diamonds! Isn't it exciting?!"

* * *

The screen I was watching clicked off. There was no telling whether they had me on some sort of schedule or if video tech was so ancient to them, they couldn't keep it powered up. They probably got the screen - an old desktop monitor a little thicker than I was used to — from an antique store.

Honestly nothing bigger would fit in the cell they had me in. Sorry, 'residence' is the word they used.

Truth was, it was like living in a cubby hole. I couldn't even sit up all the way, had to slide out. And then I was in the tight hall, which led to other empty 'residences' and locked doors.

But it was only for a couple nights. Soon enough, I'd compete in their game. I'd make a good show but get out early.

Then he said he'd send me home. But why would I trust him? I didn't care if he was old and decrepit and in a wheelchair. I didn't care if he called himself "The Gatherer" now. And I didn't care how much they said they used the game for good now.

I would never trust Todd Fowler again.

Even if he was the only person I knew in the future.

Even if he was my only way to get back home.